"KID, GRAB YOUR GUN!"

But the hands of Clancy were employed in negligently juggling a pebble. "If you draw a weapon," he said, "I'll kill you, Mister Kensing, and heaven have mercy on your bones."

"You? Devil take . . ."

And he reached for his gun. There is no word for what happens when a gunfighter reaches for his Colt. A light winked at the hip of Bill Kensing, and the gun exploded at the same instant, but it was fired too soon. It merely kicked up the dirt at the feet of Clancy. As a matter of fact, the trigger had been pulled by an involuntary contraction of the finger, which occurred as a forty-five-caliber slug from the gun of Clancy crashed home in the body of Kensing. He stooped forward out of his saddle, landed like a professional tumbler on the back of his shoulders, and lay still. The mustang he had been riding was not frightened. It merely stepped a curious step forward and sniffed at the face of its master. Then with a squeal of terror it wheeled and fled wildly down the road.

D1002440

MAX BRAND

THE ABANDONED OUTLAW

LEISURE BOOKS   NEW YORK CITY

TABLE OF CONTENTS

The Gold King Turns His Back

Frederick Faust's original title for this short novel was simply "The Gold King." The title was changed to "The Gold King Turns His Back" when it appeared in *Western Story Magazine* (4/28/23) under the byline John Frederick. Many times titles have been altered by the editors of fiction magazines to conform with one kind of editorial agenda or another. However, in the present case, the title change does, indeed, have a significance in terms of the story.

Chapter One
"The Gold King"

She rode her horse with precipitation around the corner of the shed, and this brought a fresh roar of laughter from the cowpunchers. Once under cover from their eyes, however, Miriam indulged in a chuckle of her own. No doubt her father was rather provoking, but he was also very funny. Whenever he mounted his old cutting horse, there was always the same performance, and there was always the same appreciative audience.

In the meantime her father, Judge Arthur Standard, was continuing the show. His horse was a sixteen-year-old gelding, as wise a mount as ever cut a calf from a herd. He could dodge like the cracking end of a whip, and his sprinting speed for a hundred yards might have been the boast of a mountain lion. Otherwise old Jip was simply a plain cow pony, with a liberal dash of mustang blood. That mustang blood made him want to get the stiffness out of his joints and the meanness out of his disposition by doing a little bucking every morning. But the judge did not like the idea.

For a dozen years he had gone through the same performance at least twice a week, and yet the show lost none of its novelty for the cowpunchers.

For the judge was not at all at home on the back of a bucking horse. He had come late into the cow country, and although he was honored and respected far and wide as a type of all that was best among the big ranchers, yet he had never been able to teach himself the nice balance and the careless ease of a born horseman. He was well enough at home on a slippery pad, to be sure, and he did not mind a horse of spirit that simply heaved and reared and snorted and did more harm to the air than to his rider. He was not troubled to stay on the back of such an animal, but one of these little wild-headed Western brutes could tie itself into a thousand knots and flip a man out of the saddle, ten feet from earth, as a boy squeezes a wet watermelon seed from between thumb and forefinger. Once or twice the judge had received bad falls, and he kept the memory. Then, to crown all, he had lost his heart to Jip on account of the wise head and the marvelous cutting qualities of the gelding, and Jip had that bad habit of warming up to each day's work with a little bucking.

It was a beautiful sight to see the judge in his saddle, very straight, very tall, with his magnificent mustaches down like two long white sabers, his face full of solemn consciousness of his own dignity and importance, and then watch him change when Jip began to sidle and bunch his back and lower his head.

There was no chance for Jip to begin bucking, however. The judge was out of the saddle in a flash and running at the side of the horse, jerking at the reins and crying: "You, Jip . . . you old fool, Jip . . . are you trying to pitch with me? Who's been riding this horse of mine? Who's been letting my horse buck? Sam Carter, you've been riding this Jip of mine!"

Happy Sam would indignantly deny that he could have corrupted the manners of the judge's horse.

"Jip is jest nacherally a bad 'un," he would say. "There ain't no way of trusting that hoss. He's a killer, Judge. He'll be doing you harm one of these days that the doctors ain't going to be able to help none."

"Dog-gone it, Sam," the rancher would answer, "I believe that you're right. There's a devil in this horse. But I'll have that devil out of you, Jip, you old scamp. I'll have that devil out of you, d'you hear?"

By this time the old cow pony, having enjoyed the first stage of his caper, would pretend to grow interested in a wisp of grass near at hand, but from the corner of his eye he would watch the judge mount again. No sooner was the latter in the saddle than Jip started again, bunching his back, lowering his head, and moving along at a sidling trot. But the judge sat crouched low, a hard pull on the reins, one hand clutching the pommel of the saddle, and terror making his eyes huge.

"Now, Jip . . . now, Jip, now you old fool! Jip, haven't you any sense? Are you going to pitch with me, Jip?" Then out of the saddle and another run at the side of Jip, jerking at his reins. "Don't you pitch with me, Jip! Curse your old hide, don't you pitch with me!"

This proceeded for some ten minutes, while the cowpunchers hastened from far and near. It was folly to think of trying to get work out of them while this show was going on. And the beautiful part of the show was that for ten years Jip had never pitched once. A few steps of this bluff bucking, then a shake of his head, and he was done with his wildness. However, it was quite sufficient to frighten the judge. A little later he was in the saddle again, and, as his voice died down, Miriam knew that her father had finally mastered his mount. She was about to turn her horse and ride out to join him, when she saw that she had been watched.

Yonder was the pale face of the new hand whose silence had already won him the name of Noisy Joe Hanover. He

11

was watching her steadily with a faint smile that broadened to a cordial grin, as his eyes encountered hers. He tipped his hat, but Miriam was too embarrassed and angry to make any answer to that salutation. She had been laughing at the antics of her own father. No doubt that tale would be passed around the bunkhouse by Noisy Joe, and then her dignity would be ruined forever in the eyes of the men.

So she began that morning's ride in very bad humor. For the main reason that she had come to the ranch was to impress the 'punchers and everyone else with her efficiency and dignity. Judge Arthur Standard was growing old. He had married quite late. He was already forty-three when his sole child, Miriam, was born. Now he was sixty-five, and the doctor gave him reasons why he could not live a great many years more. So he had sent for Miriam. She must decide on one of two things: either to manage the ranch, or else sell it at once and retire to live in some city.

The mind of Miriam was made up before she arrived from Paris. Music was well enough, but it was only a toy. Miriam felt that she needed a place and a career in the world. And what better than to be the queen of this little empire? Her father had been a supreme ruler all these years. Why should she not be the same?

She bought a number of books on ranching and ranch methods. From Havre to New York, from New York to the ranch, she was deep in the print. By the time she got off the train she knew the names of more fertilizers and the soils on which they did best, more breeds of cattle and the environments for which they were best fitted, more faults of stabling and shedding, feeding, branding, more diseases of horses and cows than her old father had ever heard of. She had prepared a list of questions, too, that she intended to ask her father in order to improve her knowledge, if he could answer them, and to show her knowledge, if he could not.

Before she got off three of the questions, her father had declared that he did not wish to be bothered with a lot of tommyrot which meant nothing, except when it was left buried in print.

"I'll tell you what the cow business is, Miriam," he had said in conclusion. "It's a gamble. You've got your land and your cows on one side. The other side is competition, weather, plagues, prices. You chuck in everything you've got. You wait for the wheel to stop spinning. When it's stopped, you know whether you've won or lost. And there you are, Miriam. All this book talk ain't going to help you. It'll just confuse your hands. And that ain't worth doing."

Miriam was an exceptional girl. She knew when she had run into a stone wall, and she stopped talking at this point and appeared to listen amiably to the advice of her father. But all the time she was making up her mind that, when the reins were in her hands, the ranch affairs would be driven in a different direction and at a different gait.

All of which has some bearing upon her anger when she found that her laughter had been spied upon by one of the hands. She gave the fellow another look, however, as they started off on the gallop. Noisy Joe Hanover made one of the party, Lefty Gregory was a second—both of them riding perhaps half a dozen lengths to the rear, so that the rancher and his daughter could talk in some privacy. The judge was accomplishing a double purpose in this tour of the ranch. In the first place he wanted to initiate a new hand into some of the mysteries of his range, and also he wanted to impress Miriam with the size of the domain that was to be hers before many years. It was his secret hope that he could induce Miriam to leave the management of the ranch entirely in the hands of the present foreman, Charlie Bender.

They left the plain; they climbed into the hills; and it was already nine o'clock when they saw the wild herd. The keen eye of Lefty distinguished them first, and his cry raised the heads of the others in time to see a cream-colored stallion, with a mane and tail of silver—a very painting and picture of a horse rather than matter-of-fact horseflesh—drive around the corner of a hill, and with a thundering of hoofs, sixteen or twenty mares and colts followed at his heels.

With a yell the judge jerked to get his rifle out of its case, but Miriam clung to his arm and prevented him, while at the same time her frantic orders forced the two cowpunchers behind her to lower their weapons. And the mustangs flashed on. The cream-colored leader was working like a captain in command of the troops. First he showed the way, ranging in the lead with matchless speed. Then he swept around to the rear. A lumbering colt tasted the teeth of the stallion, and a slow-footed mare was likewise punished, until she closed up the gap that was growing between her and the band. So, rounding up the laggards like a good shepherd, he brought his band out of view among the hills, with a final neigh of mockery and challenge.

It had all happened in a few seconds, and Miriam released the arm of her father, who was now in a raging temper.

"It was The Gold King," answered Lefty sadly. "And we were all in good range. I think one of us might have knocked him over, Judge."

"Might have knocked him over?" raved the rancher. "Might have? My God, Lefty, if I couldn't have filled him full of lead with my own rifle, I'd have left the range."

"Do you really mean it?" cried Miriam. "You would have shot that beautiful creature? I don't believe it!"

"She doesn't believe it," echoed her father to Lefty. "She doesn't believe that I'd shoot a thief that's run off with a thousand dollars' worth of mares for me in the past two years. She doesn't believe we'd shoot that devil of a horse and collect a twenty-five-hundred-dollar bounty on his head! Miriam, sometimes you talk so plain simple that I can't believe you're my daughter."

"I can't help what you think. I say he's the most beautiful horse I've ever seen."

"You keep going by your eyes, Miriam, and you'll lead a mighty unhappy life in this old world of ours. It ain't what you see, but what you know that counts. That same stallion has raided the ranches of fifty men, up and down the mountains. They've chased him fifty times, run down his herd, and had him go right on and collect a new gang to follow him. He likes company, curse his yellow sides!''

''I'd give a year of life,'' said Miriam obstinately, ''to sit in a saddle on his back for five minutes.''

''That's a safe offer,'' said her father dryly. ''The only way they'll ever catch The Gold King will be with a rifle bullet . . . and a lucky one at that.''

''I mean it,'' she said, going from obstinacy to emotion. ''I . . . I'd marry the man who'd bring me that horse to ride.''

Chapter Two
"A Promise Is a Promise"

They reached the ranch house again by noon. That evening, after dinner, the foreman came in from the bunkhouse to report that the new cowpuncher, Noisy Joe, had disappeared.

''He was just one of these bums,'' said Charlie Bender, ''that hear a lot of talk about the easy life on a ranch and come out to take a chance at it. He didn't know nothing. He could stick in the saddle pretty fair, but he didn't know a rope from the handle of a frying pan. What he wanted was a full belly. He's got that, and he's gone.''

This was all that was said about the disappearance of Noisy Joe Hanover. In the bunkhouse, to be sure, there were occasional references to his silence. But in a day or two he was forgotten.

As for Miriam, she was too busy to think of any of the incidents of that first day, except to be vaguely grateful that the man who had seen her laugh had disappeared before he had had a chance to spread the story among the other 'punchers. The memory of his pale face became like the memory of a dim ghost. In the meantime work poured in and filled her hands. She started at the bottom and wanted to learn everything. She would rise at five and go to bed at midnight and never stop striving for an instant in between.

"Engines in her are too big for her beam," said her father unpoetically.

She was rather a pretty girl than beautiful. For beauty, after all, is usually spoiled by action, at least by action of the mind, and Miriam's mind had never been still. There was a wrinkle marked straight up and down between her eyes. Her lips were habitually a little compressed. A shadow of purple underlined her eyes, and little crow's feet were beginning in the corners. All these things were apparent when she was in repose, and one could understand why her friends said that "poor Miriam is throwing herself away." Indeed, she was playing the spendthrift, and what a treasure she had already spent could be guessed when she laughed and talked with enthusiasm. For, then, she was truly beautiful. The charm, the thrilling illusion was there for an instant, and then the drab commonplace returned. And men said frequently: "What will she be at thirty-five, if she's only twenty-two now? Besides, she knows too much."

Which was perfectly natural as a remark, because in this age, when woman strives so gallantly toward mental strength, men hate brains in women more and more. Particularly they hate the sort of brains and ambition that belonged to Miriam, for she was eager to do anything and everything. Nothing could be beyond her reach. If a man did it, she could do it. She never talked about men and women and their differences—she talked about people, human beings. Within a month from her arrival she had roped and tied a steer; within six weeks she had received a round dozen, hard falls from bucking bronchos, and had finally ridden one of the worst horses on the ranch. Within three months from her coming, she walked with a limp, was tired of eye, brown of skin, and braver than ever in her smile.

The cowpunchers admired her courage, but they were a little afraid of her. Somehow they felt that she represented a new type of woman, fiery, resistless, ready to push man off his pedestal, where he had been posing through the ages as the builder, the maker, the pool of strength. This wisp of a girl who stood five feet and four inches, with a little, round waist hardly as big as a man's thigh, was doing as much work—even physical work—as the stoutest of the cowpunchers. Moreover, she worked as though it were a game. Wild wind and fierce weather did not dismay her. She went happily on. So that the fear of her and her kind grew up, side by side, with the admiration which she collected. And eventually the fear grew stronger than the admiration.

Even her father began to feel it. He had always been very fond of Miriam. And he had been inclined to laugh her down when she first came out to the ranch, full of theories and talk. He had not really dreamed that she had the courage and the nerve power, to say nothing of the sheer physical strength, to do what she was accomplishing. She worked all day and studied all night. And, from time to time, she cornered him in an argument, and he suffered shame and fear, as he began to perceive that she was learning more about cattle than he had ever known.

Sometimes, when he was protesting that she must not throw away her youth and her beauty in this fashion to do a mere man's work, he felt that he was talking in the defense of his sex. And she would always answer, with a sort of fierce conviction, that beauty and youth meant no more to her than beauty and youth mean to a young man. All that

17

she prized, she declared, was her good health which enabled her to work hard. As for looks, at fifty, she was fond of saying, there are only two things that are attractive in any woman, and these are health and physical agility. As for the cowpunchers, they would have worshipped her had they not been in such awe, and a man cannot love a thing he fears.

So they came to an evening three months later. The June sun was rolling down toward the horizon, but was still bright. The wind was moving in slow puffs, as warm as human breath. At one end of the verandah Charlie Bender was conversing with the judge concerning a fencing problem, and Miriam was sitting alone at the farther end, reading a treatise on the Hereford.

Charlie Bender spoke first—a sharp exclamation. Then the judge stood up. Finally Miriam looked down the hill in the same direction and saw what seemed a moving blotch of gold, coming along the road. She looked again. It was a horse, and the rider was pushing him at a steady canter.

"What a magnificent animal," she said. "D'you recognize that horse, Father?" She spoke with a careless enthusiasm. "Or do you know the rider?" she continued.

"I don't know," said her father, strangely excited. "By the Lord, Charlie, do you think that it can possibly be?"

"I can tell a man a good way off by his way of riding," remarked Charlie Bender. "And I noticed him most particular. He had a way of shoving his whole left side forward. Rode sort of twisted."

"Who did?" asked Miriam.

To her astonishment they both turned upon her abstracted glances and then turned again, without a word of answer, to watch the approaching horseman.

"There ain't any doubt about the color," said Charlie Bender.

"The color of what?" asked Dent, coming through the door. Charlie Bender gave him a glance of utter disgust and was again silent.

Indeed, every cowpuncher on the place hated Dent. He had known Miriam in New York and Paris. Therefore, he was welcome at the ranch, but nevertheless they hated him. For it was plain that he had no interest in anything on the ranch, or in the entire range of the mountains, except Miriam. She was the only person who could not see that he had come to marry her, not to enjoy a rest in the Wild West. He went about his object with perfect precision. He pored over the books about cattle that Miriam had recently bought, and, though he could not distinguish a Durham from a Hereford, he had so far progressed that he could talk about them glibly.

His name was Manning Underwood Dent, and the unlucky combination of initials, seen on his trunk, had gained for him the nickname of Mud from the cowpunchers. Had he lived through a hundred years of heroic life in the West, he could never have changed that name with them. Instead of that, however, he was known among them on second thought as an effeminate fortune hunter. Not a man on the ranch but would have made him eat dirt with the most reckless enthusiasm.

As for the occupation of Manning Underwood Dent, he had been at turns musical critic and writer of travel sketches, in which he described fishing villages in Sicily and peasant towns in France, illustrated with the work of his own brush. He had once written both the words and the music of a song. In fact, he could talk fluently of any art. He was a man of imposing presence, rather tall, exceedingly slender, with an enormous, bulging forehead, a head of black, curling hair, a close-cropped mustache, and a pale-olive skin. The pupils of his eyes were a little yellowish in tint. Altogether one could not tell whether he were a little sick from too much study or from a weak constitution. He stood now behind the chair of Miriam and gazed down the road with the others.

"On my honor," he murmured, for he made it a practice to speak always softly, "on my honor, the horse seems to be actually made of gold."

"Good heavens!" cried Miriam and started to her feet.

"My dear Miriam," said Mud, "what have I done? What have I said? You are upset."

He laid a quieting hand on her shoulder. He was fond of saying that his touch was soothing. But Miriam brushed the hand away and looked back down the road. Then she stared, appalled, at her father. That gentleman had also risen and was staring down the road with such emotion that his saber-like white mustaches worked.

"Of course, I'm seeing a ghost," said the judge.

"It can't be!" cried Miriam.

"He's spent three months doing it," said the foreman, "and here he comes back on the jump."

All the breath went out of Miriam's body. She had not dreamed that anyone else could have known about her foolish remark when she first saw The Gold King disappearing among the hills. She had thought that it had fallen upon her ears alone. But plainly either Lefty or Noisy Joe Hanover must have been told the tale when they returned from the morning ride.

"Good heavens," repeated the girl. "What does it mean?"

"I dunno," said Charlie Bender gloomily. "I figure that your father knows a pile more law than I do. Why don't you ask him?"

She turned to her father. His long mustaches were still working.

"I can't be bothered with questions," he said. "You run on inside the house."

Miriam obeyed without a word, but at the door she hesitated and glanced back down the road. Then, with a sort of groan of despair, she disappeared into the house, and they could hear the rapid beat of her feet up the stairs, and, finally, the slamming of a door which showed that she had gone to her room for refuge.

Manning Underwood Dent, in the meantime, would have

gone mad with curiosity had he not been too conscious of his own importance to speak quickly. But finally he was forced to murmur: "Miriam seems completely upset, Mister Standard."

"She does," said the judge without turning his head.

"Girls," pursued Dent, "have the strangest way of going off at tangents from the circle. Excitable and. . . ."

"I suppose you want to know what this is all about?" asked the judge finally, as though he saw that this was the easiest way of avoiding a long conversation.

"Naturally," said Dent.

"Three months ago Miriam saw a wild stallion . . . an outlaw horse . . . and she said that she'd marry the man who could bring that horse to her. Well, Mister Dent, there comes the horse, and the man on his back seems to be a fellow who used to be an old cowpuncher on the place."

Mr. Dent was staggered. But almost at once he was able to laugh.

"A very good joke," he suggested. "A poor ignorant cowpuncher actually aspiring to the hand of Miriam Standard."

This description of cowpunchers in general brought a glare from the foreman, but the foreman was of a social class so far below Dent that it never occurred to Dent that Bender might resent his remarks on the subject of cowpunchers.

"Why a joke?" asked the judge sharply. "A promise is a promise, and, by the living God, a promise that a man could give serious thought to is a promise that my daughter shall consider serious, also."

"Good Lord," gasped Dent.

"Exactly!" stormed the judge.

Mr. Dent dropped into a chair and sat there sprawling.

Chapter Three
"Miriam's Predicament"

Life returned only by the slowest degrees to the small, yellowish eyes of Mr. Dent. Eventually, however, he was able to sit up, just as the stallion was halted under the lee of the verandah wall. He *was* a glorious animal, not tall, but made as a jeweler makes a watch. He had strength enough to dance on the wind. That also was apparent. He was perhaps an inch above fifteen hands. He seemed even smaller, so exact were his proportions. His body was of molten gold cast into a mold. His mane and tail were solid silver, on which the sunshine was dazzling. And his four little feet were stockinged in black.

This was The Gold King near at hand. But, no, this was not all of him. Where is the poet to sing in wild rhythms all the fiery life which trembled in his body, or set his nostrils quivering, or blazed out at his eyes? He could not be still an instant. He was as restless as a new-caged tiger, or—to vary the simile and make it just as exact—he was as restless as a hungry puppy. In fact, in spite of all his beauty and his strength, he did not aspire awe so much as affection. When Noisy Joe Hanover dropped out of the saddle, the eyes of the stallion became soft at once, and he nibbled at the brim of the cowpuncher's hat.

When Noisy Joe rambled idly on toward the verandah, the golden horse followed until his master went up the steps.

There the stallion paused, with his front hoofs resting on the lower step and his eyes fixed upon Joe. Even Mr. Dent grew excited and arose from his chair again. As for the rancher and his foreman, they were struck dumb for a moment, and, when they regained their voices, they were only able to whisper.

"It *is* Noisy Joe," murmured Charlie Bender.

"It's him!" gasped the rancher.

"Joe, how did you do it?"

Noisy Joe sat down upon the railing of the verandah and, before he answered, drew forth tobacco and brown papers, offered them carefully to each of the three listeners—was introduced to Manning Dent during the same process—then rolled himself a smoke, lighted it, blew forth the first long, blue-brown cloud of smoke, and proceeded to deliver himself of his thrilling narrative: "I followed the old horse, got him, and we've been living together ever since."

He went on smoking and looking down the verandah, as though he saw something of surprising interest on a distant treetop.

"But what did you do? And how did you do it?" begged the judge, who loved a good story as a child loves Christmas.

"I just followed along and waited to grab him," said the cowpuncher. "When the lucky day came. . . ."

"Ah, yes, tell us about that day, Hanover."

"When the lucky day came, I nabbed him, and there he is. Mighty good-natured horse, Judge."

The judge used up some of his excess of disappointment and anger by jabbing his pocketknife into the wooden railing. "Well," he said to the foreman, "did you ever see a man like him?"

The foreman, however, was grinning broadly and looking over the truant cowpuncher with the most friendly eye in the world. The unsightly pallor was gone from the face of Noisy Joe. He was now as brown as a berry, and from the color of his skin as well as the ragged condition of his clothes—

23

which were simply a mass of patches held together rudely with twine—one might judge that the horse hunter had spent every hour of the past three months out in the open. Indeed, his very eyes were changed. The weary sadness was gone from them, and a pair of bright lights looked out upon the world. Here was a 'puncher worth having on the ranch, and, even if he knew nothing about the management of a rope, he could learn that in time. Indeed, whether he ever learned to use a rope, it would be a credit to the outfit to have the captor of The Gold King in their employ.

"I've got something to talk to you about, Judge," the returned cowpuncher was saying to the older man.

"About what?" asked the judge.

"About Miriam," said the other.

Even Charlie Bender was agape. He used that name with as much fluent ease as though he had been raised with the girl. It was suddenly and sickeningly plain that he had, indeed, taken her at her word that day three months before. What manner of man could he be? A child? No child could capture The Gold King and make a pet out of him.

"Miriam?" breathed the judge, his eyes starting from his head. "I . . . come this way, Joe. Come right into the library with me." And he fairly scrambled out of his chair and led the way into the house.

"Most amazing, by heaven," murmured Mr. Dent.

On most occasions Charlie Bender would not have stopped so far beneath the sense of his own dignity as to exchange opinions with Manning Underwood Dent, but today he was fairly stunned by what had happened, and speech was necessary.

"What the devil got into the judge?" muttered Bender.

"As though," went on Dent, growing a little pale, "he were actually taking this 'puncher fellow seriously."

Here his words were punctuated by a night-black glance from the foreman, but Dent went soberly on: "He changed color when he heard this Hanover fellow speak. What could possibly be the meaning of it?"

"You being kind of strange to the country," remarked Charlie Bender, "most likely you wouldn't know. But I'll tell you. Out in these parts, when a man or woman makes a promise, it's a sort of an unwritten law that they got to keep their word. That ain't like the East, is it?"

"Certainly not," murmured Dent. "A purely conventional exclamation of an impulsive girl turned into a whip over her head. I've never heard of anything like it."

Charlie Bender was silent. Even to him it was so amazing that he did not know what to make of it.

"I understand now," cried Dent at last. "Mister Standard is very properly buying the fellow off. No doubt the present of a good saddle would mean as much to a cowpuncher as the present of the most charming wife."

Charlie Bender groaned with impotent rage. To their very tips, his fingers ached to be at this man.

"Of course, that's it," said Dent. "By this time they've reached an agreement. Eh? Listen to that."

A door had opened, and the voice of the judge was heard flowing smoothly on and on.

"The law is a fine thing," said Charlie Bender reverently. "It makes a gent know how to be a fine persuader. Listen to the old judge sing."

Now heavy footfalls came down the hall. The voice of the judge was raised loud and high in the inner hall.

"Miriam! Oh, Miriam!"

Her answer tinkled in the distance. From the verandah they could hear another door close softly in the upper part of the house.

"Yes, Dad," answered Miriam from the head of the stairs.

"Come down here, girl."

"Very well."

The chill in that phrase was easily understandable. She had just seen Noisy Joe Hanover standing beside her father in the lower hall. Nevertheless, down she came—slowly, in the most sedate fashion. One could tell that by the regularity with which her heels tapped the stairs. Each of the men on the verandah listened agape, with their heads canted sideways and their eyes rolled up in an effort of listening and of conjuring up the picture of the scene.

She was at the bottom of the stairs.

"Now, Miriam," said the judge, "I been talking things over with Joe Hanover."

"Talking what things over, Father?"

"Listen to her," declared Bender to the thin air. "Ain't she the game little four-flusher?"

"*What* things?" thundered the judge. "Don't try to pull the wool over my eyes, young lady. We're talking over the statement you made three months ago in the hearing of three men. You said that you'd marry the man who could bring The Gold King to you to ride."

Dent and Bender came out of their chairs, as though unseen hands had lifted them.

"I'm not going to *try* to understand what you mean," asserted Miriam. "It was just a chance exclamation. It might have come from the lips of any girl. Dad, are you *wild* to call me to task for such a remark as that?"

"Look here!" exclaimed the judge. "You've been talking about the duties of a man and a woman being the same, and that a woman that tries to shove all the hard work and the worry of life onto the shoulders of a man is a coward and a sneak. Well, Miriam, go a little further and tell me what you think of the woman that has no sense of honor. Tell me that, Miriam!"

"Father," answered Miriam, "are you really serious?"

"I am," said the judge, and the two listeners on the verandah started. "This man has poured out three months of his life . . . three months of hard labor . . . he's gone starved . . . he's risked his life . . . he's worked like a dog for three months. Now he comes back, having done a miracle. He captured The Gold King. He brought you the thing you wanted, and now he demands that he have the bargain fulfilled. It's logical, just, and right.''

There was a little silence, and Miriam herself could not have started with more horror than did the two on the verandah.

''Aw,'' muttered Charlie Bender, ''it ain't going to come to nothing. Noisy Joe may be a queer one, but he's a 'puncher, and there never was a 'puncher since the beginning of time that would take advantage of a woman like that.''

The same thought must have been in the mind of Miriam.

''Of course, this is all part of a great hoax,'' she was saying stiffly. ''I appreciate that it is very funny, Mister Hanover. And I know that Western cattlemen are a thousand times too chivalrous to dream of such a thing as you are thinking of doing. You cannot hold me to the result of a careless, random expression.''

''Careless . . . nothing!'' exploded her father. ''You said the words, didn't you? You've been out here for three months, finding out how little your father knew about the cow business and wondering why he didn't go broke long ago, with his old musty methods. Well, dearie, no matter what any man may say, the first thing that a man has got to have in the cow business is a name for being a man of his word. And nobody's going to say that his daughter don't keep her word as well as her father.''

There was another deadly little pause, one of those intervals which say so much more than words can possibly do.

At length Miriam replied: ''Mister Hanover, I am going to stop talking to my father and ask you, face to face . . . do you intend to hold me to this shameless contract? Can it really be for an instant in your mind to force me to do such a thing? What under heaven, Mister Hanover, could make you dream that you and I might find any happiness together? Have we received the same education? Do we enjoy the same things?''

The reply of Hanover was wonderfully terse and to the point.

"Lady," he said, "you asked for the horse. I got the horse for you. That's my side of the thing." With this he was silent.

"Isn't that manly and fair and square?" asked the rancher.

"He's gone mad," whispered Dent.

"Shut up, Mud," breathed the foreman.

"Oh," came the wail of Miriam, "I've never heard of such a thing." And her footfalls pattered rapidly up the stairs.

Chapter Four
"Noisy Limbers Up"

"You'll hear some more of the same tune, though!" called the rancher up the stairs. "You're not through with this yet." Then came his assurance to the cowpuncher. "You'll find that I'll fight this matter through to the bitter end, Hanover. The honor of the Standards is a flawless honor until now, and a flawless honor it must remain."

He came stamping out onto the verandah, with his heavy hand clapped upon the shoulder of the cowpuncher. As for the foreman and Dent, they regarded the captor of The Gold King with frozen eyes. Charlie Bender finally rose and walked hastily for the bunkhouse. But the ranchman had passed into an ecstasy over The Gold King. The mustang was, he declared, the finest specimen of horseflesh he had ever seen. There might be Thoroughbreds of more beauty and worth, a greater price on a race track, but there was nothing in the world, he vowed, that combined such great speed and endurance, and there was no sire that would be the foundation of a line of more peerless cow ponies.

Charlie Bender heard the last part of the enthusiastic outburst. Then he hurried on for the bunkhouse. It had been a long, hard day. He found Happy Sam Carter sitting in the doorway, playing softly and sadly on a harmonica. The others were scattered about, waiting for the time to go to bed, smoking cigarettes, until the bunkhouse was a blue haze, and talking in weary voices. The foreman waked them up, as though he had announced a fire.

"Noisy Joe is back," he called from the doorway, "and he's got The Gold King and wants to trade him for Miss Standard."

Through the blue-brown smoke mist the 'punchers swung to erect positions. There was a machine-gun fire of questions, and the story was hastily told. No decorative details were left out, for that matter, and the case was made out black, indeed, against Joe Hanover.

"I heard her say them same words," announced Lefty Gregory. "Meant no more'n it'd mean if I was to say I'd give ten years of life for a drink of red-eye. It was just the same sort of a remark. Didn't mean nothing, matter of fact, and nobody but a fool like Noisy Joe would have took her serious."

"What's come over the old judge?" asked the chorus.

"The judge is sore at Miriam because she knows more'n he does. He wants to hold her down with a stupid husband."

"Noisy Joe is worse than that," declared Bender with a growing warmth, as the full horror of the situation dawned upon him. "I figure that he's sort of a simple-minded guy. Ever notice that flat, dead eye of his and the way he don't say nothing?"

Of course, all of this had been noticed.

"It's an outrage!" cried Lefty.

"It hadn't ought to be allowed," called another.

"Say," said Bender, coming sharply to the point, "let's all take a hand and bust this here thing all up. We can do it. We can give this here Hanover such a riding that he'll skin out from the ranch and never show his face within ten miles of it again. Let's get ready for him when he comes in from the house, packing his blankets. We'll fix him up with a night that he ain't going to forget, if he lives a hundred years."

With loud acclaim the thought was accepted. Charlie Bender was immensely popular with the men who worked under him, but he had never made a more popular suggestion than this. They began straightway to prepare for the reception. It was necessary that a great deal should be done. In the first place, everyone wished to salvage such perishables as he owned and put them in a safe place, because in the approaching rough house there was apt to be much damage done—at least, if Noisy Joe put up a stern resistance.

There was a brief dialogue on his possibilities as a fighter. It was agreed that his lean arms and shoulders might be furnished with muscles of excellent qualities, even if of small compass. But it was agreed, furthermore, that he was too slow to use his strength to the very best advantage. For this reason they made their preparations less elaborate than they might otherwise have done. It was decided that all should be a scene of peace and harmony, with some of the men in bed and apparently asleep, while others should be sitting about idly mending clothes or reading magazines.

Undoubtedly this would lure Noisy Joe straight into the bunkhouse and toward his old bunk. But when he made toward it, he would at once be tackled from the side by Lefty, who was a man of might. After the tackling, the others would arise. And when they were through with Noisy Joe, it was strongly surmised that the 'puncher would desire permission to depart for regions unknown more than to remain even to marry Miriam and become the heir to Judge Standard.

This was the scene, then, upon which Noisy Joe actually

looked when he reached the door of the bunkhouse. The sun was down, but the sky was still brilliantly red, and the long June evening was just beginning. Yet half of the men were in bed, and the others were preparing to retire. Upon this the silent man gazed for a time, and then, instead of entering, he stepped back and turned away.

There was a busy exchange of glances and whispers the moment he had disappeared.

"Has he smelled a rat?"

"The only rat here is himself."

"Let's go get the hound and bring him in."

All of these ominous whispers were drowned out by the commanding gesture of Charlie Bender and his murmur: "Be still, all of you. He'll hear something."

So they fell back into their former attitudes of quiet. One impulsive genius in a corner of the room even began to snore loudly, which started the others shaking with silent laughter.

"Gents," drawled the rare voice of Noisy Joe from the outside, "I wonder if I'd disturb you much if I was to limber up my old gat for a minute? I'm all out of practice."

"Help yourself, Noisy," answered Bender with the greatest good cheer. "Help yourself. We can stand it, if your target can."

With a wink at the others he stepped to the door to watch the performance. Two or three others also crowded their heads to the door to watch. And this was what they saw: Noisy Joe had found a large tin can which he placed on its side on the flat of the ground. Then he retired a distance of perhaps twenty paces—a good, long range for quick and accurate revolver work—and slipped from his holster a long, blue-barreled Colt. No one of the other men had ever paid much attention to the weapon before this. For Noisy Joe had been so inoffensive that no one had connected him with a deadly weapon.

However, it was patent that he had handled the gun with the most practiced ease. It flowed into his hand, as though it were a feather's weight, and, hardly glancing at his target, he began to stroll forward, firing once every time his right heel struck the ground. And the can, as if drawn by an invisible string, was jerked away before him, so that it remained an even twenty paces in the lead. He took six steps and six shots. As he walked, the shots were plunging into the ground close to the rolling can, and the spray of dust and gravel kicked the can along. This was more difficult work than it appeared to be. Not only was it necessary that each shot should be extremely close to the can, but it was also imperative that the can should roll straight. It angled to one side or the other with every shot, and it was important to correct the angle by placing the next shot a little to one side of center.

The six shots were fired, and then, as the Colt was dropped into the holster, another revolver was produced from somewhere in the clothes of Noisy Joe, produced as smoothly and swiftly as though it had been hanging in a holster at his hip. Now with his left hand he pumped six more shots into the dirt behind the can.

Presently the can reached the edge of a sharp, little slope and tumbled away out of sight, while Noisy Joe deliberately cleaned and reloaded his guns. There was perfect silence from the door of the bunkhouse for a time. Each man was watching with wonder.

"How much practicing do you do?" asked someone in a tone of greatest respect.

"Once a month," answered Noisy, and walked slowly off toward the corral, where The Gold King was idling back and forth along the fence, as though he were fretting at his cage.

"What I want to know," said Charlie Bender slowly, when he had turned away from the door, "is this . . . did he smell a rat when he came in and then go out to do that shooting stunt to take the wind out of our sails? Or did it just happen?"

"I dunno," said Lefty. "I sure dunno what was in his

mind, Charlie, but I know what's in my mind right now."

"What's that, Lefty?"

"The wind has been all took out of *my* sails. If the rest of you want to haze Noisy Joe, go ahead and have your party, but lemme sleep quiet in my bunk."

Charlie Bender was shocked. For Lefty was a known man of war. He loved a hard battle more than most men loved a square meal, and it was like a contradiction in terms to hear Lefty speak of withdrawing from a combat.

"I'll tell you why," he explained, as he removed his boots and dived into his bunk. "These gents that go along so smooth and easy and shoot straight are mighty dangerous to stop. They don't ask no questions. They just unlimber a gat and start in to work. I'd rather play tag with a basketful of rattlers and tickle the nose of a bull with a red rag than fool with this Noisy Joe. That's only my way of looking at it. A lot of you other boys may be braver than me. Go ahead and have your little party. But I'll sit in the gallery. That's me."

After this announcement there was no more thought of a rough house for the benefit of Noisy. That worthy entered the bunkhouse after a time and went quietly to bed in his old accustomed bunk, and not a voice or a hand was raised. Silence settled over the bunkhouse. There was no last-minute story, as boots were being drawn off. Had they all been prisoners in a jail, there could not have been a more solemn quiet. But once in a while, as Noisy methodically made down his bunk, glances were stolen at him. And it seemed to the others that he must have grown during the chase of the stallion. Certainly his shoulders were much broader.

Chapter Five
"Reckless Dent"

In an ecstasy of horror Miriam remained in her room for a long time after that interview with her father. She did not come down until dinner. At the table and in front of their guest, Dent, she was certain that she should escape from the further development of the subject. But in this she underrated her father. He went blithely ahead from the point at which he had left off during their conversation in the hall.

He had often noticed, he declared, that girls start life with a superior belief in their own powers and a contempt for the abilities of men. He had seen the same tendencies exhibited in Miriam since her arrival at the ranch. She had declared more than once that she wished no quarter as a woman, that she desired only to take what came to her as a human being. Now, declared the rancher, the time had come for her to show her true colors. Here was a promise that she had given. The promise was now waiting to be redeemed. But at this point the rancher made the mistake of appealing for judgment to young Dent.

"By no means, sir!" cried Manning Underwood Dent. "Allow me to assert my conviction, sir, that such an alliance between two people so mismated is, I am certain, nothing else than a sacrilege."

"Since when," growled the rancher, "has my daughter been a saint?"

"Ah," jumped in Manning Dent, seizing greedily upon the opening, "there is something sacred in every woman."

"Romantic rot," growled Standard.

"Divine truth," answered the other.

Here the arrival of the roast stopped the talk for a moment, and the rancher was very grateful for it. He felt that he had raised fire instead of an ally.

It was the rashness of Dent that brought on the next explosion.

"But, of course, sir," said the younger man, "we know that it is all a great hoax . . . and very admirably carried out, I am willing to admit."

"The devil you are!" roared the rancher. "You are sure it is a hoax? By the Lord, sir, if my daughter is not married to Joe Hanover before the month is out, my name is not Standard!"

Miriam folded her hands and looked down the table at her father. The sight of her white face struck him like a blow, but he hastened on to beat up his fury, simply because he was afraid that the sight of her distress might make him weaken.

"And every word of that is gospel!" he thundered. "You write it down in red and remember it!"

"Sir," she said, "you forget that we are not alone."

"Ma'am," he answered, "I don't care if the whole world flocks around and hears what I got to say to my daughter. I'm tired of these new women. I'm going to be obeyed in my own family, and I'm going to teach my own daughter that. . . ."

"That her happiness means nothing to you."

"That her happiness is nothing compared with her honor!" he roared. "Chalk it down in red, I say. If I have to drag you into the presence of the minister with my own hands, I'll do it rather than see you foresworn!"

He had gone much further than he intended to go, but he was made of inflammable stuff. When a spark touched him,

35

he was instantly at white heat. This was not all, however. An hour later he would give a great deal to retract what he had said in excess of meaning. But then, since he had once committed himself, he would throw his entire strength into the breach and fight to make it good. His daughter was as well aware of this as he was himself. If he could have been kept calm, all might have been well, but now he had been driven to a violent assertion, and he was sure to be equally violent in his deeds to make them match his words.

"Father," she breathed, rising from her chair.

"Don't stare at me with that white face, Miriam," he cried, sick at heart for what he had said, but brazening it out. "I'll have you know that I dispose of the destinies of my family."

She stood back from her chair. "I'll have you know, sir," she said, "that I am a free creature."

"School talk . . . school nonsense," he bellowed. "No meaning in those words at all!"

"You shall see."

"Of course, I'll see. Don't be an idiot, Miriam. You're going to do what I tell you to do."

"I'd rather be dead first."

"What?"

"I mean it. I'd rather die than be the wife of a horse tamer . . . a common, lazy, ignorant cowpuncher."

"How do you know he is? Have you talked to him?"

"Oh, I don't need to. I have *looked* at him!"

"I tell you, I've talked to him, and I respect him. He's a shrewd, wide-awake fellow."

"Father, good night."

"Look here, Miriam, this is war."

"If it has to be war . . . then let the war come."

"Stuff! You've been reading silly books. Why, you little rattle-headed child, I could cut you off without a penny!"

"Do it! Do it!" she cried. "Do you think I live for money or by money? It's dirt . . . it's nothing! You've worked all your life for the sake of dirt. Now do you think you can buy my obedience with it? I tell you that I scorn such a thought. It's base and low and worthy of a slave, not a free American woman."

"Go to your room," he gasped.

Miriam turned and walked slowly out. She had no sooner disappeared than the rancher ran after her, paused with his hand on the knob of the door, and then strode anxiously back and forth across the floor. Manning Underwood Dent knew well enough that he should have left the room before the argument had grown as heated as it had. But to him it was more thrilling than a play, and he could not leave before the curtain had dropped. Now, however, he rose with great dignity, bowed low to Mr. Standard, and began to leave the room.

"Sit down! Sit down!" shouted Standard. "What the devil? Are you going to let the silly ranting of a girl spoil your appetite?"

Dent hesitated. He was very hungry, and the beef was very good. But he had never before had such an admirable opening to take the center of the stage.

"Sir," he said, "I am sure that you will prefer to be alone to think over what you have just said, and I am sure that I wish to be alone to try to forget what I have just heard. I bid you a very good evening, sir."

He left the rancher, gasping, and went up to his room, tingling with his little triumph. For some time he walked up and down on the floor, rehearsing the manner in which he had delivered this speech and the change which it had worked in the face of Standard. It pleased Dent immensely. On the whole he felt that he had never appeared to better advantage in his life.

In the meantime Miriam was shrinking into a chair in her chamber. She was one of those who are seldom very angry, and, when she was carried away by a moment of rage, she suffered for it afterward. It was as though an axe were laid to the very root of her strength. She was sick now. For her own part, she was more than willing to retract every word she had said that could have offended her father. But she knew his pride was iron, and, having announced himself in such unmistakable terms, it would be strange, indeed, if he altered his mind. *What did it mean?* She, of course, could not give way. It was sure to create an estrangement between them. She could not live in this house without obeying him. And if she ever left this house, she knew her father well enough to guess that he would never take her back again. At least, this was a point on which she was sure enough.

Certainly no girl was ever placed in a more unfortunate position, or one which required more diplomacy in order to extricate herself. After a time she heard the door of the dining room open and the step of Manning Dent go softly up the stairs. He had probably offended her father before he left, and she would have to suffer for this, also.

Presently she began to feel angry at Dent. Anger, however, served to fix the idea of Dent in her mind. She did not dislike the fellow as her father and the cowpunchers did. He impressed her as a rather entertaining man who had been a great many places, known many people, done many things, and who could fill in a dull moment with pleasant small talk. Besides, he had the graces that every one else around her lacked. These things underlined all of his good qualities and minimized his bad ones.

She began to think of him now as the only person who had spoken a word for her in the midst of her present trouble. This thought grew until she eventually opened the door of her room and listened to make sure that no one was near enough to spy upon her. There was no sound in the house except the steady and measured beat of her father's familiar step, passing up and down in the library. This was his way when he was greatly moved. This was his way of grinding home a grievance until it was printed in the blackest ink in his heart of hearts. He would keep on in this fashion until he had beaten all his father's love for her out of existence. Then he would give her again that brutal alternative of marrying the cowpuncher or leaving her home.

It was like a fairy story, such cruelty as this, and a little thrill of self-pity brought the tears to her eyes. Then she stole down the hall and tapped at the door of Manning Dent. He was dressed as if for riding, she discovered, when the door was opened by him. He had a hat clapped on his head, his coat buttoned tightly, and on his bed was thrown a bag, strapped and ready for departure, as well as a rolled blanket with a slicker around it.

"By Jove!" exclaimed Dent. "I'd thought that I'd be in time to come for you, but here you've come for me, Miriam. I'm terribly ashamed."

"What do you mean by that?" she asked, frowning in her anger. "And why in the world are you in your riding togs? Have you quarreled with Dad about me?"

It was a new angle, and one which was not unwelcome, from his point of view.

"I couldn't help it," he said. "Mister Standard let his tongue get quite away from him, Miriam. One can't stand up and hear such things, you must admit."

She could not help smiling. He was so slender and pale compared with old Judge Standard's bulk and bronze. Yet, she liked him better than she had ever liked him before. There was a certain quiet gallantry about him and his defiance. All at once she found herself pitying him with a warmed heart, and liking him very much.

"You quarreled with Dad, and so you were going to ride away from the ranch, Manning?"

"Of course, but not alone."

"What?"

"Come, come, Miriam. Of course, you're going to revolt at such usage. And, of course, you're going to leave home, and, of course, I'm going to take care of you. Isn't that all simple?"

She swallowed another smile. It was rather odd that she should be facing elopement with Manning Underwood Dent.

"You're a desperately reckless fellow," she said.

"Well, well," he answered, "I see that you're going to have your laugh at me. I don't mind. I'm too fond of you to care about the little things, Miriam."

He said it so simply that his words struck noon in her heart again.

"But then you knew. I've never said it, but you've always known that I loved you, and that I was hanging about, ready to be used."

"You dear, old thing," murmured Miriam. "I didn't know anything of the kind. But *will* you take me away, Manning?"

"This instant."

"Not until I get my hat and coat."

She whirled to run down the hall, but then the excitement caught hold of her, and half in friendship and half in fun she leaned quickly to Manning Dent and touched his lips with hers, a kiss which poured the brain of that young man full of rose-tinted visions, in the midst of which she departed down the hall.

Chapter Six
"A Piece of Rope"

No sleep came to the eyes of Charlie Bender that night for some time. At length, he decided that he would stay awake and strive to puzzle out the bewildering problem of the strange cowpuncher. He had seen enough now to allow him to put certain of the details together. There was silence, expertness with a gun, great ability to trail and handle horses—as certainly was most conclusively proved in the capture of The Gold King—and finally there was the pale face with which he had originally appeared at the ranch. Such pallor, for instance, grew rapidly in shade—never in sunshine. That the pallor was not natural with Noisy Joe Hanover was amply proved by the bronze skin with which he had returned from the chase of The Gold King. Where and how had his skin become white?

There was a sharp and shocking answer for that. *No shade is so deep as a prison shade. And what but a prison could have kept from the sweep of the sun and the wind such a lover of horses and guns?* Charlie Bender nodded to himself. This was a thought that might have come in the nick of time. Certainly, if there was a shadow of a truth in it, he could crush forever the absurd pretentions of Noisy Joe to the hand of Miriam. He decided that, when the morning came, he would ride to town and send out a few inquiries by wire, which might bring in replies that would make Noisy Joe strike out for the tall timber.

This conclusion had soothed Charlie Bender to such a point that his eyes were closed, and he was about to sink into sleep, when a shadow crossed his face. He did not open his eyes wide. Fear prompted him merely to peer up through his lashes; what he saw was the face of Noisy Joe leaning close above him and studying his features, with a most intense interest by the dim light in the bunkhouse. So dim was that light that he himself could barely make out the outline of Noisy's face. But what he could see convinced him that there was a devil in the mind of Joe this night. The brow was scowling, the jaw of the cowpuncher thrust out, and it seemed to Charlie Bender that a dangerous gleam of light was in his eyes. In a moment, whatever was the purpose that had brought him to lean over the foreman, he was apparently satisfied, for he turned away. He stole across the floor of the bunkhouse, and that floor, which squeaked and protested even when a man shifted his weight in a chair, remained utterly noiseless under the tread of Joe Hanover. It seemed to the foreman that this was the final and crowning stroke of mystery. It spelled only one thing, and that was the training of a thief, for only a thief could have moved so like a shadow.

Now Noisy Joe was sitting on the step at the door of the bunkhouse. He rolled a cigarette and lighted it, and Charlie Bender swore that he could not hear the scratching of the match. Not only that, but the flame of the match and then the glow of the cigarette were both so carefully masked by the deft fingers of Hanover that only the fragrance of the burning tobacco, blowing back into the room, made Bender sure that the cowpuncher was, indeed, smoking.

This went on for some time, and all the while the heart of the foreman was increasing its heat. What manner of man was this who worked all day and then sat up most of the night in silence, covering the glow of his cigarette with an instinctive caution?

All of this would bear examination, and examination it should certainly have, as Bender was now promising himself, when the cowpuncher rose from the step, jerked his hat lower over his eyes, and disappeared.

Bender did not wait long to make sure whether or not Noisy Joe would return. After a moment he slipped out of his bunk and stole to the door. There he saw Noisy Joe walking down toward the corral, with saddle and bridle caught over the crook of his arm. In that corral he saddled and bridled a horse which even at this distance and even by the starlight was recognizable as The Gold King. He did not waste time by lowering the bars, leading out the horse, and then putting them up again. Instead, he sent the stallion at the fence and took it at a great, easy leap. He was in no pressing hurry, however. Instead of sprinting the stallion across the hills, he jogged away and disappeared by slow degrees in the dimness. Then Charlie Bender acted. It required one minute for him to equip himself. The loud snoring of Lefty in one corner of the room masked the noise of his preparations. With his gun belted on and his bridle and saddle over his arm, he left the bunkhouse and ran down to the corrals.

The tall brown mare, the one he himself had broken and exclusively used for the past three years, was caught up. He tossed the saddle on her and in another moment was flying through the night on the trail of Hanover. He found that, easily and smoothly as The Gold King had rocked away through the night, he had nevertheless opened up a very considerable gap. He put the brown mare, Nan, to the top of her speed. They shot over the swales and into the hollows until the sand, which flew up from her forehoofs, cut and stung his face. At length, he was rewarded by a distant sight of the wanderer. The color of the stallion made it impossible to conceal her even in so feeble a light as this. One might as well have tried to cover from view a great spot of burnished gold.

They were deep in the hills by this time, so that he lost sight of the yellow horse most of the time. In fact, there was one interval of a hundred yards during which the stallion disappeared. In the fear that the night wanderer might have changed his course, Charlie Bender pressed ahead with all speed and shot the mare down a narrow gully. Where, indeed, could Noisy Joe Hanover be bound?

It might even be that he had sensed the new suspicion which had formed in the mind of the foreman, just as he had been able to sense, by a single glance into the bunkhouse, that a strong-handed reception was waiting for him there. So, knowing that Bender would not rest until he had unearthed the truth about Noisy Joe, the latter had fled in the middle of the night and taken with him the horse which, as he pretended, he had brought down for Miriam Standard.

No wonder that Charlie Bender spurred hard to get up with

43

his quarry. When he reached the other, there would be trouble, of course, but Charlie Bender was unafraid. He had used a Colt before this, and he was ready to use one again, if the worst came to the worst. The facts about Noisy Joe Hanover must be his.

He shot down to the bottom of the gulch, whirled the big brown mare around a corner of the rocks, and then he saw, topping a rise just beyond, the form of The Gold King, crisply cut against the starry heavens. He drew in on the reins, but, before the mare could slacken her pace, Charlie Bender was caught across the breast, flicked out of his saddle, spun thrice over and over in the air, while the stars became sparks of fire from a pinwheel, and then he landed solidly upon his face.

If he had not regained consciousness at once, he would have died by choking, for every spoonful of breath was knocked out of him. But the stabbing pain from a cut on the forehead roused him, and he began to fight for a breath. To the uninitiated it may seem that to be out of breath is nothing. To men who knew of it only by being hit in the stomach when they are boxing like boys, and to women who know of it only when a morsel goes down the wrong way—being out of breath will seem a trivial thing. But Charlie Bender did not find it so. It was as if the foot of a mastodon, covering his entire body, had pressed down just far enough to collapse completely the bellows of the lungs. When he strove to get air back into the cells, he could not do it. He wriggled around on his back, like a fish out of water. He gnashed at the air, as a wolf bites at raw meat. He felt the veins of his face swelling, until it seemed that the skin must burst. And so at length, having passed through the drawn-out tortures of a dozen deaths, he could draw a free, long breath. On shaking arms he supported himself and dragged down the priceless air. He had never before known that mere breathing could be a delight. Finally his head was cleared. He rose, weak and unsteady, and, having gained his feet, bound up the bleeding wound in his head with a bandanna and began to look about for the cause of the trouble. The big brown mare came back to stand by and watch, as though she, too, wished to learn the meaning of this mysterious and most rapid dismounting.

It was childishly simple when he found it. It was simply a rope tied across the trail from a rock to a tree. Trembling with shame and anger, he untied the rope and examined it by the light of a match. Yes, it was the rope of Noisy Joe. He himself had given the new hand that rope and taught him some of the ways to use it.

Bender gnashed his teeth with rage. He dared not go back to the boys at the ranch and tell them what had happened. It would make him appear in much too undignified a light. No, he must keep his grievance to himself, and, when the occasion came—if ever he could lay eyes on Noisy Joe Hanover again. . . .

He gave himself up to an ecstacy of prospect. He saw himself landing a hard fist squarely on the point of Noisy's jaw. He saw Noisy fall. He saw himself mopping Noisy's face against the splintered floor. His ears drank in the sweet music of Hanover's yells for mercy. But in the meantime, what was to be his next step? He could not follow blindly on through the night. He had lost priceless time through this accident, and it would be folly to attempt to trail the matchless speed of The Gold King any more this night.

So he climbed reluctantly into the saddle again and swung Nan off the hill trail and to the south, a shorter cut back toward the ranch. If that story ever were told, how the 'punchers would laugh. They would say that Noisy Joe could do nothing with his rope except to make it fight for him. Bender himself grinned like a goblin of fury as the thought came home to him.

Chapter Seven
"Into the Lion's Trap"

The back stairs of the Standard house were steep and narrow, but they did not squeak. Therefore, it was down this exit that Miriam went, leading the way for her hero, and Manning Underwood Dent followed softly behind her. They went out the back, where the screen door mercifully did not screech. Chung Li was never able to touch that door without sending a knife edge through the ears of everyone in the house.

In the open, Miriam felt more relieved; half of the thing was done. She talked the rest over on the way down to the corral.

"Where do you think we'd better go, Manning? We're out of the lion's trap. But where shall we go now? We can't drop into a hole in the ground, you know."

"Well," said Manning, "I've always noticed that something happens. One never starves. Something always pops up. It will for us, too, old dear."

Miriam grinned through the kindly dark. There was a delightful childishness about Dent. He was like a fresh wind in the face after a night of sweltering heat. She could think better when she had him as a background or an audience.

"But where are we *going*, Manning?"

"Oh, somewhere."

"What does that mean?"

"Well, we can just light out and keep right on going until we hit some place that looks comfortable."

"Hmm," said Miriam. "We could ride our horses to death in some directions around here before we reached any comfort. We must find something more concrete than that, Manning."

"Yes, one thing, of course."

"And that?"

"We'll have to find a minister before we go far."

"Minister?"

"Isn't that reasonable?"

"Minister," she echoed.

"Because I can't be wandering around all night with a girl. Not at night, Miriam. It might spoil my reputation . . . and yours. I've certainly never done anything like that before."

Miriam laughed, but there was no mirth in the sound.

"After all, I think you're right. We *can't* rove all over the mountains without being married." Here she turned and shook her fist fiercely in the direction of the ranch house. "It will serve him right!"

"What will?" asked Manning.

"Nothing. But did you ever hear of such madness, Manning? Did you ever hear of such a thing?"

"As eloping the way we're doing?"

"No, no, no! I mean he swore that he'd make me marry that Hanover creature, if he had to drag me to the altar with his own hands."

"What a horrible catastrophe! You wouldn't have been able to marry me, then."

"Not without breaking the law." Miriam managed to laugh again.

"I don't understand you, Miriam. Laughing at such a time. Think of being a cowpuncher's wife."

"If I don't laugh, I'll cry. And now I'm going to marry *you*, Manning."

47

"Are you going to cry or laugh about *that*?"

"What in the world are we going to live on?"

"Why . . . why . . . of course, your father . . . he'll make some reasonable provision."

"Not Dad. You don't know him. He won't find a penny for us. He'd turn me away from his door if I were starving, after tonight. He's as proud as the gate of the other world, Manning."

"But . . . well, there are ways of picking up money. You have that collection of engravings, you know, in your own name. That would bring something."

"Of course."

"And then your father can't live forever."

"I hope he does. I wouldn't take a dollar of his money, except to give it to charity."

"Miriam, what nonsense."

"Let's get our horses. I don't want to talk any more. And for heaven's sake, don't get me angry, Manning."

He knew her well enough and long enough to understand the full weight of that threat. So he went on to the corrals, and they soon had secured two horses and climbed into the saddles. Then they struck away for the trail through the hills. At the top of the first rise Manning Dent drew rein for a moment.

"Dear heaven," he murmured. "To think that I'm rushing on toward the step from which I can never draw back. To think. . . . Why, it turns me positively cold, Miriam."

"Bah," said Miriam.

"What did you say, my dear?"

"I said let's find a minister and get the party over before I change my mind. And then, when Dad hears, let him rave and swear. It'll be no use . . . it'll be no use."

She repeated the last phrase in a tone between sobbing and rage. And Manning Underwood Dent felt that it might be very wise to ask no questions, but simply to ride on through the night, as fast as possible. And this was what he did for a full half hour. No matter what Miriam might think about an agreement and compromise with her father, Manning Dent had ideas of his own. Let her talk as much as she pleased before their marriage, but afterward it was to be otherwise. He would be the lord and the master, and his word would be the law in their household. It would be very strange if he could not, at the worst, shame the rancher into making an adequate provision for the household of his only child. On the whole Manning was very well satisfied. His long sojourn among the wilds of the West, if they made him the heir of the rich Standard, had been distinctly worth while. In addition to the money, Miriam was a wonder.

This train of thought amused him so completely that he did not need to speak, and they had ridden on for thirty or forty minutes, when Miriam called softly to him and then stopped her horse. He followed that example at once.

"Manning," she said, "have you a gun?"

"A g-gun? Of course not!"

"Can you *use* a gun if you have one?"

"I . . . I. . . ."

"Are you afraid?" she asked in sudden disgust.

"But why are you asking all these questions about guns? I'm not a particularly martial character. . . ."

"We're being followed," she explained. "That's why I'm asking queer questions."

"Impossible! Who would follow us . . . your father?"

"It's not he. Get off your horse and put your ear down low."

"Why waste time, if we are being followed?"

"Because we can't get away from the horse that's coming. Do as I say!"

He obeyed. Now he heard, far off and each second drawing nearer, the rhythmic beat of a galloping horse's hoofs. It required only half a second for Manning Dent to leap into the saddle.

"Let's ride on, Miriam."

"We'll never get away from that rider."

"But how can any one dare. . . ."

"This isn't Forty-second Street and Broadway, Manning. A lot of things are dared out here that would make your hair stand on end, and my father is the very man to do the daring. But what sort of horse can it be? It's coming like the very wind."

"Can you stop to think about a horse at such a time as this?"

"God willing, I hope I'll never be too busy to think about horses. Listen to that wonder tear."

The hoofbeats were purring like sticks on a drum, and the sound flowed out of the night upon them. To the excited imagination of Dent it seemed that the noise swallowed them up with its power.

"L-l-let me have that revolver," he breathed.

"I'll keep it myself, Manning," she answered. "And I think you'd better let me do the talking, too, in case the rider is really coming for us. In the meantime let's go on at a slow trot."

Dent did not reply, and they started ahead. Now little shivers wriggled up and down the back of Dent. A voice behind them spoke: "Miriam!"

"Oh, Lord," groaned Dent. "They are after us."

A small, strong, little hand gripped the sleeve of his coat and jerked it.

"Listen to me, Manning."

"How can I listen, when . . . ?"

"If you show yourself a fool and a coward now, I'll kill you myself. Do you hear?"

"What are you saying? Have you gone mad, Miriam?"

"I say, that if the people knew that I've eloped with a coward. . . . Manning, for heaven's sake, be a man. Nobody is going to eat you."

"Halt, there!" called the voice that was running up from the rear.

There was nothing for it but to halt.

As they swung around, Miriam saw the rider coming swiftly through the starlight, and on the sleek body of the horse the light glistened, as if on a lake of gold. It was The Gold King, and this was the man most detested in the world by her.

"Manning," she breathed, "we've just gone out for a midnight ride because neither of us could sleep. You understand? A midnight ride . . . intending to come back."

"Yes, yes," chattered Manning.

If only he would be a man. But there was no hope of that. In another instant the voice of the rider barked at them: "Hands up, Dent!"

And up were flung the arms of Manning Dent.

"For heaven's sake," he screamed, "don't shoot!"

Chapter Eight
"Hanover Explains"

For the moment Miriam was blinded with shame. Then, when she was able to see, she took note that the newcomer had not drawn a revolver to enforce his command. No, he simply cantered up to Dent and now ordered him to hold his hands behind his back.

"Don't do it, Manning!" she cried. "He has no right. Who are you to give such orders, sir?"

"I'm unarmed," whined Dent. "How can I resist, Miriam?"

And, putting his hands behind his back, they were instantly and deftly secured by the stranger with a few twists of a short tie rope.

"Then," exclaimed Miriam, "if you can't help yourself, I'll help myself and you, too! Mister Hanover, I think I recognize you."

"Thank you, ma'am," said the man of the night. "You're uncommon quick to recognize voices."

"Then put up your hands, Mister Hanover. Put them up, sir. I'm armed, and I'll use my weapon rather than. . . ."

"Tush, tush," laughed Joe Hanover. "I don't think you're ready to work a killing. That's even ahead of your advanced spirit."

Without haste he reached out, took her revolver by the muzzle, and removed it from her hand with a twist so gentle that she hardly realized that he had used force.

"How detestable you are," gasped Miriam. "And . . . and why didn't I press the trigger?"

"Because it's a hard thing, ma'am, for a woman to kill her future husband."

She groaned with her fury. "What do you intend to do?"

"You'll understand in another moment."

He had slipped to the ground.

"Mister Hanover. . . ."

Her cry of alarm and anger came, as he slipped the noose of a tie rope over her foot and lashed it into the stirrup.

"What do you mean . . . ?"

"Sit quiet, ma'am! There'll be no harm to you if. . . ."

But Miriam was desperate. She swung down and grasped at the butt of a holstered gun, only to have her hand caught and then her other hand. In a thrice they were tied together. She could not dismount, with one foot lashed into a stirrup and her two hands bound together. He deliberately passed around to the farther side of the horse and tied the other foot into its stirrup, exactly as he had done the first. Not only this, but he passed another rope beneath the belly of the horse and bound the two stirrups together.

In the meantime the tongue of Miriam was not idle. She told him in detail all the terrible things that were destined to happen to him in the immediate future. She vowed a vengeance so great that the falling of the heavens would be as nothing compared with her wrath. But he went calmly on with his work, and, when he had secured her to his satisfaction, he proceeded to tie poor Manning Underwood Dent into his saddle in the same fashion.

"My dear fellow," wailed Manning, "what can possibly be in your mind? Do you know what you're doing, and to whom you're doing it? Do you know what any court in the land will do, when a free citizen . . . ?"

"Listen to me, son," said Noisy Joe Hanover. "I'm going to give you a free-for-nothing description of yourself. You ain't a free citizen . . . you ain't even as good as a coyote. You're a hybrid cross between a skunk and a snake. You take a girl away from her home and her father at night, and you run away with her because you figure that marrying her is an easy way of making a living. Is that the straight of it? Then you have the nerve to step up and call yourself a free citizen. Son, if you open your trap again, I'll drop a chunk of lead down your throat and see how it rides in your stomach."

This brutal outpouring of words completely spiked the guns of the worthy Dent; they even accomplished something with Miriam. In the first place, she was exceedingly surprised that Noisy Joe should have spoken at such length and with such force. In the second place, she began to see that there was point and substance to the things he had said. It was assuredly not the most honorable thing in the world for a man to run off with a girl by night, even if she were a willing partner—or more than willing. There was nothing to call it except low.

She could hear Dent murmuring softly to himself. The

53

fellow was in a white panic. A sharp word might have made him faint.

In the meantime their captor was proceeding with his work which consisted in tying the bridles of Miriam's and Dent's horses together. That done, he attached a lead rope to Dent's horse, swung into his saddle on The Gold King, and started off down the trail. Once he paused, turned back, and touched the rope that tied her hands with his knife.

"I hope that rope hasn't hurt your wrists," he said.

She would not speak. Her fury was so great that she was afraid sobs instead of words would break forth. When he saw that he would get no answer, he calmly laid hold of one of her wrists. His grip was not hard, but, when she wrenched against it, it was like pulling at a glove of iron. He now lighted a match, examined the skin carefully, and announced that the wrists were simply chafed.

"And mine are, too . . . terribly," cried Manning Dent.

The answer of the cowpuncher, however, was brutally curt and to the point.

"It will do you good," he said, and went on ahead with The Gold King.

They continued in this fashion for some time, not a word being spoken on either side. As they swung out from the hill trail and started across a region of deeper sand and fewer trees, heading straight back to the ranch house, a horseman with a leveled gun plunged suddenly out of a thicket.

His challenge brought up the hands of Noisy Joe quickly enough. And Miriam, her heart swelling with gratitude, recognized the voice of the foreman, Charlie Bender. If she could not with a single smile bend that man around her finger and twist him into foolish knots, she would foreswear all pretense at knowledge of men.

"Keep your arms straight!" Bender was commanding. "And who's back up there? Miss Miriam? What, you infernal rat, have you been up to, and where are you taking them?"

But the infernal rat did not answer. In fact, he did not speak again during the rest of the night until the dawn had come.

"Now keep quiet, while I get this gun out of your holster," began Charlie Bender. "You dirty dog, you played me a trick tonight that I'll make you sweat for. You played me a trick that I'll write into your hide for you, so's it'll be easy to remember. When. . . ."

He got no further. Noisy Joe, sitting straight as a ramrod in the saddle, suddenly swung the foot that was farthest away from Bender over the neck of his horse and jammed the high heel of his riding boot squarely between the eyes of the foreman, as the latter leaned to reach for the gun.

There was only one possible result. Charlie Bender dropped out of his saddle, as if he had been shot. By the time his senses returned his hands were bound securely behind him. Then he was assisted to his feet and helped back into the saddle. His head was still reeling, while he was secured to the stirrups, just as the other two had been. Then a handkerchief was tied around his bleeding forehead, and his horse was secured to the saddle of The Gold King. When all this was done, the procession started on once more.

Miriam had something to say now. The foreman, as his brain cleared, had still more to remark. But they received no answer from Noisy Joe. The latter held steadily on his way until he reached the crest of a hill from which they could all look down on the ranch house. There he dismounted and sat cross-legged on a rock, smoking one cigarette after another. In this fashion, two mortal hours passed.

Whoever has had to ride steadily for two hours over rough and smooth will testify that a saddle becomes an uncomfortable seat long before the end of that period. But far worse than any riding is to sit motionless in a saddle during such a length of time. There were many groans from poor Manning Underwood Dent before the time had ended, and Miriam more than once thought that she would faint from sheer exhaustion. Yet their complaints did not receive the slightest answer from the cowpuncher.

It was not until the dawn began to turn the mountains gray that he rose and climbed into his saddle. But still he lingered until the sky was rosy, and then the rim of the sun pushed up in the east. As soon as that happened, he began a leisurely progress down the hill.

At last, his course was clear to the others. He had waited until he could bring his procession of captives in the full light of day. He had waited until there would be not a shadow to conceal their shame and their fury from a score of curious eyes. The ranch houses were laid out before them as clear as a picture. And now in the distance they could see the cowpunchers coming out of the bunkhouse.

Suddenly there seemed to be an alarm. There was a scurry for the corrals. The form of old Judge Standard could be made out, leading the way. In a trice saddles were clapped on horses. And then someone saw the fugitives returning.

There was still time, however, to escape from the wretched position in which they were. Charlie Bender was the first to make an appeal. He saw for himself the most horrible ruin. It seemed to him that he had been attacked by a man with the power of a very devil. Now he was to be exposed to the eyes of his men, knowing that his reputation would be blasted forever by what they saw of him—led like a horse with a halter, tied, helpless, a fool before the eyes of the world. Charlie Bender, therefore, was the first to break down. He begged the cowpuncher by all that was holy to cut his bonds and make him a free man. He swore to him undying friendship and affection. He would toil and moil in the service of kind Joe Hanover, swore the foreman. To the end of life he would never show the slightest malice for what had happened on this strange night. Besides all of which, he had in his pocket fifty dollars in currency that he would be only too happy if Joe Hanover would accept it.

Joe Hanover did not hear. His dreamy eyes were fixed far

off among the hills. And then the girl wakened to the full understanding of what was about to happen. If it was disgrace for a mere foreman to be seen in a ridiculous situation, what would it be to her, who expected actually to own that ranch and to direct the men who were working on it?

Miriam glanced aside to Manning Underwood Dent, and there rose in her scornful lips the cowpuncher's nickname: Mud! He was just that, a shapeless, lifeless lump of humanity. The long wait, sitting motionless in the saddle, had been hard even upon Bender and Miriam, though they were used to riding. But for Manning Dent it had been almost death. He slumped over now with a pale face, gaping mouth, coat bunched around the shoulders, necktie awry, hat on the back of his head, and his hair streaming down toward his eyes. And this was the fellow who would be pointed out as the lover of Judge Standard's daughter. This was the man the cowpunchers would remember thereafter. She could already feel their smiles eating into the small of her back. She had two desires. The first was to kill Noisy Joe Hanover and feed his body to the coyotes; the second was to melt away into the earth and be seen by no eye. She would have paid five years of life for five minutes of invisibility.

And Noisy Joe Hanover? He seemed quite unchanged by the night of action that had just been spent. His shoulders were just as thin as ever, his body was just as slender, and his eyes not a shade more weary.

For a moment even her hatred for him was swallowed up in an overwhelming wave of wonder. What was there in him that made him such a master? He had gone out alone and captured a wild mustang that had been chased in vain by many men, with parties of hunters, for several years. And now, tonight, he had mastered her and Dent, and, though Dent was nothing, the manner of Hanover had led her to think that a much greater opposition would have been of no avail against him. She must strike now, or forever give up all hopes of becoming the actual manager of the ranch. That

57

disgusting betrayal of her weakness before all the 'punchers would make it impossible for them ever to take her seriously. And, knowing this, she was fighting for existence itself, when she begged, and then commanded, Joe Hanover to set her loose from her companion.

But Joe Hanover did not even take the cigarette from between his lips. He merely turned his head, regarded her with dull eyes for an instant, and then continued on his way. It was a hopeless battle, and Miriam resigned herself as well as she could.

Here came the men of the Standard forces. They poured around her. They sent a great volley of questions from a distance, and then, sweeping up, they saw the picture in detail and were struck dumb. Here was their foreman, their strong-handed, hard-headed leader who had so far raised himself above their level that it was commonly believed throughout the range that the judge intended to take in his foreman as a junior partner with a small interest in the firm. And here he was with a bandaged head, his hands tied behind his back, his feet lashed into his stirrups, and upon his face black blood and dust and a yet blacker frown.

But, far more wonderful, behind him came that proud young lady, Miriam herself—tied into her saddle, while her horse's bridle was tied to the bridle of the man they delighted to call, in their scorn and their anger, Mud.

Standard himself had a late start, but he arrived an instant after the main body of his men, in time to hear the foreman calling: "Lefty . . . Mike . . . a couple of you kick that swine, Hanover, out of his saddle and cut these ropes . . . then I'll finish him up piecemeal."

"Wait a minute," commanded Standard. "I'll have a look into this."

He paid no more attention to Miriam than if she had not been there. He pushed his horse straight up to The Gold King and confronted Hanover.

"What the devil is the meaning of this outrage, Hanover? Explain yourself!"

"Only this," said Noisy Joe, and he reluctantly took the cigarette from between his lips. "Only this . . . I'm not particularly happy about having the girl I'm going to marry gallivanting around at night with something like this."

He indicated Mud with a jerk of his thumb over his shoulder. And the latter straightened feebly and made a vain effort to become dignified.

"So I just went after them," went on Noisy Joe, "and I brought them back and asked them to do their riding by day. This other one"—and here a similar gesture indicated the foreman—"started bothering me, so I had to bring him along."

Chapter Nine
"Bender Changes His Mind"

That brilliant, if erratic, genius, Jacques Casanova, has pointed out that a guilty man has usually more chance of receiving a lenient sentence, or even acquittal, if he tells the plain truth without distortion than if he tries to wash his hands white and protect himself from danger with a great barrier of lies. For once a lie is known, all he has said is equally damned, and his entire effort falls at a blow to the ground. But if the truth is so powerful to win sympathy, an understatement is still more mighty.

Had Noisy Joe Hanover poured forth a denunciation of

Manning Dent because the latter had attempted to steal away the rancher's daughter by night, had he heaped the shrinking rascal with abuse, perhaps Dent would have been thought sufficiently punished. Or, if he had attacked the foreman himself with smarting words, it was more than probable that the cowpunchers and the rancher would have felt their own dignity impeached by the treatment their foreman had received. But the mild understatements of Noisy Joe seemed hints at greater things. The men grew angry because this dull fellow had not seemed to understand just how near that night had brought Miriam to a catastrophe. Elopement with such a man as Manning Dent! It made their blood run cold.

The rancher saw their mood at a glance. He had Dent freed and turned him over to his men to be escorted to the nearest railway station. To that point, accordingly, he was taken, but, by the time he arrived, the wheat of his manhood had been winnowed away and only the chaff was left. His blood was hardly warm before he got back to the roar of Manhattan, and the wounds that cunningly welded quirts had cut across his back did not heal for many a day after that.

It was only one of many steps in Manning Dent's long career of intrigue, which at last landed him the desire of his life—a rich wife—but it was the step that clung longest in his mind. And to this very day he had rather lift a rattler by the head than smile at a woman whose birthplace is west of the Rockies.

Dent was disposed of in this satisfactory fashion. There remained the foreman and Miriam. The problems here were different. What Standard wanted most of all, it seemed, was to uproot her old ideas and purpose of running the ranch, when it came into her hands; but, though the adventure of the night shook her, it did not break her will. Father and daughter straightway indulged in a long and fierce verbal battle that lasted the rest of the morning. She insisted upon two things: the discharge of the wretch who had dared to handle her as Noisy Joe had done, and the discharge, also,

of all the cowpunchers who had witnessed her shame. To
these demands Judge Standard replied with laughter. And
when she pressed the point, he informed her curtly that, if
he had intended before to see that she fulfilled her promise
of marrying Noisy Joe, he would now never be content until
he had accomplished that object.

It was a subject that brought into the face of the girl an
expression of frightened horror.

"I know it's only a way of yours to plague me," she cried.
"But when I hear you talk that way, Dad, it makes me cold
to the heart."

"You take all this for a joke?"

"Don't I know that you're every bit as proud as I am . . .
and much prouder? You'd rather see me in my grave than
married to a stupid, uneducated, soulless cowpuncher . . . a
man as blunt and thick-skinned as the cattle he herds."

"Is he all that?" asked her father. "He seemed to me
rather a remarkable chap, Miriam. In the first place, the capture of The Gold King is a good deal more than it may sound
to be. Fifty men have chased that mustang, I imagine.
They've done it with bands and gangs of horses. Noisy Joe
did it by himself."

"By working three months! Who but a brute would give
up three months of his vital life to the capture of another
brute?"

"D'you mean that, Miriam?"

"Of course, I do . . . every word of it. Father, do you think
that I'm mad?"

"A man that would give up three months to capturing a
horse is a man after my own heart. Besides, Hanover was
doing a good deal more. He was capturing a wife at the same
time . . . and you might admit that some wives are worth
three months' trouble on the part of a man."

She bit her lip. There was about her father such an air of
mingled good humor, mockery, and determination that she
quite failed to make him out. Had he simply opposed her

61

anger and resolution with anger and resolution on his own part, she would have been at home in fighting back. But this poised surety was something new. It was as though the rancher were playing with marked cards that made Miriam a mere helpless dupe.

"And, besides the capture of the horse, there was the capture of you the other night, Miriam. You must admit that's something worthwhile."

"If the man riding with me had been anything other than a coward and a fool. . . ."

"But, suppose, Miriam, that just to spite me and prove yourself independent you had married this coward and fool, as you call him?"

She started. She had not looked upon it from just that angle. There was enough justice in the remark to make her very angry.

"But, of course, I never intended to marry him," she declared.

"Of course not," grinned her father.

His mirth at this point was so out of place that she stamped her foot and cried: "What in the world has happened to you, Dad?"

"It's a game, dear," said the judge. "You've been too much for me all your life. I've fought and sworn and laid awake at night trying to think of plans of getting around you. But I always lost. You were too quick in the brain for me. Now, Miriam, the tables are turned. I sit back at my ease and watch another man lay the net around you, and I know that you cannot escape."

Something akin to fear rose in the heart of Miriam.

"What utter nonsense," she breathed. "Why, Dad, don't you know that I have only to say one word to free myself from any man in the world? I have only to say no. Isn't it true?"

He shook his head, grinning again.

"Not true with Noisy Joe. He seems to be of different metal from your other suitors."

It swept her back to the tales in the fairy stories of young girls forced to marry—or almost forced to marry—against their wills. And she studied the face of her father with a new and profound interest. She thought that she was beginning to see new things in his eyes—a certain hardness, an ability to put himself at a distance from her and consider her not as his daughter, but as a human being quite unattached to him. It increased the fear that had been growing in her heart like shadows in the corners of a twilight room. He had become so strange that she was beginning to feel different herself. All the world was gone mad, and she was mad with it.

"If you persist in letting that man hound me," she stated, "there is only one thing I can do."

"And that, my dear?"

"I . . . I'll ask some of the boys to dispose of him . . . to get him out of the way."

"Ask some of the boys to get him out of the way?" echoed the judge, and then, exploding into tremendous laughter, he threw himself back in his chair and filled the room with the thunder of his mirth.

"That's rare . . . that's good," he said at last. "You go ahead and ask some of the boys to get him out of the way, and then you just wait and see how far they move him."

"All those men in the bunkhouse?"

"Even all those men in the bunkhouse."

"Dad," she murmured, struck with awe," if he's such a terrible man, who is he? What has he done? What do you know about him?"

"Terrible man? Rot! I know that he's manhandled you and two men on the same night and caught The Gold King all by himself. I say that one man like that can't be handled by twenty ordinary cowpunchers. Took all Europe to beat Napoleon, Miriam."

63

"I see that there is going to be nothing for me to do except to leave the ranch and go to Paris again."

"Miriam, I'd a lot rather have you in Paris than on this ranch, if you're going to be a cattle woman."

It was perfectly true, and she knew that she would be simply playing into his hand if she executed her threat. It made her silent, and silently she left the room.

She sat down in the library, and, there, with her face in her hands, she tried to think her way through the entire puzzling tangle. While she was there, she heard the voice of Charlie Bender in the room where she had left her father.

He had come to resign. He spoke in a rather high, monotonously sharp key. He appreciated the kind treatment and the great confidence that the rancher had given to him, but he could no longer stay on a place where the men did not respect him. It was in vain that the rancher argued. Miriam heard him put forth a long string of promises—heard him tell how necessary Charlie had proved himself on the place—how lost they would be without him—but there was nothing strong enough to shake the resolution of Charlie Bender. His dignity had split upon a rock, and it would never sail the seas again.

"Besides," he concluded, "I want to be a free agent when I fight it out with Hanover."

"Fight it out with him?" roared the rancher in horror.

"Just that. D'you think I'm yaller, Standard?"

"Wait! Wait!" cried the judge, and his voice at once fell into an indistinguishable murmur, from which Miriam could understand nothing, no matter how she strained her ears.

Suddenly the foreman shouted: "What? You don't mean it."

"I do, though. I swear I do, Charlie."

Five minutes later Charlie Bender, his resignation apparently withdrawn, was swinging out of the house and whistling joyously on his way toward the bunkhouse.

What was the secret which the rancher had told him? What

had removed all his shame and made him suddenly so happy?

Once more Miriam felt the skin of her back pucker, as with cold.

Chapter Ten
"A Dash for Liberty"

Of course, she was accustomed to difficult problems, for all her life she had been studying at one thing or another, but here was a difficulty rather larger than usual. Other things could be puzzled out if one used patience and brain power lavishly enough. But to attack the conundrum of Noisy Joe Hanover was like trying to unriddle the smile of the sphinx.

What could it be about him? What was the fact which, when mentioned, had taken all the sting out of the shame of the foreman? What had made him leave the house singing and laughing? But certainly Noisy Joe was not entirely a joke. She remembered the easy efficiency with which he had disposed of Charlie Bender that night. Charlie was a big man, and she had heard her father say more than once that he was worth his weight in wildcats, when it came to a fight. And yet the slender cowpuncher had crushed the larger man without effort. He had moved, indeed, so casually and smoothly that she could hardly conceive of any force great enough to stop him. He had seemed to be striking with a lazy leisureliness, and yet there had been a blinding speed that had paralyzed the efforts of Bender.

A sphinx, indeed! For here was the granite power and the smile behind the force. Of course, she told herself, something would happen to keep her from the horrible fate of becoming this man's wife. Something was sure to happen—she had rather die than submit. And yet, when she remembered how he had been twice successful against great odds, the old horror swept back over her. If it had been something known and acknowledged—something definitely to fight against—she would not have budged. But there was nothing in plain sight. Certainly there was no possible way of explaining that maddening certainty of her father's that she would have to marry the cowpuncher in the end. And, because there was such a mystery about it, she decided that she could not stay. The ranch was like a great trap to her. She had to leave.

She spent the afternoon in sleep to make up for her lost rest of the evening before. At supper she put on a cheerful face, and, afterward, she sat in the living room at the piano and sang the "Raggle Taggle Gypsies" and other favorites of her father, as long as he cared to ask for them. But when he had gone up to bed, she retired to her room and made her preparations for departure. There would be no one with her this time, and, therefore, the alarm of her father must be of a different nature. She rather cruelly rejoiced in the fear that must prey upon him the next morning when her absence was noted.

Forty miles due north lay the ranch of the Sigmund Jones family. She was an old playmate of Harriet Jones, and to Harriet now she intended to flee. On the way she would have time for speculation, and on the way she would be free from the attendance of Noisy Joe Hanover on The Gold King.

So she stole out with her pack made and the food supplies taken from the larder in the kitchen. For, if something happened to delay her in the journey, she was too wise a mountain girl not to know that food must be a part of her equipment.

Down to the corrals she went, took a saddle, and started

for a horse. Of course, The Gold King was the mount she needed, if she expected to outstrip all pursuit. But though he had been made a present to her, she had not yet introduced herself to him. The horse was as gentle as a child with Noisy Joe Hanover, but he was as wild as a lion when any other human being approached him, unescorted by his first master.

The Gold King she could not take, but he should not be used by Hanover to ride up her trail, when the morning came, or to follow her this night, if it happened that he was lurking around, as he had been on the preceeding evening when she had started away with Manning Dent. She lowered the bars of his corral. Instantly he was out in a yellow flash under the stars and dipped into a gully so swiftly that the beat of his hoofs was like a single roar, like the falling of water.

After all, the mustang had been given to her, and why should she not return the stallion to his freedom, if she so chose? Yet she shrank inwardly, as she thought of the grief and the rage of her father when he learned that the famous horse had been turned into the wilderness. Let him grow still more angry, however. She carried her saddle around to the rear of the big shed where, luxurious in a box stall, stood the favorite mount of Judge Standard. It was not the old gelding so serviceable on the range, but the horse on whose back he sometimes put one of his old English saddles and posted down the road, with all the airs of a gentleman taking an airing in Central Park. He was perfectly useless for working cattle, this tall chestnut, but he had the spirit of a tornado and the speed of the same. Certainly if she sat on his back, even The Gold King would have had a hard time to come into the dust of the chestnut, Danny. And with The Gold King gone, no other could hope to live with the big gelding for a moment.

She saddled Danny, led him out, mounted, and was off like a streak. She had never backed the big fellow before, and perhaps this was the first time he had ever heard the rustle of divided skirts, which was the range style for women in the saddle. He flattened his ears, straightened his neck, and, as Lefty would have said: "Did the first mile in nothing." That spurt, however, took the edge off his desire for running, and he went on at a moderate gait.

There was need for a conservation of strength, indeed, for most of the forty miles that separated them from the Jones Ranch consisted of mountain going. She rated the gelding along at an easy pace, and soon they struck the hills. After that, their progress was slow enough, for Danny was not at home on the slopes. His long legs were meant for speed over the flat; yet, by the time the dawn came, the constant plodding had brought them so far along that they were in the thick of the peaks.

She dismounted at a pool, gave Danny a few good swallows, and ate an early cold breakfast, while Danny munched grass here and there. Then she mounted again and went on. She was hardly in the saddle, however, when she heard a noisy roar of falling stones, as though a landslide were starting behind her, and, looking back, she saw in the rose of the morning light a yellow horse plunging down a long slope, braced on stiff forelegs, and coasting like a boy in the snow.

It was very daring work. Her admiration of both horse and rider made her draw rein and stare until they came out on the level at a gallop and made toward her. Then she realized what she might have known before at the first glance—that this was The Gold King, and that on his back sat no other than the man she most detested in all the world—for it was Noisy Joe Hanover himself.

Chapter Eleven
"Invincible Logic"

He was not riding with a saddle. Instead, he sat like an Indian on a blanket that was strapped around the back of the stallion, and, since his feet were not supported, his long legs dangled far down, and his back was more bowed than ever. He looked like a hunchback, as he came up to her, with The Gold King neighing a greeting to the other horse.

Miriam was speechless. Fear had been the first emotion, then helpless surrender, and then a wild anger. She waited until he was close and then gave him the first volley.

"Will you tell me what you mean, Mister Hanover?" she asked. "Will you tell me what you mean by daring to follow me up here? Haven't I the right to privacy?"

He considered her for a moment with his eyes. Then, as though words were a foolish and unnecessary effort, he shrugged his shoulders and occupied himself with the rolling of a cigarette.

"This intolerable persecution, Mister Hanover," she went on. "It isn't possible, and yet I see you here with my own eyes. Have you no shame?"

"I thought a horse thief must have turned The Gold King loose," said the other. "So I came along to find him."

Her anger abated for a single instant in her wonder. She had last seen The Gold King loosed from the string and bound for his old wild freedom. How had the man been able to trail him and find him so quickly, with a blanket and bridle thrown over his shoulder, as he ran, and how had he been able to entice the famous mustang to his hand, once he was in sight of the fugitive?

She recovered from her wonder to discover that Joe Hanover was viewing her patiently through a smoke screen that he was casting up from the cigarette.

"Now that you have found out that no horse thief did that," she said, "you may go back."

He shrugged his shoulders again, and his carelessness brought a vicious thought into her mind.

"Is The Gold King mine?" she asked suddenly. "Did you really mean it when you said that you brought him to me?"

"I did," he nodded.

"Then get off his back and turn the horse loose. The Gold King is mine. I choose to set him free."

He dropped obediently to the ground and stripped off blanket and bridle. The Gold King followed cautiously behind him as he approached Danny.

"That's fair enough," said the cowpuncher. "I'll take Danny, then."

"What are you talking about?" demanded Miriam.

"Is Danny your horse?"

"He belongs to my father."

"I'll take him back to your father."

"This," cried Miriam, "is the most insufferable effrontry I have ever encountered."

"I'm sorry," said Noisy Joe.

"Stand out of my way," she ordered, husky with anger, as he came in front of the gelding. Yielding again to a wild passion of temper, she gave Danny the spurs.

He leaped forward like a rocket. And then the hand of Noisy Joe shot out, fastened on the rein close to the bit, and Danny was halted with such suddenness that Miriam was flung forward on the neck of the horse. She recovered herself slowly, gasping to get back the wind which had been knocked out of her lungs. It was very much as though the cowpuncher had struck her with his hand. It was not only terrible to her, but it was horrible, also. She was both frightened and disgusted.

"Will you take your hand from that rein?" she demanded.

He smiled. The cigarette had not been dislodged from his lips. And Miriam jerked up her quirt.

"Let the horse go," she commanded.

"Don't do that," urged Noisy Joe. "Please don't do that."

The quirt fell idly to her side. She felt that she had been about to strike an unchained tiger with her whip.

"What earthly right have you to stop me here?"

"What earthly right," he answered, "have you to run away with Judge Standard's horse?"

"My own father. . . ."

"I'm working for him," said the cowpuncher, "and not for you. I catch you thirty miles from the ranch at dawn on one of his horses. It's the second time you've tried to run away. I've turned The Gold King free. You're welcome to ride him if you can. I'll take Danny home with me."

There was an invincible logic in this. Any court in the land would stand behind him.

"Besides," went on Hanover, "a wife has to learn to be obedient. It's going to be a job to teach you, and I might as well start before the marriage ceremony."

Was he serious? It seemed to her that there was a faint twinkle in his eye. And once more the sight of his amusement filled her with dread more than the thought that she was in his hands.

"You are quite mad!" she managed to breathe. She added: "Take The Gold King then, and let me go on my way."

He stepped back, placed the blanket and bridle on the stallion, and, as she watched him, she followed a foolish impulse and sent Danny away at the top of his speed. Never had Danny worked more valiantly, but he might as well have tried to escape from a cloud shadow blowing across the sur-

71

face of the mountains. The Gold King drifted up beside them, dazzlingly splendid in the morning light, burnished with sweat. And Miriam drew rein again with a sob.

"Do you intend to follow me?"

"I have to," said Noisy Joe. "I can't let the girl I'm engaged to wander around like this."

"Oh," she moaned. "I'm losing my mind."

And, dropping her face in her gloved hands, she broke into tears. It was only an instant of weakness. She recovered self-control again, but she knew that she had thrown away her strength. Her first glance at him was stolen, expecting to find that he was grinning at her. But, to her amazement, he had sent The Gold King on a little ahead of her, and, with his back turned and his arms folded, he was looking down from the brow of a mountain into the valley to the east and far beneath. This certainly was a delicacy such as she had not expected from him. Then, banishing her shame, she rode up beside him and said: "Mister Hanover, we have to come to an understanding. I think I know what has happened. My father has hired you particularly to be a plague to me. Confess that's it."

He turned a little toward her in the saddle, and into his eyes, like lightning through a fog, came a flash of emotion.

"Good Lord," he murmured, "how perfectly blind you are. Do you think that I would do such things for anyone but myself?"

Chapter Twelve
"The Gold King Understands"

There was something in his manner of saying this which made the celebrated Judge Standard seem like nothing at all—a mere name without a body attached.

"What do you expect me to do?" asked Hanover. "When a man worships the very air a girl breathes . . . what is he to do about it?"

"Do other men act as you act?"

"Other men have a thousand pretty things to say to girls. I'm not like the rest. I'm not a pretty man, Miriam, and I can't talk out of character. Will you try to understand that? I had to make you notice me, and I've tried to do it."

"You've made me hate you!" she stormed.

"God knows how sorry I am for that," he said soberly enough.

Her rage had been so perfect a little time before that she had not dreamed that she could wish him anything but a wretched end. But now she felt a small, keen pang of pity.

"Will you let me tell you something?" she said.

"A thousand things."

"I think I know what you are," she said. "I've seen that you are brave and strong and patient . . . that you can fight, and that you can wait." She paused. All of these things were true. And yet it was a much more flattering picture than she had intended to draw. "After what has happened," she contined, "I can never look at you with patience. You've shamed me . . . laid me open to scorn and. . . ." She paused again, as emotion choked her. "If I knew you three years instead of three months, I could do nothing but wish I had never seen you. Go where you'll be appreciated, Mister Hanover. Go where you will find people like yourself, silent and strong and ready to appreciate silence and strength." Here she paused. "There is a man in the valley who would like to have a man like you, working on his ranch."

She pointed down into the valley. It was a beautiful picture. It might be ten miles long and half that distance in width, partly rich bottom land and partly rolling hills. Cattle and grain must be raised there, thick and fast. The river streaked through the midst of it. They could make out the small blotch which must be a mighty grouping of trees and ranch buildings.

"There is the man for you."

"Tell me about him. Why would he want me?"

"His name is Warner. He's a hard man like you, Mister Hanover. He was trapped and saddled with a crime that he hadn't committed when he was a boy. They drove him away from his home. They hounded him for ten years, I think. He became an outlaw. Of course, you've heard of Warner."

"Not in this way," he said, shaking his head.

"He was a terrible fighter. He seemed to *wish* men dead when they stood up to him. His career was as wild as the wild. Then . . . I think it was two or three years ago . . . it was found out that the first crime had really not been his . . . that he had been forced by that false accusation to lead the life which he had lived. The governor sent for him. He was pardoned. That was three or four years ago. And since then, everything Warner has done has been prosperous. He has made money out of mining, out of oil farther south, and now he has bought this whole valley. He's very rich, very powerful, trusts no one, and likes to have strong men around him. Go down to his place, Mister Hanover. He'd be glad to have you. If he has a daughter, perhaps she *would* be the one for you."

"But he has no daughter," said Noisy Joe solemnly.

"You know him, then?"

"Very well. And he hasn't been prosperous in everything, Miriam."

"Where has he failed?"

"He loves a woman," said Hanover, "and she'll have nothing to do with him."

"That," said the girl, nodding, "proves that you really don't know him at all. That man would *make* a woman love him. Nothing can stand before him when he makes up his mind."

"Perhaps," said Hanover, "we are not speaking of the same man. What are the initials of your Warner?"

"J. H. Warner," she said.

"J. H.? And what do the initials stand for?"

"Joseph," she answered, "Joseph Hanover Warner . . . oh." She clasped her hands against her cheeks and stared at him.

How clear it all was. This, then, explained why her father had been persuaded by the obscure cowpuncher that the daughter of Judge Stanford was not too good to be his wife. This explained why Charlie Bender had been able to swallow his humiliation and leave the house, whistling—because it was no shame to be defeated by such a man as this. This explained, too, all that dread she had felt from the beginning. This explained the power she had sensed in him, the inescapable thing. She could remember so many little details. His English, for instance, had been purer than that of any cowpuncher she had ever heard talk before. And now that her eyes were opened, the impassive expression that she had thought stupidity, spoke of dominant and unquestionable mastery.

· "Oh," she murmured, "you . . . *you* are Joseph Warner."

"Will you let me explain why I came as I've come?" he pleaded.

"For heaven's sake . . . tell me everything . . . quickly."

"I saw you in town when you got off the train. I was waiting to take a train east. But after I saw you, Miriam, I bought a horse, got a cowpuncher's rig, and hired out on the ranch. I knew that if you understood what I was and had been, you would detest me. I knew that you could have no use for a person who had been reputed to be a killer. I hoped that I could hide under a new name . . . or, rather, part of my true name . . . and that I might finally win your attention. So I tried playing this strange part, and I have lost.

"But it's been a good fight, after all. I've done my best. I've played all my cards. I'm simply beaten. And so, you see, I was right when I said that Joseph Warner was unhappy in one thing."

There was a little interval of quiet.

"At least," said Miriam at last, "you can't argue me down. I think he is only *foolish* in one thing."

A bird darted up from the ground, whistling wildly and well. Surely it could not be a lark on the top of so high a mountain.

"What," asked Joseph Hanover Warner, "do you mean by that?"

"The Gold King," answered Miriam, "seems to understand."

For the yellow stallion, reaching for a spray of bunch grass, had turned his back squarely upon them.

The Three Crosses

Of all of Frederick Faust's early themes in his Western fiction the psychological principle of breaking the spirit of a man, or an animal, would be one that he varied most often, and always to a powerful dramatic effect. It is at the heart of "The Laughter of Slim Malone," first published in 1919 and collected in *Tales Of The Wild West* (Circle Ⓥ Westerns, 1997), but nowhere perhaps is such a scene as fully realized as in the confrontation between Barry Home and Stuffy Malone in "The Three Crosses" which under the by-line George Owen Baxter first appeared in the January 23, 1932 issue of Street & Smith's *Western Story Magazine* more than a decade later.

Chapter One
"Average"

Before narrating the strange events that befell Barry Home, the best thing is to get pretty close to the man, because he was a good many jumps from any young girl's ideal of youth and beauty. As for looks, he was about the romantic height of six feet, but his weight was not a pound over a hundred and sixty. He was not small boned, either. There was plenty of substance to his wrists and feet and shoulder bones, but the muscle was laid sparingly on top of this frame. It was tough stuff, very enduring and surprisingly strong. He was not a very powerful man, but, like a desert wolf, though he looked all skin and bones, he could run all day and fight all night. His legs, there is no doubt, curved out more than a shade. That curve helped to lock him in place on any horse, large or small. But it was not beautiful, and neither was the distinct stoop of his shoulders that threw his neck forward at an awkward angle and made his chin jut out.

These curves and angles made a slouchy man out of Barry Home, and his clothes were not worn with any attempt to rectify that impression. At the moment when important events began to happen to him, he was dressed in common or garden overalls that were rubbed white along the seams and that bagged enormously at the knee. He had on a flannel shirt of uncertain color, and a badly knotted bandanna was at his neck. Because it was cold, he was wearing a coat, too. It was the sort of coat that seems never to have been a part of a suit, but, coming singly into the world, it had simply been a coat from the beginning. There was a great oil spot on the right shoulder. The left elbow was patched with a large, triangular section of blue jeans, and this patch had not been sewed on well, therefore, the cloth of the sleeve was pulled quite awry.

Sagging well below the bottom of the coat appeared the gun belt, so loose that it appeared about to drop over the narrow hips of this man. And far down on the right thigh there was the holster with the flap buttoned over the handles of the gun. To look at that arrangement, one would have said that the gun was worn for the purpose of shooting snakes and vermin, rather than to rough it with other men. And that, in fact, was the case. It was a hard-working gun, part of the proper equipment of a hard-working man. When he was in town, he thought a revolver was a burden and a bore. But when he was on the range, he would have felt rather naked and indecent if he had not had the familiar lump and bump hanging down from his right hip.

Another conclusion about the dress of Barry Home would have been that he was absolutely free from vanity. But, when one came to the boots, there the opinion stuck and changed, for they were the finest quality of leather and made to order so that they fitted as gloves should fit, and shoes so seldom do. But more amazing than the boots were the spurs, which were actually plated with heavy gold—gold spurs to stick into the hairy sides of bronchos on the range.

Perhaps that set Barry Home a little apart from the others?

Perhaps it was that. It was certainly not his superiority in the matter of personal habits.

Your ordinary cowhand will sweat and get dust down the neck for six days or so. When the seventh comes, he lugubriously begs a small quantity of boiling water from the cook and pours it into a galvanized iron washtub, adding not very much more cool water. Then, he peels off his clothes, takes a scrubbing brush, and gingerly enters the bath with a chunk of laundry soap. He looks, then, like a cross between a starved crow and a restored statue, the original bronze being cut off at the nape of the neck and the wrists, and the torso being restored in shockingly bad taste to the purest white marble.

This bathing is not a pleasant ceremony, and the boys do not like it. Generally they get through it once a week. But sometimes they do not. This is a sad thing, but the truth must out. You who have a steam-heated bathroom at your convenience—how many baths would you take in a bunkhouse refrigerated by hurricanes at twenty below zero?

Well, Barry Home was not one whit better than the average. In addition, he had other unclean habits. For instance, the paper tag of a package of high-grade tobacco was generally hanging out of the breast pocket of his shirt and the soiled yellow strings of the little sack, as well. He was always rolling a smoke, and letting dribblings of the golden dust fall into the wrinkles of his coat and the pockets. He had a way, too, of removing a cigarette from his mouth and sticking the butt of it on the first convenient surface, he hardly cared where.

On winter evenings, Barry Home was fond of smoking a pipe in the bunkhouse. His pipe was black. The forward lip of it had been pounded to a decided bevel in knocking out the ashes. In the back of the pipe there was a deep crack, and Barry Home kept the old pipe from falling to pieces by twisting around it a bit of small-sized baling wire which often grew hot enough to burn through even his thick hide. Every winter Barry Home decided that he would have to give up that battered excuse for a pipe and get a new one. But when he remembered how a new pipe parched the throat and scorched the tongue, he always weakened. Besides, the old pipe was endeared by the many lies he had told around the stem of it, breathing forth clouds of smoke and sulphurous untruths.

For he was a great liar—on winter evenings. In fact, he preferred always the most roundabout way of getting at a thing. The truth was to Barry Home like a glaring, noonday sun, and he preferred the mysterious half-tones, the twilight glories, and profundities of the imagination.

To continue the list of his bad habits, it must be admitted that he chewed tobacco, though this was strictly a summer vice. He had an idea that a quid of tobacco stowed in one cheek keeps the throat moist in the most acrid August weather. He even believed that if one stowed the quid far back in the pouch of the cheek, and took a drink of water from a canteen, the water so flavored had tonic properties.

So, from time to time, he would buy for himself a long plug of good chewing tobacco, each cut of which was ornamented with a tin star stamped into the hard leaf. This tobacco was sweetly flavored with molasses, and it was kept neither in a pouch nor in a metal case, but simply in a hip pocket, so that it was generally much battered against the cantle of the saddle and was compressed on the rims.

To continue the discussion of Barry Home along equally personal lines, his talents were such as one often finds on the range. In no respect were they exceptional. For instance, with guns he had much acquaintance, but he was by no means a great expert. His rifles had killed for him a good many deer and one grizzly bear. He was very fond of talking about that bear, and the story grew more extended and the action of it was more dangerous with the passage of every year.

But he was not a dead shot. He could not bring down the

body of a running deer, blurred with speed, as it shot through the brush four or five hundred yards away. He had heard of a good many men who could do that trick every time, but he never had seen the trick done, and he never had met a man who personally claimed that he could do it.

With a revolver he also could hit a mark, if it were not too far away, and if it obligingly stood still. He did not fan the hammer. It is true that he stuck to the old-fashioned, single-action gun, and he was quite skillful in cocking the hammer with his thumb, but the trigger was not a hair-trigger, and neither was it filed away. In common with many other fellows, his peers, he had had plenty of fights, but they had all been with fists. He never had pulled knife or gun on any man. If he had to do such a thing, he would play slow and sure, trying to get close to his mark, and settle the affair with one well-placed slug of lead. But he did not relish the thought of gun fights. The idea of them frightened him.

He was a good rider, as a matter of course. But he was not a flash, fit to win the blue ribbon and the highest prize at a rodeo, where professional horsebreakers exhibited their uncanny skill. He had broken a great many tough, bad mustangs, but he did not do it from choice. When he selected his riding string, he sacrificed a good deal both of beauty and speed for the sake of the large, quiet eye that is apt to bespeak horse sense and good nature. Even so, every year he would be bucked off, three or four times, and he hated that. Whenever he felt a horse arching its back under the saddle, he grew a little cold and sick in the pit of his stomach. He would shout loudly and jerk on the reins to distract the mind of the pony. And he was almost devoutly thankful when such an ordeal ended with his feet still securely in the stirrups.

With a rope he could do the ordinary work, but he had no fancy tricks up his sleeve, and never, never did he uncoil a rope except when the season required work of that sort. Personally, he preferred the light, forty-foot, Texas rope, for he had learned with that kind. Now he was much farther north. He had to swing sixty feet of heavy lariat. That was necessary because the cattle were much bigger—a Texas pony would hardly hold these huge steers, and the bigger, clumsier horses one found on the northern range could not maneuver as close to the target as could the Southern mustangs, quick-footed cats that they are. One needed that sixty-foot length of rope. Sometimes one wished for the strength of arm and the dexterity to throw one of a hundred feet.

In conclusion, one must add, among the talents of Barry Home, that he was a first-rate cowman; that he generally held his jobs for a long stretch at a time; and that he was quite generally liked and respected. He was a veteran and had campaigned in this frontier cattle war for fourteen years. He was referred to as an old-timer—he was called Old Man Barry Home. He was, in fact, of advanced years, having numbered thirty-two of them, all told.

He was a fellow of some education and could talk book English well, but ordinarily he spoke a vile lingo of the range. If he could understand the other fellow and make himself understood at the same time, he was contented.

This Barry Home, here truthfully portrayed, was nevertheless the central figure in the remarkable events which are about to be described. And I dare say that even in daydreams, he never imagined himself accomplishing such things as now fell to his lot. Perhaps a shrewd judge of character might have expected a good deal from him, once the blue, steady fire began to burn in his eyes and the long, lean jaw to set.

Chapter Two
"The Palmist"

It was Doc Grace who started the ball rolling. He was mis-named. He was not a doctor, and there was no grace about him. He was a work-dodging, shiftless, lazy scalawag, and he did not confine his lying to winter evenings. He loved all excitement for which he did not have to work. His chief delight was to start trouble and then stand by and watch it roll downhill, growing bigger and bigger, involving many people in its fall. This was his idea of a rip-roaring good time.

On the morning when this narrative begins, the cook had just shouted: "Turn out, you lazy bums! Turn out! Come and get it! Come and get it!"

Hardly any other cry, not even that of "Indians!" could have roused those 'punchers from their blankets under their deep tarpaulins. But now they struggled to sitting postures and, grunting, cursing, pulled at their boots. Many an aching one of them would hardly have cared if the drizzly rain had been a mist of dreadful fire falling from heaven, except that they had been through just such times before.

There was the flare of the big fire, that the cook had fresh-ened when his cookery was ended. That heat and blaze of light called to them as to so many moths. They dressed, they rose, staggering, uncertain, and felt their way toward the warpath. There they stood shuddering, heads bowed, coats shrugged high about the shoulders.

It was supposed that spring was beginning, but, though it was time for the dawn to begin, the sky was only lighted enough to reveal its darkness. For vast clouds poured across the zenith and let down shadowy arms that struck the earth as rain, or flickerings of pale snow, or sudden beatings of hail that danced for a moment on the ground.

No wonder those 'punchers were a gloomy lot. But they were young, and they were tough. Presently food began to cheer them. It was substantial food. This breakfast was exactly what lunch would be, and lunch was the twin brother of supper. Namely, there was beefsteak, boiled potatoes in their jackets, vast hunks of cornbread, and a swimming of molasses for dessert, and black coffee. The beefsteak was cut thin and fried gray. It dripped with grease. The potatoes had raw streaks in them, and many were frostbitten yellow. The cornbread was heavy as mud. The molasses was of the cheapest and the sharpest sort. The coffee would peel the tongues of ordinary people like you and me. But there was plenty of everything. These men had to have fuel if they were to keep up steam for fourteen or fifteen hours of hard riding. Therefore, the cook stood by the cauldron of potatoes and the big pan that was heaped with slabs of steak, and anyone who came within reach was sure to receive another width of steak, pitchforked onto his plate whether he wanted it or not. The potatoes were there for the taking, and coffee for the dipping. Not a one of the men complained of the quality of the food. In fact, it was felt that this camp fed well.

Of all the crowd, only Barry Home shuddered, suddenly, with more than cold. He took one chunk of the soggy cornbread and one cup of the bitter black coffee. The stuff flowed like a rapid poison through the veins of Barry. His heart fluttered, and climbed into his throat. He threw the unfinished part of his coffee into the ashes of the fire, and the ashes hissed.

The Three Crosses

The cook marked that act. He was more like a butcher than a chef, this big-barreled, wide-shouldered man, and though he was generally good natured enough, like all cooks he sometimes flew into a passion. He flew into one now: "Hey, you, Barry Home," he shouted. "Whacha mean by wasting good coffee? I gotta mind to put you on bread and water a coupla days!"

Barry Home looked back at him with a sardonic smile and answered nothing. One does not talk back to a camp cook. For the whole camp has to suffer if one man throws the cook into a fit of bad temper. If there is any unwritten law of the range, it is that a cook must be respected. No *prima donna* is more spoiled, flattered, and coaxed than is the cook of a range outfit.

Barry Home turned his back on the big fellow, his great shoulders and his scarred face, and spread his hands toward the fire.

It was then that Doc Grace dropped the spark into the powder magazine. Doc was squatting nearby the stand of Barry Home. He had a nearly finished plate of potatoes and beefsteak on his knee. His coffee cup stood on the muddy ground beside him. His hat was pushed back on his head, so that his stiffly twisting forelock was liberated and stood up. Above the round, fat face of Doc Grace, his pudgy nose and his pale eyes, that forelock stood up like a hand, to warn people that the evil one sometimes took up his residence in the cowpuncher.

Now Doc Grace rose suddenly to his feet, leaned, and stared at the hands of Barry Home.

"Great, sufferin' Scott," he murmured, and squatted again.

"Not clean enough to suit you, Doc?" asked Barry Home, in an ominous tone.

If there was a gay demon in Doc Grace, there was a growling, snarling, black-browed one in Barry. He did not turn his head as he spoke, but the sound of his voice alone was enough to make other 'punchers, nearby, take note and look curiously from one of the pair to the other.

They were generally companions in mischief, bedeviling some one or other of the men. It was a pleasant thing to most of them to hear this ghost of discord rising between the two.

"Clean enough?" said Doc Grace. "They're clean enough, all right. I wasn't thinking about that."

"No?" asked the gloomy Barry Home. "Don't start thinking, Doc. It's not your long suit. Do anything else rather than start thinking. It makes me pretty blue when you begin to think, Doc. It takes you a long time to recover . . . it's worse than a morning after, for you."

"All right, Barry," said Doc Grace gently. "That's all right. I don't mind what you say. It just gave me a sort of a start to see. . . ." He stopped himself short.

"To see what?" asked Barry Home, surprised by the mild tone of his friend.

"I mean, in your hands, to see the sign of . . . oh, nothing." He paused again, as though embarrassed. And that seeming should have been enough to warn Barry Home and put him on his guard. For he might have known, if embarrassment had seized on Doc Grace, it was for the first time in his life.

But the mind of Barry Home was not quite clear. A before-breakfast discontent still persisted in him, and just now a shower of cold rain flogged his shoulders and sent a chill down his spine.

"What sign did you see on my hands?" he asked.

"Oh, nothing," persisted Doc Grace. "You know, Barry, I worked for years fiddling around with palmistry. I guess there's nothing much to it."

"I never knew that you worked on anything but cows and crooked poker," said the other sourly. "Whacha mean, you worked on palmistry?"

It seemed impossible to offend Doc Grace this morning. Now he merely said: "Oh, you know . . . spent years on it when I was a kid. I used to get the books and read them. They're a lot of bunk, mostly. It's chiefly faking, all that Gypsy business. Maybe there's something behind it . . . anyway, it's been going on for thousands of years. But you know, Barry, you know how it is. You never learn anything straight that's good news. It seems to be all bad. The future always seems to be pretty rotten.

"I gave the game up . . . I got tired of looking at the hands of people . . . it's years since I read a palm, because it always just gave me the blues. I used to see so many bad things ahead, that I always had to lie to the people. And it was kind of a shock to me, just now, when I looked at your hands and saw for the first time . . . you know, there's nothing in it."

"What did you see for the first time?" asked Barry Home.

"I don't wanta talk about it any more," said Doc Grace. "Forget it, will you, Barry, old scout?" His voice was gentler than ever, rich and tender apparently with affectionate sympathy.

"There's nothing in that palmistry lingo," declared Barry Home. "Not a damned thing."

"Sure, there isn't," said Doc Grace heartily. "Not a damned thing. You stick to that, Barry. I wouldn't want you to believe. . . ." He paused, stopping short again.

"Well, you wouldn't want me to believe what?" asked Barry Home.

"I must have been wrong anyway," said Doc Grace in a murmur, as though to himself. "I couldn't really have seen. . . ." He rose, put down plate and cup, and leaned over once more to stare at the hands of the other. He took hold of them, turned them from the growing light of the day to the brighter, rosier light of the fire. Suddenly he caught his breath and exclaimed. He started to let the hands of Barry Home fall, while he looked up with amazement and with wide eyes of horror at the taller man. Then, shaking his head, he quickly turned the long, bony hands of the other palm upward and stared again.

"It's true!" he breathed again. He abandoned the hands of Barry, gripped him firmly by one hand, and stood close to him, looking up into his eyes with commiserating pity, with friendship, with a sort of despair, also.

"Come on," said Barry Home. "This is just a lot of bunk. Don't you try to make any game out of me."

"Me, try to make game out of you about a thing like this?" exclaimed Doc Grace. "What sort of a hound do you think I am, Barry, anyway? What sort of a low hound d'you think I am?"

"You're kidding me, brother," said the other calmly.

"Kidding you?" echoed Doc Grace. "Look here, Barry, you know there's one thing that nobody ever kids about."

"I don't know. What is it?" asked Barry.

"Death," said Doc Grace.

Chapter Three
"Fate"

No sooner had that word left the lips of Doc Grace than he clapped his hand over his mouth, like an Indian registering astonishment. Then, dropping his hand, he exclaimed: "I'm sorry, old man. I didn't wanta say that. I'm damned sorry. It just slipped out."

"Did it?" said the other, managing a rather sour smile. "You mean I'm gonna die sometime, don't you? Well, I could've guessed that myself."

"Yeah, that's all I mean," said Doc Grace. "I didn't mean

anything but that.'' And, dropping the subject with a well-pretended gladness, Doc picked up his coffee cup and went to get it filled. Then he carried his cup to another part of the circle of men, warming themselves at the fire. Shortly, a hand, which he had been expecting, fell on his shoulder. Of course, it was Barry Home, but Doc Grace did not allow his smile to appear.

"Look, Doc, what's all this bunk about?'' asked the 'puncher. He added, rather shamefaced: "I don't believe in any of that stuff, of course.''

"Well, neither do I,'' agreed Doc Grace.

"But,'' said Barry, "I don't look at a new moon through a glass or throw salt over my left shoulder, if I think in time . . . and I don't walk under a ladder, either. You know . . . a fellow sort of takes the superstitious stuff a little seriously. Just lukewarm, eh?''

"Yeah, but don't pay any attention to it,'' said Doc Grace. He laid his grip on the arm of his companion and muttered: "I'm sorry I said a word. It just sort of popped out, you know, seeing the same sign on the outside and the inside of the hand. That was the funny part. That was what sort of staggered me, and the word just popped out. You're not going to die. I mean, not so quick as all that. Maybe.'' His conclusion was a little shaken and weak.

"You mean,'' said the other slowly, "that you pretend my hand shows when I'm going to die?''

Doc Grace laughed a little, a very short, dry, unmirthful laugh. "You know, old son, that life line business. Some of the books say that you can measure off the years. Well, I don't know. But this is a joke, this time. You know, a joke! Because according to everything I can see . . . wait a minute. You mind if I look again?''

"Aw, no,'' said Barry Home, attempting a large and careless attitude. "I don't mind.''

He held out his hands. The other took the left one and examined the back of it.

"That's what I saw first," he murmured, as though to himself. "That dent, behind the little finger. It's not only there, but it's deep, too. Poor old Sam Waller had the same dent there," he added, his voice now so low that Barry could hardly make out the words.

However, he remembered that Sam Waller, the year before, had been thrown and trampled to death by a vicious wild-caught stallion. Barry Home thought of his string of riding horses at present. The gray had a Roman nose that promised mischief, and there was that quiet mouse of a mare—with eyes that were always flecked with red, and some day there might be murder in that mare. He cleared his throat. All was decidedly not well with him.

Doc Grace had turned up his friend's palm and was peering at it. He traced the life line with his forefinger. Once, twice, and thrice he repeated the operation, muttering, shaking his head. "No," he said, "I give it up. There's nothing in it. But I never saw the signs clearer."

"That there life line," commented Barry Home, with as much calmness as he could maintain, "looks to me good and long, if you ask me."

Doc jerked up his head and nodded. "Sure it's long," he said. "It isn't the length that counts, though. It's the breaks in the line. What's a line, anyway, but a wrinkle made by shutting the hand? There's that break, and you look close . . . you see those three crosses beside the break?"

"No, I don't see them," said Barry Home. He was beginning to sweat a little; yet he was colder than before. The fire could not warm him.

"Here . . . get the light on your hand. You see 'em now?"

"Hold on," exclaimed Barry. "Yeah, I see 'em now, all right."

"Well," said the other, "when I saw those, it flattened me. That was what made me talk like a fool. Three of 'em! You might get by one danger, but not three . . . not three all in a row, like that. That wouldn't be natural."

92

"Wouldn't it?" said Barry Home, his voice very faint, indeed.

The zeal of the palmist, the interest in the occult, seemed to sweep Doc Grace away in a stream of excitement, making him forgetful of the dire messages he was conveying to his friend. He was saying: "Not with a break like that in the line. That's sure proof. No racettes, either. That's another good proof. I never saw anybody in my life, before, without a single racette."

"What's a racette?" asked the feeble voice of Barry Home.

His friend did not seem to hear, but, pouring on with his words, he said: "Then the three crosses, almost hitched together. Why, it's like three red lights in a row along the railroad track. Danger! That's what it is. Only, nobody can dodge the danger that's hid away in fate, like a bomb in the dark. Three crosses, yeah, like they were at the head of three graves. They're faintly marked, but that doesn't make any difference. But it's damned lucky that one thing puts it all out." He dropped the hand of Barry Home and nodded and smiled happily, with a brightening eye. "I've measured it all out," he said. "I might be wrong by a couple of years, one way or the other. It's not as exact as all that. But this just goes to prove how far palmistry can be all wrong."

"Does it?" said Barry, warmth flooding through his heart again.

"Of course, it does," said Grace, with increasing cheer. "You see, according to the time you've lived and according to the signs in your hand, why, you're dead already, Barry!" He laughed as he said it.

"Am I?" said Barry Home, grinning at last. "Well, that's rich, all right."

"Sure," said Doc. "It's a joke. It just goes to show that palmistry is a superstition. That's all it is. According to the lines and crosses and breaks, and everything on your hand, you're dead five, six years ago."

"Tell me how you make that out?" asked the other, now so much at ease that he began to roll a cigarette.

"Why, here you are thirty-seven or thirty-eight years old, but, according to your hand, you're dead at thirty, maybe thirty-two at the latest."

He laughed again, happily.

But Barry Home dropped the unfinished cigarette to the ground. His lips parted, but it was a long time before the ice of them thawed enough for him to enunciate.

"Doc, I'm exactly thirty-two!"

"Hold on," said Grace. "You don't mean that, do you?"

"I look older," said Barry, in a hollow voice. "But I'm just thirty-two."

The solemnity of his utterance brought all talk between them to an end for the moment.

Then Doc Grace, blinking and shaking his solemn head, observed: "Are you just exactly that? Are you just exactly thirty-two?"

"Just exactly," said Barry Home.

Doc Grace shook his head and shrugged his shoulders. "I know that there's nothing in it all!" he exclaimed finally. "But . . . but . . . Barry, tell me what to do to help?"

"Why," said Barry Home, "what can I do and what can anybody do? If the cards are stacked, the game's lost, and that's simply all there is to it."

Doc Grace said: "You know, Barry, that there's hardly any game that can't be beaten."

The other answered: "Doc, you can't cheer me up. If I'm to get the knife, I'll take it. That's all right. Only, in the time that's left ahead of me, I'm going to stake the easy line. I've worked long enough. If there's a jumping-off place ahead of me, I'm going to ride and coast the rest of the way." With that he turned on his heel and walked together with other figures through the murky light of the morning toward the corral.

Very strange things were happening in the mind of Barry.

He got saddle and rope and bridle, went to the corral, and entered. Before him the horses milled, sometimes dashing back and forth like liquid shaken to froth in a shallow pan, and sometimes they swerved around and around the corral in one mass.

Into that mass the 'punchers worked, cautiously—cautiously, because many of those half-wild mustangs would have enjoyed nothing so much as an opportunity to put teeth and hoofs to work in stamping out the life of any human. But, now and again, a rope shot from a clever hand and found its mark, and the selected horse, well knowing that no folly is greater than running against the burn of a rope, would throw up its head, halt from its gallop, and a moment later it was snubbed against a fence, waiting for the saddle.

Barry Home saw many of his own string in the unhappy light of that dawn. He also saw the only horse he owned. He had taken it the week before from young Hal Masters in payment of a poker debt. It was a five-year-old stallion graced with the beauty of a fiend and the temper of the same deity. It had been an outlaw from the first. It had maimed three men and nearly broken the neck of a fourth. It was worth exactly the price of its hide and hoofs. But now, when Barry Home saw its dark head shooting by, lofty in the throng, its ears flattened, its teeth agleam as it snapped tigerishly right and left at the other mustangs, a slight shudder ran through his body.

Fate was inescapable. If it was his fate to be slain by the black horse, why should he attempt to put off the inevitable moment? Was it not fate, now working in him, that made the rope leave his hand and shoot, swift and sure, for the head of the horse?

Chapter Four
"Just Riding"

As he finished saddling his own horse, big Bull Chalmers turned and saw the big, black, evil beauty snubbed against an adjoining fence, fidgeting a very little, its ears pricked forward, contentment in its eyes.

"You ain't drunk this early in the morning, Barry," said Chalmers. "You don't think that you're gonna ride that man-eater, do you?"

"I'm not thinking," said Barry. "I'm just riding."

He unloosed the head of the great horse and swung into the saddle. A small man stood a little farther down the fence, laughing silently in the brightening dawn. That was Doc Grace, and one glimpse of him would have been enough to snake Barry Home out of the saddle with the realization that he had been made the victim of a peculiarly cunning, practical jest. However, his head was not turned that way, and a moment later it was turning all ways at once. For the black horse did not wait. Like a good musician, he played his best piece first, and that piece was so full of action that he seemed to be climbing the air and disdaining the earth. The shocks of that convulsive bucking kept the head of Barry Home snapping to one shoulder or the other, or throwing it back, or jerking his chin against his breast.

He lost both stirrups. He clung by the golden spurs, sunk in the girth. And he was not in doubt, now. He was certain that it was the end of life for him. Fate? Yes, and he had rushed forward to meet it. *But who can deny his doom?* So thought Barry.

Straightway he swung his quirt in the air and brought it down full length along the satin, tender flank of the stallion. Blackie was in the midst of a fine operation that was designed to pitch his rider into the heart of the sky, out of which he might pick him again with his strong teeth, as the man descended. But when he felt the whip, nature reacted involuntarily, and made him fling far forward. As he landed from that mighty bound, the whip cut his opposite flank, and he leaped farther forward than ever.

It was very fast running, but more straight racing will not shake off a trained cowpuncher. Barry Home got his feet instantly in both stirrups, and gave Blackie the lash on each shoulder, alternately. Blackie screamed like a lost soul with rage and hate. As he ran, he turned and tried to get the knee of the rider in his teeth, but a bludgeon stroke across his soft muzzle changed his mind about that, and he flung himself to the ground, sidelong, spinning over and over again.

Not skill, but the mere force of the fall disengaged Barry Home from the saddle. He got up, sick and dizzy, and climbed onto the back of the horse as Blackie surged to his feet, a little dizzy in his own turn, and more than dizzy with amazement to find the man still with him. It was years since he had felt the whip. Riders were too busy pulling leather with both hands to get a free arm for wielding the lash. But now the horrible serpent with many tails rushed through the air with a whistling sound and beat on the flank of Blackie again, urging him to get to his feet once more, urging him to run, to buck, to do what he pleased.

Blackie obeyed the first impulse. He tried to blow this man out of the saddle by the terrific force of his gallop, but still, as he raced, the whip burned his hide. He was pulled to the right, and, in his blindness, he obeyed that pull. As though in reward, he was not punished. He was drawn to a trot. Still the whip did not fall. He halted. Then the voice told him calmly to go on. In reply, he tried to kick a cloud out of the dark sky and, with his heel still in the air, turned his head again to get the right leg of the master. For answer, the tails of the quirt, swung by the practiced strength in the arm of Barry Home, cut Blackie across the face. He began to run again. But he was thinking now. His whole body burned with the pain he had endured. His whole soul ached with bitter revolt. But if he obeyed instructions, the pain ceased.

After all, a clever horse need not depend upon bucking only. There are such things as braining a man while standing in a stall, or kicking him through a barn wall, from the same happy post of vantage, or rushing him with gaping mouth as he comes to the hitching rack. Blackie knew some of these devices, and he gave up the bucking contest, but not the entire battle.

It had not lasted many minutes. Now Barry Home came riding back to the camp.

The day was rapidly growing brighter, and it was high time for the 'punchers to be off at their work, but still they lingered. They had seen some riding that was worth while, and many of their throats were aching, so very loudly had they been appealing to the cowboy to ride him.

Barry Home found the foreman, Pemberton, sitting on the pole of the cook wagon, drinking coffee. He was a sour, little man, an excellent cattleman, without a human weakness or a kindness in him.

"I'm going to town, Pemberton," said Barry Home.

The little man did not look up. "If you go to town, you don't need to come back," he said.

"That's no news to me," said Barry.

"No?"

Pemberton looked up now with a start. "What's the matter?" he asked.

"We don't feed him good enough," the cook said. The angry cook was sneering. "He won't eat the meat I cook for

him. He throws my coffee into the fire. I ain't a fancy enough
cook to suit him!'' He stood, vast and threatening, his fists
planted on his narrow hips, his shoulders thrown forward,
unhumanly broad.

Barry Home looked at him with a curious eye. He had
always feared this man because of something brutal, both in
his reputation and his face. The ugly scar was light upon his
soul, as it were. But now Barry feared him no longer. When
a man is face to face with his doom, and the doom itself is
unknown, why should he feel fear? A wild horse, a brutal
fellow like this with a cleaver in his hand—either one of the
two was enough to end his days, but not unless it were so
fated. It was very odd. Like a Thoroughbred freed from the
grip of the cinches and the burden of the saddle, he was
lightened; he felt free as he never had been before.

Now he stripped the glove from his right hand. He raised
that hand a little. He pointed the forefinger at the cook.

''Your cooking is well enough,'' said Barry. ''It's your
foul mouth that the 'punchers can't stand.''

''If you want . . . ,'' began the cook, with a roar. Then he
changed his mind. He had been on tiptoe to charge, but the
steadily pointed finger of Barry Home reminded him that
there were such things as guns about a cow camp. Such a
thing as death, in fact, might not be so far away. So he
changed his mind, turned on his heel, and strode off, muttering something about fools stewing in their own folly.

With a mild and yet a deep surprise, Barry looked after
the man. He had not dreamed that it would be like this. He
had expected the rush of the man like the rush of a bulldog.
He saw the foreman nodding.

''Yeah, he's that way,'' said the boss. ''I wondered how
long it would take the boys to call his bluff. But somehow
I didn't reckon that you'd be the first one. You're mostly
peaceable, Barry. Now, you tell me, what's the matter with
you? There ain't anything wrong with the chuck we give you

99

up here. I work the boys pretty hard, but not worse than other outfits. Just want a change?''

"That's it," said Barry. "I just want a change."

"You've got thirty dollars, minus the price of some tobacco, coming to you," said the foreman. He stood up. He brought out his wallet and counted the cash into the other's hand. "Common or garden cowpunching ain't after your liking, Barry, is that it?''

"It's all right. I just want a change," insisted Barry Home.

"Well," said the other, "if I'd known what was eating you, I might've given you a chance at . . . look here, Home. You've got the right stuff in you, and the old man wants eight men to go over to his new piece of range and take charge of the herd he's sending in there. Why can't you take the job?''

Barry remembered once more that there was no human kindness in Pemberton. The welfare of others never had meant the slightest thing to him. Then, wherefore should he show all of this concern and kindness? In its small way, this was one of the most amazing things that ever had befallen Home.

He said: "That's fine of you, Pemberton. I won't forget it. But I've got to get away to a new start."

Pemberton was not offended. "I know," he said, with actual sympathy in his voice. "You've got growing pains. Well, go on and grow, Home. You've got the stuff in you. This here world is tool-proof steel, but a diamond point will cut it, all right. So long. I've got to be riding.''

He went off to get a horse, walking slowly, limping a little. Barry Home, still amazed, watched him go, and presently saw him turn to look back. As though ashamed of being caught so, Pemberton waved a hand in renewed farewell and walked on. Barry went on in a dream to his blankets, made up his roll, and then climbed into the saddle on the back of Blackie.

The black horse was shining with sweat, and the long

welts of the whip strokes were entangled across his body. The continued pain of them made his tail keep switching back and forth. His lip twisted in a sneer, like that of an angry man, when the master approached, but he did not attempt to snap. Something held him back. Perhaps it was the calm curiosity in the eye of Barry Home and the steady step with which he approached the big fellow. Unhindered, he mounted, and moved off across the fields.

Chapter Five
"Funeral Activities"

Barry Home went on to town. For that section of the range, town was Twin Falls, where the Crane River and Yellow Creek dump their waters over a bluff within a hundred yards of one another. The town itself is farther down the narrow valley, but the sound of the tumbling, breaking water is in the air day and night, all the year long, except that in September and again in January, for opposite reasons, Yellow Creek sends only a small trickle over its cliff. But there is always a considerable stream rushing down the valley and under the bridge at Twin Falls. As soon as he came over the ridge, even while a grove of trees still shut him out from a view of the falls, Barry Home could hear it in the mournful distance, and he told himself that this was fitting music to accompany his last day, or his last days. Men who are about to die should listen to the most eloquent sermons.

Now he came through the trees and saw the little town

itself, strung out long and narrow in the bottom of the gorge, and he looked toward the flashing faces of the falls, and then up to the blue sky and the white clouds painted against it. He asked himself if it could be true—could death really be approaching through such a scene as this? He was more than half doubtful. He stripped off the glove from his left hand and looked again at the lines and the wrinkles that had told so much to young Doc Grace.

It was a very strange thing that men could pretend to know so much from the examination of a hand. And yet, after all, was it not an ancient science? Yes, there are mysterious things in this world, decided Barry Home. Wise men heed them; fools laugh at them; and those who are neither very wise nor very foolish are likely to regard the mysteries with gravity and speak of them not at all. He felt that he belonged in the third class. But to pretend to measure the actual time at which events would take place? Well, why not even that?

Taking the life of a man to be threescore and ten, why could not one estimate quite accurately—yes, even to the very year. He felt that Doc Grace had certainly been honest. He had seen Doc in all of his veins of jesting, but he had never seen him wear such a face as he had worn when examining his own hand. More and more, his conviction increased. Besides, and this was the clinching point, Doc Grace had actually withdrawn from him and striven, in this manner, to break off the conversation rather than to give such bad tidings of the future. And then there was the matter of his age. Doc apparently had taken him for thirty-seven or eight. Could he have known the truth? Looking back, Barry Home could not remember that he ever told a man in that camp his correct age.

No, when the things were fitted together, one by one, it seemed certain that Grace had not been talking through his hat. There were the three crosses, faintly lined, to be sure, but entirely discernible, once the eye knew where to look for them. Barry Home sighed and drew on his glove again with a melancholy thoughtfulness, now growing deeper.

For had not Doc Grace said that a man might escape the danger implied in two of those signs, but never in the third? That would be the fatal one. Of course, he could not tell how often danger had come near him this year. There was the time the big boulder had bounded down the hillside and missed him by a yard or so. There was the time he fell, and the mules had galloped over him without touching his body. There was the time when he was nailing up shakes on the roof of the big hay barn, and he had slipped and skidded clear to the rain gutter, before he saved himself. That fall, for instance, might well have broken his neck.

This very day, from Blackie and the cook, he might well have been said to have had narrow calls. Before the night closed upon the day, was it not possible that he would have closed his eyes to this world forever? The thought became so vivid that it was no longer a mere thought—it was a conviction. It was too deeply graven in him to be expressed by fear, and as he sent Blackie ahead down the slope again, he laughed a little, seeing the dainty ease with which the stallion, in spite of his great size, picked his way among the stones, surely judging the uncertain footing from the safe.

Men could say what they pleased, but just as a wild-caught falcon had powers of flight that no eyes could ever rival, so a mustang that had been allowed to reach maturity among the dangers of the desert wilderness, saving itself from famine and the storm and heat and freezing, and the hunting of wild beasts—such a horse would have, Barry Home felt, thews of body and sinews of the brains, which no animal reared in domesticity could ever be expected to rival.

He was pleased with the stallion. Though he knew that the horse was not pleased with his master, it was perhaps not because of the identity of the man, but because all masters would be alike hateful to the great horse. But what a throne for any rider to sit upon. If he, Barry Home, were to die this day or the next, at least he hoped that death would find him on horseback. It was that thought which kept his head high, as he rode into the town.

In fact, he was quite changed. He passed, lounging on a street corner, old Dick Wendell, and he waved and called to him cheerfully.

Old Dick had hated him for years. Now he drew himself up and stared without making a gesture of response. But what did that matter? Let bygones be bygones. Was it not better to be remembered, even in death, even by such a fellow as Wendell, in a final gesture of good will? Barry Home felt that it was.

He got to the hotel, put up his horse in the barn, and then stopped at the store to get a clean shirt, some socks, and underwear. The sombrero would do. And he had in his roll of blankets a suit of clothes that only needed some pressing. He picked out a necktie with care.

The clerk, who knew it, said: "You're turning yourself into a dandy, Barry."

"A fellow has to dress for weddings and funerals," answered Barry Home.

"Who's getting married?" asked the clerk.

"Oh, I don't know," said Barry Home.

"Somebody just died?" asked the clerk with interest.

Barry Home merely laughed. He could not explain. He never would be able to explain to anyone. People would write him down as a fool in the first place, or as a more confirmed practical jester than ever in the second place. Why not that, then?

So, still laughing, he said: "I'm dressing for my own funeral, Bud."

"Are you?" asked Bud, laughing cheerfully in turn.

"That's it. Dressing for my own funeral."

"What's going to kill you?" asked Bud, grinning broadly.

"Oh, a horse, a man, a gun, or a brick on the head. I don't know what. Plenty of things to kill a man, Bud."

"That's true. Where did you find out you was going to die? In the newspaper?"

"I had my hand read," said the other. "I went and had my palm read, and the reader said that my life line was right up against the rocks. Not enough left of that life line to daub on a cow . . . not enough of it to go and tie the heels of a yearling." At this, Bud laughed very heartily.

"That's dog-gone funny, Barry," he said, when he could speak. "You're certainly a great one, you are. This is worth telling, all right." Then, he added: "I'd like to see where the line wrecks."

"It's right here," answered the 'puncher amiably. "Wait a minute till I get the light on it right. You see the break in the line and the three crosses."

"I see the break, all right," said Bud, poring and peering. "I don't see the crosses, though."

"Right off to the side, like little wooden head pieces for three, little graves."

"By Jiminy, I see 'em, all right. Poor old-timer, it looks to me like you've got to die three times in a row."

"Yeah, it looks that way, all right," said Barry Home. "It's what I call hard lines. If I were a cat, I wouldn't mind so much. But one life is about all I can afford to spend at once."

Bud roared louder than ever. Tears were actually on his face, but still laughing he said: "Hold on, Barry. You loaned me twenty dollars last year. I never paid you back. You'd better have that money, if you're getting ready for your own funeral, eh?"

"Never mind, Bud," answered Barry Home. "Why should you waste your money on me? You drop a check for it in my coffin, and we'll call it square."

The idea amused Bud more than ever. Still laughing, he clapped the 'puncher on the shoulder. He followed him to the door.

"You're all by yourself, Barry," he cried after him. "I'll be seeing you soon. So long, old man."

And Barry Home, faintly smiling, but only very faintly indeed, went down the street, bound toward the hotel.

That was the best way. He was getting ready for his funeral. Everyone might know that. They would excuse his little eccentricities of the moment by attributing them to the completion of the jest.

Chapter Six
"Pawnshop Purchase"

Down the street, on the way to the hotel, he came to the pawnshop of Solomon Dill, and paused to look into the window, crowded with cheap jewelry of all sorts and fashions, some of it valuable enough, most of it utterly worthless. There is no more melancholy thing in the world than a pawnbroker's shop, for every article in it, well-nigh, represents the sorrow of someone. Nothing, at least, can make one smile, except some of the lurid designs in jewelry.

In this window one could find everything from guns to spurs, watches of all sorts, belt buckles, ornaments for the hatband or the trouser seams. There was a host of fine Mexican silver and goldwork in which Mexicans are so cunning. Altogether there was quite a blaze from the window. It was set off by a little fanfare of light in each of the four corners, for in each of these were three Mexican knives, with their points stuck into wood and their handles thrusting outward.

Those handles were brightened with big, red pieces of glass, set in the butt, or perhaps the stuff was a cheap red stone.

Even Barry Home smiled in earnest, when he saw this glittering ornament. Where would one find even a Mexican who might wish to carry such a gaudy thing as this? No, hardly even a Mexican, certainly not a man who was about to dress for his own funeral.

Then, still laughing, he nodded his head. After all, there was a grim pleasure in this game. It would make Twin Falls laugh heartily for a day or two before the odd coincidence of his death set some of the wiseacres to shaking their heads and remembering that Providence should not be tempted.

He opened the door and went in.

Young Isaac Dill was behind the counter, improving an idle hour by polishing some silver. He rose at once, quietly, respectfully, attentively, and stood with his hands folded on the edge of the counter. Young Ikey had made up his mind, years before, that he would not be a snarling brute like his father. He would follow the same business because he loved it and had a real talent for the thing. But he would not allow himself to become a wild, savage creature, hated by all men.

Ikey never raised his voice, never sneered, never loudly debated prices. He had decided, instead, that it was better to have a fixed price system. Once his father was dead, Ikey would set a price tag upon every article in the shop. He would make each price, in every instance, a little better than a good bargain for himself. However, he would prominently display, from time to time, a few objects that would be real cost price bargains for the public. Even the easy-going people of Western towns, he felt, are likely to love and recognize a real bargain, now and then, and what is better for a shop than to have the ladies of the town dropping in just to look things over?

Yes, Ikey had many ideas locked within the narrow range of his low forehead. Strangely enough, he had red hair. His eyes were blue and small as the eyes of a ferret. His face was utterly colorless. It was like a translucent stone.

"Hello, Ikey," said the 'puncher.

"How do you do, Mister Home," said the boy.

"Come, come, Ikey," said the other, "we know each other better than that, don't we?"

"Of course, Mister Home," said Ikey, "it's a pleasure to me, I'm sure, to be known by my first name to gentlemen. But it's just a little more proper, sir, for me to remember titles, don't you think?" He bowed across the counter to Barry Home and smiled.

Ikey was educated. He had fought for that education, raged, starved, and labored for it. He had it, now. He felt the grace of it like an invisible mantle of dignity thrown over his shoulders. Ikey felt that worth would find its way in this world, even from a pawnshop, upward.

"All right," said the 'puncher. "Lemme have a look at one of those knives in the window, there, will you?"

"Yes," said Ikey. "Certainly, Mister Home." He slid open the inner window.

"One of those with the red stones in the handles," said Barry Home.

"Ah?" said Ikey, and he flashed a glance at his companion, as though waiting to see a smile.

"Yeah, I want one of 'em," declared Barry Home. "I'm going to a funeral."

"Are you?" smiled the clerk. "Well, if it's that sort of a funeral, take your choice, Mister Home." And he picked out the whole dozen knives from the wooden blocks in which they were stuck, and laid them carefully in a row upon his counter.

Barry Home handled them one by one. He could see that they were cheap stuff. These blades were not steel, hardly better than cheap iron. The thin gilding that brightened the blades was rusting through in little spots, here and there.

"Good hunting knife, this would be," he said.

Ikey bowed and said nothing. He was always willing to

smile at a joke, though jokes were things that he rarely understood.

One of them was a little heavier than the others in the handle.

"This is the king of 'em," said Barry Home, making his choice. "Not such a big piece of red glass in the butt of it, but the glass is redder a lot. I'll take this one. How much, Ikey?"

"Why, those knives were just a window decoration, Mister Home," said Ikey. "A dollar is all we charge for them."

"A dollar for this?" said the other. "A dollar for this piece of junk? Well, it's good enough to wear at the funeral. I'll take it. You don't need to wrap it up, and here's the dollar."

Ikey went with his customer to the door. "Whose funeral, sir?" he asked, graciously interested.

"My own," said Barry Home, and stepped out into the street.

The thought of his last purchase kept him still with that faint, amused twinkle in his eyes when he reached the hotel. And there he was hailed by Tom Langley with a great shout.

"Hey, Barry! What's this about a wedding? What's the truth about that, eh?"

"Wedding?" said Barry Home, smiling again, and wondering at the speed with which the slightest rumor travels in this world.

"Yeah, that's what we hear."

"Funeral, I thought it was," said Barry Home.

"What funeral?" asked his friend.

"My funeral," said Barry. And his smile went out as, entering the door of the hotel, he heard a loud, appreciative roar of laughter behind him.

But that was the better way, after all, he decided, when he got to his room. Better for them to keep laughing until the trick was turned, and knife, bullet, rope, or disease ended his days. In the meantime, he must make himself decent for the end. He remembered having read, sometime, somewhere, words that went something like this: **Nothing in his life became him like his leaving of it.** Well, he would try to make those words fit him.

He thought, as he was busily scrubbing in the bathtub, of the past years of his life. He frowned as he added them up. It was true that he had not done much evil; it was true that the great, windy days of riding over the hills were very pleasant, and so were the evenings in camp, and the gay, rough talk of the other 'punchers, the sway and swing of galloping horses, the blast of cold winter, and the crisping heat of summer were merely the backgrounds against which the better moments appeared in kinder relief. After all, he had been drifting, he had been doing nothing for himself. What money had he laid up? What land had he gathered? Or had he ever brought himself to the point of asking a girl to marry him?

No, if he had done that, if he could have anchored himself to a woman and a home, then he might have accomplished something worth leaving behind him. He might have built a house no matter how small, or he might have had a child or so, to grow up and remember him. But now?

He had come to the end of his tether, the very end. It might be a day, it might be a month before he died, but death was there, waiting with its horrible smile. Well, he would not quit. He would try to put a good face on everything.

The first thing was gentleness. He would have to work on that, every day and moment. No critical sneering at other people. Who was he, a doomed man, to sneer at the rest of the world? They would still be inheriting the beauty of this glorious world while he lay in choking darkness forever. Next, just as he put away pride, so he must take on himself justice, throwing from his heart malice and envy. It was far too late for envy now. Above all, he would surely be able to show courage, now that nothing but fate itself could injure him. No bullet would strike him, except one predestined. It was a very strange feeling, indeed.

He got out of the tub, rubbed himself dry, and went to his room to dress. Then he looked at himself in the mirror. His appearance was neat enough, to be sure. But he was standing like a country gawk. His shoulders had to go back, his head had to be carried higher. What was the best way to meet death? Why, like a soldier, to be sure. He was going to execution, but not as one condemned for a shameful crime. He sighed a little. With humble, steadfast eyes he encountered the brown face that looked back at him from the mirror.

Chapter Seven
"The Piece of Glass"

Before he got out of the room, Ikey Dill came tapping at his door. He called out, and the pale face appeared, the little bright serious eyes staring at him.

"I'm sorry to bother you, Mister Home," said Ikey.

"It's all right," answered Barry Home, though he felt that he had seen more than enough of Ikey for a single day.

"It's about that knife," said Ikey.

"What? To give me a refund?" asked Home.

"Well, yes," said Ikey.

"I thought it was a high price," said the 'puncher. "How much you want to give back to me, honest man?"

"A dollar," answered the pawnbroker.

"A dollar?" exclaimed Home.

"We'll take back the knife. You know, Mister Home, any other knife would do better for you. Any other knife would

111

have steel in it. There's no steel in that thing. We'll just take it back. I shouldn't have let you take it in the first place.''

''Well, Ikey,'' said the cowboy, ''you're starting in to be a credit to Twin Falls, I must say.''

Ikey laid a dollar on the center table and held out his hand a little.

''But I need a knife,'' said Barry Home.

''Well, if you need a knife,'' said Ikey, ''I've brought some for you, some real knives.'' And he drew out three good hunting knives from his pocket.

''What price are they?'' asked Home.

''Same price, Mister Home.''

Barry was holding out the gilded imitation with the red stone in the hilt, and he felt the hand of the other take hold of it, as he leaned over the three knives which had been laid upon the table.

''Same price?'' asked Home, surprised.

For one of these knives had a real horn handle, and the blade was clearly marked. It was the best kind of English steel, and it could hardly be sold at such a low price, he felt.

''Just the same, a dollar,'' said Ikey, and tugged gently at the bit of window decoration which he had come to reclaim.

It was not overly patent, but it was patent enough to arouse a twinge of suspicion in Barry Home.

Ikey wanted that knife back, and he wanted it badly. Barry stood up and shook his head. He put the knife back in his clothes and noticed, first, the swift shadow of anger, then a pale brightness, like fear, in the eyes of the young pawnbroker.

''You know, Ikey,'' he said, ''a fellow gets freaks of fancy. I like this knife. I think I'll keep it. You're a good fellow not to want me to keep it, because it's only an imitation knife, but I knew that when I bought it. I could see the rusted spots, biting through the gilding. I bought it for a joke.''

He had made a long enough explanation, and now Ikey

gathered up the three, good knives that he had brought to make the exchange. In the center of each cheek there was a white spot. In a wide ellipse around his mouth there was a streak of white, also. Clearly, Ikey was badly upset, and now he said, taking a step back toward the door: "My father will make me suffer for this, Mister Home."

"Will he? Why?" asked Barry Home.

"Because he lost his temper badly, when he saw what I'd done. He said that I'd spoiled the window decoration. I didn't know that he put so much stock in those knives as decorations."

"He shouldn't put any stock in 'em," declared Home. "They look like the mischief. They simply tell the passers-by that everyone who tries to do business in that shop will be stuck."

He laughed a little. Ikey Dill only managed a faint caricature of a smile in response.

"It's not what's right or wrong," he explained. "It's only what's right or wrong in my father's eyes. He was in a rage. He said that I was trying to take the running of the shop out of his hands. He said that I was a fool, and he made a good many other remarks." Ikey paused, shaking his head and rolling his eyes a little. "He told me not to come back to the shop without the knife," he murmured faintly. He had reached the door, as he said this, and now he turned disconsolately through it, his head hanging.

That picture of the brutality of Solomon Dill held Barry Home spellbound for the moment. In his mind's eye he saw Solomon, the long, hanging face, the brutal mouth and brows. Yes, he would be quite capable of turning the boy out of the house for no better reason than this.

"Wait a minute!" called Barry Home.

Young Ikey whirled about, his face lighted with hope, a flame of it in his eyes. "Yes, Mister Home?" he exclaimed.

Barry Home paused. The expression on Ikey's face had changed a little too quickly. It seemed apparent that he had

113

been merely acting a sad part, overacting it a little, perhaps. And now there was scarcely subdued triumph in his flashing eyes.

In short, Barry Home changed his mind. He said, calmly: "You want this bit of junk, this knife, back. I don't know why you want it. But you want it pretty badly. Well, Ikey, I don't think that you can have it. There's a secret about it. I'd like to find out the secret myself."

The joy in the face of Ikey darkened to crimson rage. Suddenly he could not speak, stifled by the smoke of his passion. Then, gradually controlling himself, he said: "Mister Home, I know that you're a kind man. You wouldn't want to ruin me. My father is in a crazy temper, and he'll never let me come back into the business. It may not be a business that you approve of, Mister Home, but it's the one that I was raised to."

He clasped his hands together and gave them an eloquent wring as he spoke. But Barry Home was watching with a most critical eye now. He was watching for every sign of a sham, and he detected plenty of overacting in this last appeal. Decidedly and firmly he shook his head.

"I don't want to do you any harm, Ikey," he said, "and I know that your old man doesn't mean what he says. He couldn't run the shop without you, could he? Oh, no, he was simply throwing a fit to scare you. He's a bully. You go back and draw a line, and you'll see fast enough that he'll never dare to cross it. But I'm curious about this knife. I'm going to keep it for a while."

Violent trembling shook the body of young Ikey. Twice he tried to speak and could not. Then two words came in a sibilant gasp.

With a whispered curse, he slid out of the room like a silent shadow, closing the door behind him.

Nothing in that odd interview impressed Barry Home like the closing of it. Ikey Dill was famous for his humility in Twin Falls. Yet he had dared to curse a man to his face.

Barry crossed the room, opened the door, and looked out in the hallway. It was empty already. Then he came back to his table and laid the knife on it. Stare at it as he might, there was nothing about it except obvious cheapness.

He examined the handle; he examined the blade. Sometimes valuables were hidden in the handle of a knife, within the hollow of it. So he snapped off the blade at the hilt. He was quite right; it was hardly more than cheaply gilded tin. The breaking of the blade opened up the frail hollow of the handle. He could see at a glance everything that was inside and all that he saw there was a layer of rust. The answer must be in the blade of the knife, therefore.

He broke it into twenty pieces in his fingers, bit by bit, but there remained only a glittering handful of junk, which he dropped with a slight clattering into the waste paper basket. He was about to throw the handle in after the rest, when it occurred to him that the secret of the knife's importance might lie in the big, red stone that capped the butt of it. So he stared at this. It was about an inch square, and the flat light which he saw in it might be either ordinary quartz or a sign of the cheapest glass. He would pick glass as the greater probability. But suppose that such a thing were a ruby.

The very thought took his breath. Such a stone would be one of the jewels of the world, but he remembered having seen rubies many a time, and always there had been a welter of crimson flame in them, as though a fire were burning in the stone. Even by matchlight, they flared more than this big square did by the light of day. However, that lump of stone or glass, whichever it might be, seemed the only reason for the knife's peculiar value to the Dills. Unless, by any chance, there might be a meaning in the cheap scrollwork that ran down the sides of the hilt? That was a possibility. He dropped the whole handle into his pocket. He took it out again at once. The scrollwork was, it appeared, the most ordinary mechanical pattern; and yet there might be more in it than met the eye. However, he would need time to puzzle over that. In the meantime, he could find out definitely about the red stone, or glass, on the butt of the handle.

He went out at once. There was a second pawnshop in the town, and to this he went. Dutch—he seemed to have no other name—lay flat and squashy in his chair behind the counter. He took the knife handle in his big, dirty fingers and looked at it from thick-lidded eyes.

"Fifty cents," he said. "I dunno that I want it, though."

"What is it?" said Barry Home.

"Quartz, I guess," said the other. "Got anything else to hock?"

"I'm not hocking. I'm only asking," said Barry Home, pocketing the knife handle.

"Well, go on, then. I ain't got any time to waste," said Dutch.

Barry Home went on.

Chapter Eight
"Fate's Game"

He felt a strange calm that was like the languor of childhood on a sunny, lazy afternoon, with no mental care except to plan the next game. There were two important differences, however. With this calm there was no inertia. And he did not need to plan, for plans would come and find him. Fate was his opponent and would keep him well engaged.

He sat on the verandah of the hotel until supper time. Then he went into the dining room, where he sat at the long table and ate his meal with a curious detachment. He was seeing everything clearly, hearing everything with a wonderful precision. Nothing troubled him.

Tom McGuire came in and sat opposite him at the table by mistake. For they were old enemies. There had been a dispute over cards five years before, and the bad blood lingered. He saw McGuire start, scowl, move as though to leave his chair, then resolutely settle down into it, prepared for anything. He understood perfectly, watching McGuire. There was plenty of fighting blood in this man.

"Hello, Tom," he said presently.

McGuire looked up with another start and glared at Barry Home. "What's the matter with you?" he demanded.

Other people heard. They could not help hearing. They knew, most of them, all about the enmity. Now they watched the interchange of words with much interest. One never could tell. A gun play might spring out of the slightest circumstance.

Barry Home said: "Tom, why should we be growling at each other the rest of our lives just because we were a pair of fools five years back?"

McGuire was frankly amazed. He narrowed his eyes; he passed a finger under the band of his collar to loosen it. Then he said: "Whacha driving at?"

"You ought to know what I'm driving at," said Barry Home. "I know you're a good fellow, Tom. Your friends think a lot of you. I'm not such a hound, either. D'you think I am?"

McGuire hesitated. Temptation made his face crimson. His pale eyebrows lowered, and his very red hair seemed to bristle. However, he controlled himself, and said: "Maybe I ain't publishing what I think of you."

Barry Home found it possible to smile and to look unoffended, without tenseness, into the square, wide-mouthed face of the other. It might be that doom was about to overtake him even now and that presently a gun would be in the hand

117

of Tom McGuire and thin smoke curling from its lips, while he, Barry Home, fell backward dead upon the floor. But what did it matter? Nothing would happen unless decreed by fate. And Tom McGuire could shoot straight. It would be as easy a death as any.

Barry pursued: "You didn't know me very well, then. You thought I'd run in a cold pack on the game that evening, didn't you? Well, you know me better now. I've been around this part of the world long enough for the boys to know I'm not a crook. I'd have more money in my pocket if I were. We both used a lot of bad language that other night. How about forgetting it and making a fresh start?"

McGuire blinked. He even leaned a little lower in his chair, as though prepared to jump a little to one side or the other and get out his gun. Then he muttered: "You're doing all the leading, in this here."

"Sure I am," said Barry Home. "Nobody'll ever be able to say that you took the first step toward making up."

McGuire grew redder than ever. He thrust out his lower jaw. "Not that I'd be givin' a continental what anybody else might think about whether I took the first step or the last one," he declared. "It's between you and me."

"That's who it's between," agreed Home.

Suddenly McGuire grinned from ear to ear. "The mischief, Barry," he said. "I've always wanted to be friends, down in my boots. I was the leading fool, that evening."

"We were neck and neck," said Barry Home.

"Partner," said McGuire, "gimme your mitt on that!" And he thrust a thick arm across the table and grasped the hand of Barry Home with great energy.

An old cattleman at the table said: "That's a good job. Home, you're a man. You've growed up, since I last seen you kicking up your heels and breaking glassware around the town."

A general murmur went around the table. It was plain that everyone thought it was a fine gesture—and Tom McGuire above all. His eyes were shining; Irish warmth was kindling the fire.

He said: "I oughta made the first move like I made the first mean move that other time. I'm pretty damned ashamed of myself. You and me are gonna have a drink after supper, partner."

"There's nobody I'd rather drink with," said Barry Home, not quite truthfully.

The old cattleman, at the table, caressed his saber-shaped mustache, looked before him into space and said: "It takes nerve to be a gentleman. That's what we used to say about Dan Moody. We used to say that Dan was a gentleman."

"Dan Moody was the gunman and killer, wasn't he?" said someone.

"Yeah," answered the cattleman, "he killed seven men, before he died of the kick of a mule. But he was wounded every time he killed his man. The way he killed 'em, that was why we called him a gentleman."

"How did he kill 'em?"

"It was a kind of pretty thing to see," said the veteran. "It was kind of a mean thing, too. I seen the first time that he dropped a man. That was in the old days. You kids wouldn't know much about Dan Moody."

"How did he kill his first man, Colonel?"

"I seen him walk down the street. He got close to the steps of the hotel verandah when a fellow by the name of Jerry Burton come out of the door and seen him, and run down and cursed him about something.

"Well, he looked at Jerry as cool as you please, and he says . . . 'I'll tell you what, Jerry, it looks as though you or I would have to die, for usin' language like that. It's too hot to be all bottled up.'

" 'I'm ready now!' yells Jerry.

" 'Are you?' says Dan Moody. 'Well, take hold of an end of this handkerchief. That'll give us about the right distance apart. Grab it in your left hand, Jerry, and then we'll start in shooting, if it's all the same to you.'

"Jerry was game, and he grabbed the handkerchief, all right. The guns went off about the same second, and Jerry fell on his face.

" 'Will somebody call for a doctor?' said Dan Moody.

" 'Jerry don't need a doctor,' says I, because I was the first to reach the body and turn it over on its back. 'He'll never need a doctor again,' says I.

" 'I do, though,' says Dan.

"He was shot through the side of the leg!"

This story was greeted with silence, first, as each man asked himself whether or not he would have sufficient courage to grasp the proffered end of the handkerchief. After this breathing space, there was an interval of talk.

"Yeah, he had nerve," said McGuire. "I wouldn't wanta do that trick. I wouldn't wanta offer the handkerchief, either. Did he kill all his other men the same way?"

"All the same way," said the old-timer. "He killed four of 'em right in that town. It was a mean place, but after the fourth one, nobody else liked the game any more, and they let Dan Moody alone. Dan was a gentleman, he was. It was a coupla years later that he dodged too short, and a mule brained him."

"A mule is worse business than any gun, if you get the mule good and started," said someone.

"All that a mule needs is practice," said another man. "I seen a coupla starved wolves in the middle of winter try to pull down an ornery little Texas mule. That mule, it busted the back of one of them with a forehoof . . . and it took half the hide off the ribs of the other, as it jumped in to hamstring it. I never seen nothing travel like that wolf for the tall timber."

"Yeah, you say you seen that happen?" asked a cynic.

"I mean to say, brother," said the speaker, with a dangerous gentleness in his voice, "that I owned that mule, and

I'd drove it for five year, and it was the meanest demon and the ironest mouth that I ever tried to handle. And I mean to say that I seen that thing happen with my own eyes. What do you mean?''

Whatever the answer might have been, it was prevented by the commanding voice of the old cattleman, exclaiming: "You two shut up. You'll be shooting in another minute. And we ain't gonna stand it. Barry Home down there, he's taught us manners. And I ain't gonna allow no more shooting. I'm too old for it, and it hurts my ears a whole lot.''

There was more of this talk, and Barry Home thought that it was all very amusing. He felt that if he had brought about this reconciliation years before, it would have been very well, indeed. But he knew that he would never have been able to do it. Only the close presence of death had made the thing easier tonight.

Afterward, he went with Tom McGuire to Tod Randal's saloon, and they stood at a corner of the bar. Others drifted in. Presently Tom was saying: "You're drinking beer to my whiskey. That ain't very friendly, and that ain't like you, partner.''

Barry Home said, mysteriously, but gently: "I can't afford to get tight, Tom.''

"You don't have to afford it," said McGuire. "I'm buying the drinks, tonight.''

Then, from the farther end of the bar, as the door swung open, a loud voice called: "Anybody seen that hound, Barry Home?''

Barry listened without turning his head. He did not have to look in order to realize who was speaking. And he felt, with a cold and calm foreknowledge, that death had at last come surely upon him.

Chapter Nine
"Sipping Beer"

There were, at this time, nearly twenty men in the long, narrow room. Voices were loud, and the air was filled with smoke that merely helped to darken the corners, but which rose in a cone of brilliant bluish-white underneath the lamp that hung from the ceiling just over the center of Tod Randal's bar.

The voice of the newcomer rang out loudly and thrust back, as though with a hand, everyone who was leaning against the bar.

Then the voice of McGuire muttered at Home's ear: "It's Stuffy Malone! What's Stuffy got ag'in' you?"

"I dunno," said Home.

"I'll stand by you," said McGuire, with a desperate sincerity.

"You back out of this," said Barry Home, in words that were afterward remembered and repeated. "You couldn't help me. Nobody could help me."

McGuire, though very reluctantly, consulted his safety sufficiently to draw back a little from his newly made friend.

"You!" shouted the great voice. "You're what I want! You're the meat that I'm gonna chew on! You, Barry Home!"

And still Barry did not turn his head. Well, it hardly mattered. It was all destiny. If he were doomed, as now it seemed

122

certain, to die at the hand of this scoundrel, this professional murderer and jailbird, then that was the way he would fall. There was no question about that. There was no need for excitement, either. Better this than falling over a cliff, say, or being caught in a burning building. So he did not even turn his head, and, when he raised his hand, it was to lift his glass of beer to his lips.

Stuffy Malone, not unnaturally, put a wrong interpretation on the attitude of the other. He roared out: "You ain't gonna hear me, eh? I'll open your ears for you, you sneaking low-lifer, you lying hound of a played-out cowpuncher!" His stamping stride advanced down the floor of the barroom. A very odd and startling thing happened then.

Barry Home's quiet voice was heard saying: "I'll kill you presently, Stuffy, but don't bother me till I've finished my beer."

It stopped Stuffy Malone. Everything instantly was placed upon a different basis. There was no rough and tumble about this. This was a challenge given and accepted. And Stuffy Malone was not more astonished than relieved, astonished that such an observant fellow as this new cowpuncher should remain so calm in his presence, and delighted above all that now it was to be a fair fight, with warning given and taken. Then his own matchless gun play would finish the encounter in the proper way. So he halted, just on the verge of the cone of light that descended through the smoke from the lamp above.

Barry Home conjured out of the past the unsavory picture of the monster. He was worthy to figure as the illustration of an ogre in a child's fairy book. He was one of those fellows who are slim to the age of twenty-five or six, and then are swelled and bloated by steady dissipation. He was tall, but his breadth gave him the name Stuffy, his breadth and the rolling flesh of his face, whiskey-stained to a purplish-red. His very forehead was fat. Fat rolled up and almost obscured his eyes. Only his hands had remained young. He treated them as a lady of fashion might treat her hands. He massaged and rubbed and stroked them every spare moment. He wore on them the thinnest, most delicate gloves, specially made, when he rode a horse. When he came into a town, his left hand remained gloved, but his gun hand was always bare, for he never knew when he would need it. Delicate, pale, slender, wonderfully sensitive, it seemed that only this one part of his body remained what all of him might have been. It was as though all that was strong in his soul were lodged there also. Men said that his greatest sorrow was that he could not decorate that hand with rings covered with shining jewels. But rings might interfere with the drawing of a gun. He had killed many men. No one knew just exactly how many. He was only forty, but he had been a most terrible legend for fifteen years at least.

This was the monster who, as Barry Home knew, waited there on the verge of the cone of light. Yet the younger man went on sipping his beer. He looked down and saw that his hand did not tremble. Even a day before, had such a trial come, how that same hand would have been shaking. But it's only fools and knaves that tremble when they stand, at last, guiltless on a scaffold. He began to smile; he even laughed a little.

Other people shuddered then. Tod Randal, in particular, as he stood, white-faced behind the bar, his eyes staring, thrusting out from his head. He said in a shaken voice: "Boys, it's gotta be stopped. You got nothing against old Barry Home, Stuffy. Somebody must get help!"

There was no need to get help. There was plenty of help at hand. What held back those grim-faced 'punchers was that they knew the code which does not permit of interference in any personal quarrel between two men.

Now the voice of McGuire yelled, sharp and high: "I'm gonna take a hand for one. It ain't no fight. Barry's no good with a gun. It's murder . . . that's what it is!"

"I'll mind you, later on, McGuire!" said the raging voice of Stuffy Malone.

"You'll mind me, too, then," said another. More chimed in.

Then, suddenly and most unexpectedly, came the words of Barry Home, who still sipped his beer without turning his head. "You fellows all back up, please."

They paused. The murmuring ceased. Stuffy Malone, who had begun to think of retreating before such aggressive numbers, stared bewildered at his intended victim.

"Everybody stay here and see the show," said Barry Home, in the same unmoved manner. "Because it's going to be worth seeing, I think. I don't want any help. I'll tell you another thing, and that is that your help is no good to me"

Many men breathed deeply when they heard this. They could not quite understand. They could barely make out that Barry Home was actually picking up the defiance of Stuffy Malone and throwing it back at him.

And there he stood, never turning his head, sipping his beer. There was very little left in the bottom of his glass.

He said: "Stuffy, who hired you to go after me?"

"Hired me?" shouted Malone, driving himself headlong into a passion. "Was there any need to hire me to wipe such a hound off the range?"

"You don't need to yell like this," said Barry Home. "It's a small room. No need to deafen me before you kill me." As he said that, he laughed a little again.

Stuffy Malone thrust out his head in a strange manner, like a rooster, when it peers at a new object. And he said nothing at all, in response to the last injunction. He seemed staggered. His left, gloved hand grasped the edge of the bar. His lips moved, but the curses were not audible. But it was true. He had seen Barry Home laughing, as he placidly sipped his beer.

"After all," went on Barry Home, "I wonder how this thing will turn out. You know, Stuffy, that you can kill only

125

as many men as you're fated to kill. When your luck turns against you, then it's your turn to die. Perhaps tonight is the time.''

''If you're done yapping,'' said Malone, his voice strained and uneven, ''we'll get this party over with.''

''I'm not quite through with my beer,'' said Barry Home. ''When I finish that, I'll see to you.'' He stood a little straighter and pressed his shoulders farther back. He wanted to stand now as a man should stand when he was about to die. For, considering their comparative skill, he knew that he had no more chance against the huge Malone than he would have had in front of a firing squad. It would not be a battle. It would be merely an execution. What could have set Malone on the warpath against him?

He finished the beer. Then he raised his hand to his breast pocket.

Instantly a revolver flashed in the hand of Stuffy.

The bartender shrank back, with a faint groan, and threw up a hand before his eyes. His face was for all the world set as though he expected that the bullet would fly at him.

But with that long, white handkerchief, which he had drawn from the breast pocket of his coat, Barry Home was merely patting and wiping away the bit of foam that remained on his mouth after the beer.

''McGuire,'' said Barry Home.

''Aye, Barry, old son,'' came the tremulous response.

''McGuire, I've got a black stallion in the stable behind the hotel. If I'm killed, the horse goes to you to remember me by.''

''Aye, Barry,'' said McGuire truthfully, ''but I don't need a horse to remember you by. There ain't a man here that'll ever forget you.''

Stuffy Malone, seeing that he had drawn too soon, grew a dark crimson, ashamed of his haste. He put the gun away again with a well-oiled, sliding gesture of his right hand. He gritted his teeth and narrowed his eyes, then waited, tense and brittle with readiness.

"The horse is yours if I go down," said Barry. "The way to ride him is to tear into him with a whip before he tears into you. Otherwise, he's a demon and a killer, like Stuffy, here." He chuckled again, and that laughter, at such a time, froze the blood of all who heard it. "Poor Stuffy, perhaps he doesn't expect what may happen to him," he said. Then he turned from the bar, for the first time, and faced Malone, with the handkerchief still in his left hand.

Chapter Ten
"The Man Ran"

It was not planned before. It was simply that the handkerchief was there in his fingers, and that he remembered the story which the old cattleman had told at the supper table. That was enough to give him the idea. It was what the veteran had said of Dan Moody that stuck in the mind of the cowpuncher now. He was dressed cleanly; he was standing straight; he had made his will. That was the gesture of a gentleman, the old cattleman had felt, that throwing of a handkerchief's end to an adversary.

It did not strike Barry Home as being a little foolish and melodramatic. Neither did it strike any other man in that barroom as being ridiculous. They were standing on too vital a stage. And, though they were spectators, this was a play which would have only one performance and which must end in blood.

Some of those men who were looking on were frozen with dread. Others were half sickened at the thought of what might come. Others again, with cold, clear eyes, noted every detail of what happened. It was these last who gave the world the true version of the scene afterward.

The beginning had been odd enough. What followed was still more of a strain to the nerves, when Barry Home walked calmly down the bar and said: "Take hold of this, Stuffy. It will give us about the right distance," and offered the end of his handkerchief to Malone.

Stuffy took it with a grasp of his gloved hand. His face was swollen with the whiskey bloat and with diabolical passion as well. He felt that he was being put further and further in the wrong in some mysterious way. Besides, the whole conduct of this affair was unexpected. It was years since any single man had dared to stand up to him, even men of some celebrity. And what was Barry Home? Simply an obscure cowpuncher, rather well known in places for his whimsical humor and his practical jokes. Perhaps there was a joke behind his manner now. Perhaps his calm indicated that the whole scene had been worked up and carefully planned. Perhaps it meant that when he, Malone, drew a gun, by some neat device the weapon would be knocked out of his hand.

It seemed to Stuffy Malone that the people who lined the wall of the room, staring, were smiling also. Smiling at what? Why, smiling at him, at the practical joke which was about to be revealed, entirely at his expense. He wanted desperately to glance to the side and make sure whether or not he was being laughed at. But now, of course, it was too late for that. The antagonist was standing close to him, and he was anchored in body and in mind also, for he was holding the end of that handkerchief.

He wondered why he had not drawn and fired when Home turned at the bar and walked toward him. But that was not generally his way. His own skill was so consummate that he could afford to let the hand of the enemy begin to move, before his own fatal gesture flickered in and out and the gun spoke once and needed to speak no more. So he had waited in this instance, and now the fellow was close upon him.

The important thing was to get the matter over at once. "Fill your hand, you!" said Malone.

The order and the oaths that followed did not stir Barry Home. Since the only thing he was intent on was dying properly, it followed as a matter of course that he must not make the first gesture toward his gun. He must give every advantage, even to this brutal manslayer who needed no advantage. Now he actually smiled again. And the lines of humor were so well drawn around his eyes that the smile appeared perfectly genuine.

It was not easy for Stuffy Malone to have that smile so close to him. It seemed genuine. Therefore, it meant that his enemy was perfectly assured of the outcome of this affair. It meant that Barry Home knew he would come scathless from the ordeal. Very strange, inexplicable! Was it a plot, in fact, against the great Stuffy Malone? More than ever, Stuffy yearned to steal a side glance at the faces of the men along the wall. But he dared not.

It was odd, too, to find himself staring at such close range. It was almost as though he never had looked a man in the eye before. From ten yards, or even five paces, the whole man was in the picture. But at this range he saw nothing but the head and neck of the other, hardly the shoulders even. His glance was drawn hard and fast to the keen eyes of Barry Home. He could see the sun-burned tips of the eyelashes and the thin-cut wrinkles on the forehead. The bridge of the nose was high and lean and strong; the cheekbones were well defined beneath the brown skin. And the mouth was smiling. That was the horrible part of it, that the mouth should be faintly smiling. How? Well, calmly, in the first place, disdainfully in the second.

He, Stuffy Malone, was being regarded with scorn. Then a dreadful thought pierced him like a knife and rankled in his heart. Had they, perhaps, gained access to his guns the night before? Had they done that and tampered with them? He, like an utter fool, had not looked to his weapons on this day, but had taken them for granted. It was almost the first time since his days of maturity that he had done so careless a thing.

Fear widened his eyes. His crimsoned face turned pale. It glistened with sweat. That was it. They had drawn the bullets, and in his revolvers there were only blank cartridges.

The voice of Barry Home was in his ears, saying: "I don't take advantages. Not even from a fellow like you, Stuffy. Make your move, when you dare to make it."

"Go after your gun, you fool!" said Malone, showing his teeth.

He was glad to speak. Every second of silence was a dreadful weight on his heart.

"What's the matter, Stuffy?' he heard the voice of Home saying. "Are you losing your nerve? Your face is soggy . . . it's gray. Is it true that you're not a fighting man, after all? Are you just a plain murderer? Are you just a hired murderer?"

"I'll blow that question through the back of your head," said Malone.

The other actually leaned a little toward him, and a gleam, half curious and half cruel, was shining in his eyes. Very difficult eyes they were, and with every instant they were harder to endure. In their unwinking steadiness, was there the power of hypnotism? That was it! said the heart of Stuffy Malone to his struggling soul. It must be hypnotism. That was the reason behind the device of the handkerchief. That was why Home wanted to come so close, in order that the horrible fascination of his art might penetrate the mind of Malone. Had he already penetrated to the core of his mind, freezing up the power of action, enchaining the marvelous and lightning skill of the right hand of the slayer?

A third thrust of horror entered the soul of Stuffy Malone, and he drew back a little. He did not move his feet, but his body leaned slightly away, for every inch of distance from that lean, hard face was a vital advantage to him.

Yet the other would not give him this grace. Instead, he seemed to sway closer. He was in good training. He was in perfect condition. That was clear. Oh, for the days when he, Malone, had also kept in perfect physical trim, days when his own face was as lean and as hard as this. In those days, his heart had never raced, staggered, and bumped, as it was doing now. The horrible thing within him seemed to be enlarging. It filled his entire body. Breath was difficult to draw. There was no steadiness to that beat, but it raced downhill and labored up long grades again. He wanted to lie down and recover his wind. He would have been glad to lie down right there on the floor of that barroom, for two minutes, only until that heart of his was steadier. Then he would rise and kill this wretch, hypnotism or no hypnotism.

Then he saw the lips of the other moving. But he saw them only dimly. He really observed nothing except those fixed and staring and unconquerable eyes, though the lips were now saying: ''Why, you're only a fake and a sham, Stuffy Malone. You're shaking, and you're beaten. You're not worthy of a gun play. I think you never shot a man in your life, unless you had some advantage over him. You're not even brave. You're a coward . . . a murdering coward is all that you are. I give you your last chance to fill your hand. You hear me? I count to five, and if your gun isn't in your hand by that time, I'm going to kick you out of this place because you won't be fit to drink with white men.''

Actually, like the slow tolling of a bell, the steady resonant voice began to count.

Suddenly Malone knew that he was paralyzed unless he avoided the eyes of this man, at least for one instant. Freed from that terrible domination for a moment, he could then look back and strike to kill. So he dragged his eyes away and glanced toward the wall. And there he saw what he expected.

It was true that several men were white as sheets; one had actually hidden his face behind his hands, unable to endure any longer this scene of torture. But there were others who were smiling. Yes, with savage leers of pleasure they were following the disintegration of the gunman. His brutal record was well known to them, and now they reveled in the horrible spectacle so unexpectedly played out before them.

It was true, said Stuffy Malone to himself. The whole thing was a plot, and he was ruined, undone!

He heard the steady voice count: "Four!"

He jerked his glance back toward Barry Home, but a mere glimpse of those steady, brilliant eyes was more than he could stand. He could not face them. His own eyes wavered.

"Five!" counted the voice.

Inside his coat jumped his hand, reacting involuntarily, swifter than thought, and gripped the butt of the gun. Then something caught. There was a rip of cloth. His hand was still there, inside his coat, shuddering in every finger, and the wrist was numb with weakness. And there, leveled before him, was the bright length of a Colt revolver, covering his heart.

Someone leaning against the wall groaned, a long, sick sound, and then a loose body hit the floor.

He, Stuffy Malone, felt those sounds as though they came from his own throat, and the falling of his own body. Death was before him. Oh, the kind mountains and the sweeping plains, the breath of the pine trees and the flashing of distant rivers, far away from dangerous men—if only he could return to them, freed from the horrors of this moment.

He heard Barry Home saying: "I thought you were a bad one, but a man. You're only a stuffed cur. You ought to be thrown to the dogs! Get out of Twin Falls and never come back!"

132

With the hard flat of his left hand he struck the soggy face of Stuffy Malone and swinging through, struck the other side of the wet face with the harder knuckles of his fingers.

The gun slid from the nerveless hand of Stuffy. He raised both arms before his face and cowered. "Don't shoot!" moaned Stuffy.

"I swear that I'll shoot unless you run," said the terrible voice of Barry Home.

Stuffy ran, blindly, striking against the bar and then the side of the doorway, and so, staggering, out into the open of the street.

Chapter Eleven
"She Proposes"

Night had gathered, by this time, thick and complete, but, as Barry Home followed the routed gunman as far as the swinging doors, he looked across the blackness of the street, and the shaft of light from the saloon itself struck upon a familiar tall, gaunt form. He thought that he recognized the outlines of Solomon Dill. It was not very hard to put two and two together now. The knife that the pawnbroker had been so willing to exchange or to buy back, he wanted so very much that he was even willing to hire a murderer for the purpose of regaining it.

It could hardly be the merest chance that posted him across the street from the saloon. It could hardly be chance that made him turn on his heel, when he saw the exit of the gunman, and the pass that he made down the street with long, swift strides. Most assuredly there was some connection between him and the murderous design of Stuffy Malone. It was well known that Stuffy had killed for money. It was even well known that his price was not very high. In fact, the whole thing hung together like a charm.

He stood for a time, revolving the thoughts which came to him. Then he went out through the doors and walked slowly down the street.

Nothing that had happened, so far, had so fully convinced him of the insight that lay behind the predictions of Doc Grace. For certainly more had been crammed into this one day than had happened to him in years and years before. In all his life, in fact, there was nothing so terrible or so weird as that encounter with the gunman in the saloon of Tod Randal.

Thrice he was to face dreadful danger. Twice he might escape it, but the third time would be fatal. Well, it had seemed, before this evening, that the grim figure of the cook of the camp in the hills, had been one sufficient danger. The riding of the stallion had certainly seemed to be another. But both of these things now dwindled in his mind. They were as nothing compared to the stress and strain of confronting Stuffy Malone. Perhaps that was the one important crisis, and the others did not matter so very much.

Slowly he sauntered down the street, turned mechanically into an alley, and, following this, came to the verge of the town before he knew where he was. Then he saw before him a small, white cottage, gleaming here and there softly, where the lamplight from neighboring windows was streaked upon it.

It was the Sale house, to which his footsteps had brought him. As he passed through a shaft of light, a hearty voice greeted him, old Pete Sale himself, calling out: "Hello, there, Barry. About time that you looked up your old friends. Come on in here and gimme an accounting of yourself, will you?"

Barry stood at the front gate and rested an arm on top of its pickets. "I can't come in," he said. "Judy won't let me."

Pete Sale was watering the lawn, and now he swung the stream of water onto the base of the climbing vines that swarmed up over the front verandah of the little house.

"Hey, Ma!" called Pete Sale.

"Yeah?" cried a strong voice, coming from the house.

"Hey, Ma!" yelled Pete Sale again.

The strong voice of the woman reached the front door and burst upon the outer night.

"Yeah, I heard you, I heard you. You want me to fly, every time you speak. I haven't got any wings, Pete Sale, and you know it!"

He answered: "Here's somebody come to call, a friend of mine, and he says that Judy won't let him in."

"Great goodness," said Mrs. Sale. "It's Barry Home, and bless my eyes! You come in here, Barry! The Wilkins boy was just by, and told us all about how you handled that ruffian, Malone. The wicked wretch! You come right in."

He persisted at the gate. "I can't come in," he said. "Judy won't let me."

"The little vixen," said the mother. "Judy, come out here. Look, the scamp's been sitting here in the dark of the verandah the whole time, pretending that she didn't hear."

"I wasn't pretending that I didn't hear," said Judy Sale's voice, full of husky, soft, contralto music. She came to the top of the steps, a dim form.

"Now, you tell me," challenged her father, "that you had the brass to tell a friend of mine like Barry Home not to come inside this gate no more?"

"Yes, I told him that," she said.

"Hey?" yelled Mr. Sale.

"Pa," said Mrs. Sale, "you don't need to yell. You don't need to let all the neighbors know everything that happens in our house."

"It ain't any good trying to keep things quiet," answered

135

Pete Sale. "Not the way this town is. You couldn't keep a secret in Twin Falls if you dug a hole in the ground and whispered into it, and filled the hole ag'in. No, sir, a gopher would go and hear it, and tell the snake that swallered him, and the snake would go and hiss it in the ear of that hatchet-faced Missus Walters."

"Hush, Pa, hush!" said Mrs. Sale. "She'll be hearing you. You know that she always sets out on the verandah in the cool of the day."

"I hope she hears," declared Pa Sale. "It ain't the first time that she's heard a few settlers from me, the old witch! Now I'm talking about something else. Judy, I wanta know, whacha mean by telling folks they can come and they can't come?"

"I told him because I didn't want to see him any more," said the girl.

The father was gritting his teeth audibly with anger. "You told him that, did you?" he said. "You went and told him that you didn't want to see him, no more? And what about me? Didn't I wanta see him no more? Barry, you come right in, or I'll start in and raise the mischief."

"I can't come in," said Barry Home, grinning through the dark. "I don't dare. I'm afraid of Judy."

"You are, are you? You ain't afraid of Stuffy Malone. But you're afraid of Judy, are you?"

"So are you, Pete," suggested the younger man.

"Me?" said Pete. "Well, I ain't afraid of her right now. You come inside, Barry. Ma, turn off the water there, will you?"

Mrs. Sale went to turn off the water from the house.

"I can't come in till Judy asks me," said the cowpuncher.

"I won't ask you, Barry," answered the girl. "But I'll come down and talk to you at the gate."

Down she came. Pete Sale, as the sound of the water died down, no longer gushing from the nozzle of the hose, went on: "I never heard of a girl acting up like that. How much

money and time has Barry, here, spent on you, taking you
to dances and things? That's what I'd like to know.''

"Do be still,'' said the girl.

She came down the path and stood before the gate.

"Are we shaking hands, Barry?'' she said.

"I hope so,'' he replied.

He took her cool, slender hand, but he felt that he was at
a disadvantage, because the light from the open front door
streamed dimly upon his face, whereas she was left in deeper
shadow by it. It only gleamed very faintly in her hair.

"Are you in on another spree so soon, Barry?'' she asked.

"Ain't you gonna ask him inside?'' demanded the insis-
tent father.

"Come along here, Pete Sale,'' said the mother of the
family. "Don't you know nothing? Young folks have to have
their squabbles out.''

"I'm gonna get at the bottom of this,'' declared Pete Sale.
"What's the meaning of it, Barry?''

"I've been asking her to marry me about every other time
I saw her,'' said Barry Home. "She got tired of it, after a
while.''

"She's precious fine, if she gets tired of a gent like you.
Judy, I'm ashamed of you.''

"It was only by way of talk,'' she said. "Barry is one of
the men who runs dry in his talk, and he has to start a little
sentimentality or else fall into a silence.''

"That's right,'' agreed Barry Home.

"Well,'' said Pete Sale, "you kids, nowadays, you beat
me. You make me tired. I'm gonna go inside. Barry, if you
don't manage to come inside, too, I won't think you're
more'n half a man.''

He retreated with his wife, and the girl said: "You're honest, Barry, anyway. Are you having a good party in Twin
Falls this time?''

"It's not a party.''

"Wrangling around with gunmen in saloons, you don't do

137

that for fun, I suppose? It's a new angle on you, too, Barry. You're a deeper one than I guessed. I thought you kept your guns for rabbits and wolves and coyotes . . . I never knew that you would use 'em on men.''

"I don't," he explained. "Stuffy started to run over me. That was all. I didn't start the trouble."

"You finished it, though," she observed. "I'd like to read a bit deeper in your past. I'd like to find out why you have to live on the range as a common 'puncher. What have you done, Barry? Why are you afraid to settle down? What is it that you don't want people to find out about your past?"

"Are you going to make a mystery out of me?" he asked her.

"I'm not making one out of you. You've always played the joker and the harmless, happy-go-lucky fellow. But tonight people have had a chance to see that there's danger in the core of you. Why don't you tell me the truth, Barry? I don't chatter and gossip."

He looked steadfastly at her. He had always liked her better than others. It seemed to him, now, that he glanced deep into her nature and saw there something that made him love her. It was true that she did not chatter idly. There was strength and dignity about her. But how could he talk to any human being of the cause that had brought him to Twin Falls? Palmistry and a silly, tinsel knife that had been part of a window decoration—that was an odd combination. She would simply think that he was lying.

He said: "Judy, I'd like to talk to you, but I can't. I came around here tonight almost by accident. My feet took me, you might say. And I'd better get along again."

"I won't hold you, Barry," she answered.

A rush of emotion came over him. Life, of which so little remained to him, could be a beautiful thing, indeed. The smell of the wet earth, the freshness of the grass, and the perfume of the roses were only a setting for this girl who stood before him.

He leaned across the gate a little, saying: "I want to break loose. I want to tell you that I'd rather have you than . . . but I can't talk. I'm sorry I said so much. I beg your pardon, Judy."

"Wait a moment. Why can't you talk? Is there something in your past? Is there another woman tangled up in it, Barry?"

He shook his head. "It's the future that stops me. It's nothing in the past. I see the future like an open road."

"The future go hang!" she said. "You like me a little. I like you a lot."

"Don't talk any more. You're putting me in the fire, I tell you."

"You can bet that I'll talk some more," she said. "I don't know what your mystery is, but the town is buzzing and laughing about your silly remarks of dressing up for a wedding or for your own funeral and such stuff. Well, Barry, if your funeral were coming tomorrow, you could buy me right now like a horse for a thousand dollars."

"What d'you mean?" he demanded.

An odd, stifling impulse of excitement began to tremble in him and trouble his whole soul and body.

"I mean," she said, "that if you ever care enough about me to show me a thousand dollars for starting a home . . . not that I care a rap about the money, either, but it would show that you were really in earnest . . . why, Barry, I'd marry you in a minute. This silly stuff about your future . . . I'd take care of that future! You don't think a lot of me, but, once I have you, I'll make you love me or break my hands and my heart trying. I'm a bold girl. You can see that. But I'm tired of seeing my happiness drift in and out again every time Barry Home rides into town or away. I'm going to catch you, you piece of driftwood, and hold you if I can."

"Judy," he said, reaching toward her.

She caught him firmly by both wrists. "Oh, I know you're willing to slip into a little love scene," she whispered. "But

139

I'm not. I won't have it, either. But if you want me, you can have me. Bring me a thousand dollars and count it out on the gatepost here, and I'll not even go back to put on my hat. I'll march straight downtown with you and marry you, and you'll never get away from me as long as you live, Mister Barry Home. I'll make a home for you, and I'll keep you there, too. For every lick of work that you do, I'll do two, and we'll be so horribly happy, Barry, that it almost makes me cry to think about it. Good night!''

She went, hurrying back down the path toward the house, leaving a mute and trembling hero behind her at the gate.

Chapter Twelve
"Alone"

He remained there for some time, flooded with emotion that made him quite helpless. Now, as he was about to be shut away into the long, cold night of death, he saw a door open which revealed to him a whole heaven of happiness. A thousand dollars? Why, he would make ten thousand for her. He would tear the money out of the rocks. He would do it in a day. The sense of infinite power filled him.

Then he remembered. On the very wedding date, fate might come for him and take him in her inevitable way. At he thought of this, never before had the pain of life seemed so cruelly bitter to Barry Home.

He turned, at last, and went down the street. It appeared to him, then, that the very nearness of his doom was what had changed him and made all of these recent solutions of events possible. The moment he came to town, a whisper about him had passed through Twin Falls because he had changed. There was destiny working in him surely and coldly. He had been able to find the friendship of that hard-hitting, fiercely honest Irishman, McGuire. He had met and crushed Stuffy Malone. Now, finally, here was Judy Sale telling him so freely that she loved him.

She had even said that her happiness had followed him for a long time, but he discounted that, and was sure that it was what she had heard of his exploits on this one day in Twin Falls that had influenced her mind and opened her soul to him—not to the real Barry Home, the careless, worthless cowpuncher, the mere bit of driftwood, as she had frankly termed him, but a new man, remade, faced by the dangers in which he moved.

It was a sadder thought, then, that he carried with him down the alley and, moving back into the main street, he encountered Tom McGuire who seized on him.

"I been hunting everywhere for you, old son," said Tom. "Now I've got you, and I'm gonna keep you. You can't slide out on the boys this way. It can't be done. We're gonna have a few drinks in honor of you, Barry. We gotta have 'em. We're dry and thirsty to have 'em. You march with me, Barry, you damned, old, stony face. It was the finest thing that I ever seen. I wouldn't have said that any man could do it, but I seen it with my own eyes.

"And me, I felt like a hound, letting you go in alone to meet him like that. I didn't know what you were. I knew you were a good fellow, Barry. I didn't guess that even a Stuffy Malone didn't mean nothing in your young life. Oh, you've kept a lot up your sleeve for a long time, but now we've found you out, and now we know you, Barry, and we think a damned whole lot of you. Stuffy Malone is done. Kids will kick him around the lot from now on. His heart's broke for him. You come along this way, Barry."

141

He said: "Listen to me, Tom. I'd like fine to go along with you. There's nothing that I'd really like better. But I can't. I've got something to do."

"I'll help you do it, then," said the generous Irishman. "Many hands make light work. I'll lighten it for you. There's a coupla dozen of us that would like to lighten things for you, boy!"

"Thanks, Tom," said Home. He felt like an old man, as he added: "There's nobody in the world who can help me in this pinch. I've got to go at it alone. Thanks, Tom, but I've got to leave you."

Tom McGuire stepped back. "I dunno that I understand," he said. "But I know when a man is up ag'in' some things, he wants to be alone. When you're through with the pinch, we want you with us, Barry. That's all that I got to say." And he stepped back and waved his hand in what was almost a formal salute.

Barry Home went on down the street. And he said to himself that it was still true—it was not the real Barry Home they were all so fond of now. It was that new face which he had acquired, in waiting for inevitable doom.

And wait for it much longer, he felt that he could not. He would have to force himself upon it, and the only door to fate which he could think of was one that lay well before him, down the street, a door over which gleamed a dull light, and the light, in turn, glimmered over the moons of the pawnbroker's shop. Solomon Dill—through him he might come the more quickly upon the end of all things, if his guess were right.

So he marched down to the door of the little shop and paused before it for an instant, doubting a little. Then he laid his hand upon the knob and entered. The jingle of the bell above the door echoed back through the inner rooms and seemed to float back to him in a thin, dismal echo. For the shop itself was empty and, only after a few moments, did he hear a padding footfall. Then the curtain that covered the inner hall was moved to the side, and Solomon Dill himself appeared, in a round cloth brimless cap and a long dingy dressing gown, with slippers on his feet. He seemed to have been eating, and the ragged beard on the end of his long chin was still wagging a little, up and down and from side to side. He paused there, and, holding the robe together over his hollow chest, he solemnly eyed his visitor.

Chapter Thirteen
"The Pawnbroker"

This rather awful figure was greeted with: "Hello, Solomon, old son." Solomon Dill advanced a step and allowed the curtain to swing to behind him. Then he said: "Good evenin', Barry Home. What kind of mischief you up to here, young man?"

The cowpuncher smiled. "Not your kind of mischief, Solly," he answered.

"What's my kind of mischief?" demanded Solomon.

"Not murder," said the younger man.

"Murder?" exclaimed Solomon.

"Murder," repeated Barry Home. "You know . . . the worst kind . . . murder by hire, is what I mean to talk about."

Solomon Dill wagged his head. Then he sat down in the chair behind the counter and allowed his spare shoulders to fall into their familiar droop. He picked up a stained piece of chamois and with it began to fondle and fumble with a piece of silver with his gnarled fingers.

"You talk sense," he said, "or you go away. I'm a busy man."

"So am I," answered Barry Home. "I'm too busy to be murdered by your hired men."

Solomon raised his head and his voice, and said: "You say that ag'in. Now, get out and stay out. I don't want you here!"

"I know it," insisted Barry Home. "You don't want me here. You'd rather have me dead. You hoped that I'd drop dead there in the saloon, didn't you?"

Solomon Dill did not frown. He merely looked impatiently toward the door. Then he shrugged his shoulders, as one who has endured insult before.

Barry Home continued: "Take it this way, Solomon. You hire Stuffy Malone, and you think that he'll put a couple of slugs through me, and then have a chance to bend over me and wish me good bye, eh? But you forgot one thing."

"I don't know what you say," declared the pawnbroker.

"You try to think again," said Home.

"If you won't go, I've got men to send you," said Solomon, with a dark and quiet anger.

"You send me," answered the other, "and I'll come back with some of the boys of the town. I could tell them things that would make them crack you open like the shell of a crab, to eat the meat inside."

"What could you tell them?" asked Solomon Dill, not expectantly.

"That you hired Stuffy Malone."

"Me? I hire him to kill you?"

"Yes."

"That's a lie!"

"You lie yourself," replied Barry Home. "But Stuffy wouldn't have lied, too, not in the corner where I had him."

The crimson anger died instantly from the face of the pawnbroker, and left his sallowness a grayer tinge than ordinary. "What did he say?" he croaked.

"That you paid him to come for my scalp," lied Home.

"Oh," groaned Solomon Dill, "what for would anybody want to ruin an old man like me, sayin' such things?"

"That's what he said," answered Barry Home.

"The fool!" screamed Dill suddenly. "And why for would I want to have you killed?"

"For this," said Barry Home.

He held the handle of the broken knife with the red stone in the butt of it under the nose of the pawnbroker. The effect of this gesture was very extraordinary.

Like a hawk on its high post of advantage, ruffling its feathers, gaping its beak open, preparing to leap through the thin fathoms of the air and fasten its talons on its prey, so Solomon Dill in an instant mantled, showed his yellow teeth, and raised both of his skinny hands, as though to grasp the thing from the fingers of Barry Home. It was a revolting and to some extent an unnerving thing.

Barry Home put the thing back in his pocket. "That's the reason," he said. "To a man who knows what it's all about, I think that's enough of a reason to get a man killed."

"Wouldn't I say that men have died before on account of it?" demanded Solomon Dill. He added: "But there ain't no proof against me. There's no proof against me!"

"Maybe not for a courtroom," answered Home, "but there's enough proof to make some of the cowpunchers that are in this town come in here and take your dump to pieces, Solly. You're not the best-liked man in town. You make too much money, and you make it too fast. People are jealous of you. They'd like to take you apart and see what makes you tick."

Solomon Dill narrowed his eyes, and through the thin aperture between the lids he looked far out across the years and saw many scenes of violence, more vividly than they might have appeared in print or in paint. He had, to be sure, seen much of this West in the making. The violent years which had been the foundation of his fortune had also founded his understanding of the wild temper of Westerners when they are roused. More than one necktie party had he witnessed. Once those bony, old hands of his had pulled upon the rope. He liked to remember that scene, as a rule, but he did not like to remember it now.

He said: "Mister Home, old friends like we been for years, old friends like us, why for should we be talkin' so to each other?"

"Because I have a prejudice against being murdered," said Home. "You know how it is. We all have our foolish little ideas. We don't like to be killed before our time. Especially we don't like to be shot up by hired gunmen. Not for the sake of a pawnbroker."

Solomon Dill extended a long, gaunt forefinger. "You know that my fool of a son ... he never should sell you that?"

"I know he sold it. That's enough for me to know."

"He sold it. You want a knife. He sell you that! Oh, the fool! The price of his blood ten times, would it be worth that?"

A little chill ran through the very soul of Home. What could be the unique value in that piece of quartz—no, not in the quartz, but no doubt in the stamped inscription on the sides of the handle?

Then furious curiosity mastered the tongue of Solomon, and he exclaimed: "How did you know that one of the twelve knives had that?"

Barry Home countered instantly: "You tell me, first, how did you come to get your dirty hands on it?"

He made his tone loud and peremptory, and Solomon Dill shrank a little. Then he opened his crooked mouth a little and ran the red, furtive tip of his tongue across his lips. "Now, my son," he said, "the time has come for us to stop talking in anger. You want money. I want that. I give you money ... you give it back to me."

Suddenly, Barry Home was remembering the voice of the

girl, the deep and resolved note in it, when she said: *"The moment you come and count out a thousand dollars on the top of this gatepost, I won't even go back to the house for my hat."* She had meant it, too. There was no sham about her, and there never had been. He thought of her, also, not as he had been able to see her that night, but as he had seen her in the full light of the day—her rose and brown face, the steady blue eyes. The man who married her was marrying a life's work, clearly enough. But what a work, what a glorious work. Better to commence it, perhaps, even if he could not live long to finish the structure of their happiness together.

He said: "Money is always money, Solomon. What would you offer?"

Solomon interlocked his long fingers. He looked up into the face of Home with a glance filled with something like a wistful entreaty. "Why, Mister Home, I wouldn't haggle about money with you. I want it. You know I want it. I'd make you my top offer right away. I'll give you five hundred dollars."

Dutch had offered fifty cents—this was an offer exactly a thousand times as high. Barry lowered his eyes to conceal the leaping excitement in them. Then he looked up and smiled genially upon Solomon. "You like to make a hard bargain," he said. "But I'm not a fool, Solly."

Dill parted his lips a little, shook his head as though about to delay all further interest in the thing, and then, as though in his own despite, he said: "I want it. I pay for what I want. I'll give you a thousand dollars . . . in cash." He pulled open a cash drawer as he spoke, sighing and shaking his head, as though reproving himself for his own folly.

But the blood of Barry Home was racing through his veins like hot quicksilver.

"Why, Solly," he said, "I don't know what you think I am. A thousand dollars doesn't interest me . . . not considering what this is."

Solomon Dill slowly closed the cash drawer. He did not

look up again. "Well, what is it?" he asked in the dry voice of one who has no breath left.

"Come along," said Barry Home. "You know what it is, and so do I. Now, you tell me what you'll make me for a real offer. Ready to do that, eh?"

He saw a shudder pass through the body of Dill, from the shoulders to the feet.

Then the pawnbroker said: "I'll pay you five thousand dollars!"

"Five thousand?" answered Home, slowly, utterly amazed, but still ready to pursue this strange game to its ultimate conclusion. "That's almost like a beginning. But now turn loose and make me a real offer, will you?"

Solomon Dill bent back his head and looked up to heaven to witness his agony.

He said: "Ten thousand dollars."

"Bah!" snapped Barry Home. In fact, he had not breath enough to say more.

"Twenty thousand dollars," groaned Solomon Dill, "and may heaven have mercy on my soul."

Chapter Fourteen
"The Great Ruby"

Barry rested an elbow against the counter and looked down, still automatically shaking his head. He could not meet the glance of Dill, for fear that the pawnbroker would see the wonder and the delight in his eyes. In the meantime, he estimated rapidly what twenty thousand dollars would do. It would start life so well that there would be no question about the finish of it. He had always been more than an average worker, even working for others. He felt that he could take hold of the problems of life with a giant's grasp, if ever he were to work for himself and such a girl as Judy Sale. They would have land and cattle from the start, and they would make their start grow and grow.

It was not so much of wealth that he thought, but it was of a sufficiency which would enable him to build a house on a small scale and in it raise a family in comfort—brown children as strong as hickory and sound to the core, on the backs of his own horses and riding through all the weathers of the year. Well, that was all a dream. There would be no time for that—though might there not be time for the beginning? There might be another year of life left to him, and any work to which he put his hand, Judy would complete. Of these things he thought, leaning against the counter in the little shop.

Then he said: "Twenty thousand is a lot of money, Solly. But you know what you're offering it for?"

Solomon Dill threw his two arms toward the ceiling. "I know what you think!" he screamed. "If it were clear, if it were clear. But there's a flaw! I know what a flawless ruby might be worth, that size. It's my business to know. But there's a flaw. Come here. Come around here. I show you under my glass." He picked up a small magnifying glass and gestured with it toward his eye.

Barry Home went slowly around the edge of the counter, walking in a profound haze. *A ruby?* Dimly the same thought had crossed his mind's eye, but the casual opinion of Dutch had dissipated that idea. *A ruby?* It would have to be in a pendant only, or set in a king's crown. Almost staggeringly he came.

Solomon Dill was exclaiming, hastily: "I offer you twenty thousand! I don't know. I mortgage my soul and borrow all from all my friends, and maybe I'm able to raise thirty thousand for it. That's all."

Thirty thousand dollars! From fifty cents to thirty thousand dollars, and good grazing land was cheap as dirt, and Texas steers to be had almost for the asking, if one wished to ride into that Southern land and drive the lean longhorns north.

He rounded the counter. He leaned and took the magnifying glass and drew from his pocket the knife handle. He heard Solomon Dill saying in a moaning voice: "Not even my boy knew. When I got it, I hid it that way. How should I know that Satan would be sitting under your eyebrows to point out the thing to you? Twelve knives and all of them with the same sort of a silly piece of red in the head of them. I laughed when I thought of that. There would be a fortune standing behind the pane of my window. And the world would walk by and never know the truth."

Suddenly his voice rose to a whining cry: "Now, Ikey!" And he flung his arms around the body of the cowpuncher, pinning him helplessly, for the instant. Before Barry Home could act effectively, he heard a padding step behind him, the grunting sound of an intaken breath, and then a blow on his head which knocked a great shower of red sparks across his vision.

Staggering, he heard the voice of the pawnbroker screaming: "Ride, Ikey! No matter if they kill me. No matter if they send me to prison. Ride! Ride! It's worth all Hades!"

Half sick, Barry Home staggered back and forth, held in the long, strangely powerful arms of Solomon Dill, but then, half consciousness returning, he set himself free with a single gesture. He saw Solomon reel back from him, the long arms flung up to ward off the blow that seemed sure to come, but it was not of Solomon Dill that he thought. It was of the jewel, and that was being carried away by the son of the pawnbroker.

He staggered into the street and saw the fugitive rider fling out of the alley mouth beside the shop and go dashing away—not one rider alone, but two more behind the smaller figure which he identified as Ikey Dill. There was, it seemed, a bodyguard with the younger pawnbroker, and he was behind them, on foot, and in an empty street where his loudest shouts would bring him no assistance. He pulled a revolver, but something stopped him. He never had fired at a human being before, and he could not do it, even on this night. He merely ran on, blindly, with all his might, like a foolish child after a galloping horse.

He saw them swerve out of the darkness of the main street into the moonlight that came pouring down the side alley near the hotel. Around that same corner he dashed the next moment. Far up the slope of the hill he could see the trio diminishing rapidly.

It was fate again, perhaps, which led him on, but he plunged into the stable behind the hotel, and instantly had a saddle and bridle on Blackie. Out into the moonlight he brought the big fellow with a twitch and a leap. And then up the trail.

He had been recognized. Voices called out to him; men were running from the verandah of the hotel, but they would be of no use. To pause and explain would be to lose the race hopelessly, even at the start.

He had seen the three riders scourging their horses frantically forward. But he did not let the tall black run at full speed. There was no need of burning out his lungs on such an ascent. It was a stern chase and was bound to be a long one, and endurance would count for the finish. So he kept the stallion in hand, sweeping up the slope, and as he rode he reasoned.

The first impulse of those riders would be to put one or two ridges of the hills between them and Twin Falls. After that, they would cast about for the best road to their destination, since some definite goal they must have in mind. Perhaps it would be the nearest junction with a railroad. Once on the train, Ikey would be off to some great Eastern city where the gem could be priced and sold. To be sure, he could advertise it in the newspapers, but that would only cause the great ruby to be cut up and sold in fragments to receivers of stolen goods. Stolen it must be. Otherwise, why would Solomon Dill be so earnest to hide it in the cunning manner which he had chosen. How small a thing had undone Solomon Dill's plans—merely the freakish impulse in an idle cowpuncher, driven by destiny, and the chance that he noted the slightly heavier weight of the real gem. All the rest had been sheerest luck, if that were a large enough term for it.

Now, as he rode, he could bless two things—the moonlight and the early falling of the dew. It lay like a sort of bright, gray dust all over the range grass, and though, of course, he lost sight of the trail where it passed into the deep shadows of the woods, yet in the open it was easily traceable—three narrow streaks of darkness across the hills or, where they went one behind the other, one large trail.

Exactly as he had thought, the trail led straight across the ridges of the hills, until the second range was behind him and between him and Twin Falls. Then the sign failed altogether over a broad plateau where the surface was almost entirely naked rock. He groaned when he saw this. There was only one way, and, skirting rapidly around the verge of the rocky ground, he picked up the trails, one by one.

They had played safely and cleverly, too. Each trail led in a different direction: one almost straight back to Twin Falls, one off toward the Case Pass, and the third down the long, narrow valley that led toward the town of Chesterfield. He did not hesitate. For the railroad touched at Chesterfield and that, he made sure, was the point to which the man he wanted would flee. There he would overtake him, fate willing, and take back his own from the fugitive.

Down that valley he let the black stallion take wings, and Blackie ran both kindly and well, as though he realized that the time had come when it was easier and more pleasant to obey than to resist. With every curving of the way, with every lift of the valley floor, anxiously Barry scanned the distance to find a sign of the fugitive. But always the valley stretched before him, silver with dew and the moonlight, and there was only the thin trail of a single galloping horse spotted over the short grass or streaked through the higher growth.

Trees appeared in groves, here and there, and now and again were broad fields of dark shrubbery. In the distance, he began to see the windings of Chester Creek, narrow and bright. Then, rounding the shoulder of a grove, he saw that the trail had vanished before him, and at the same instant Blackie leaped to the side, dodging like a wildcat. A rifle exploded from the shrubbery at the same time, and he heard the whir of the ball pass his head as, neatly shed from saddle and stirrups, he was flung violently forward and crashed into the brush. It received him with a thousand scratches. But the little branches broke the force of the fall like so many springs, and, floundering back to his feet, he saw a form dodging off among the trees. Instantly he rushed forward in pursuit.

Chapter Fifteen
"The Return"

It was Ikey, he made sure, for the figure was of about the same height, and he thought that he could recognize, also, the furtive way in which such a fugitive would run, like a leaping, dodging little ferret. The pain still stabbed to his

153

brain, where the blow had fallen on his head, but a thousand motives of eagerness and rage made him run as he had never run before. Valiantly, the fugitive fled before him, but the long legs of Home were telling the tale, when the little man in front disappeared behind a tree, which instantly gave forth spitting bullets on the farther rim of the trunk. Home dodged behind another trunk, heard the sixth bullet fired, and was out again in a flash.

He heard a wild cry, half yell and half groan, just before him, and then, in the act of reloading a revolver, he saw a small form that suddenly flung the gun at his pursuer's head. It missed Barry Home narrowly. In another bound, he had gathered the man inside the crook of his left arm.

The fellow twisted like a wild thing. A knife flashed in his hand as he swerved about, but the remorseless pressure of the revolver's muzzle against his throat made him drop the useless weapon.

It was Juan, the half-breed, who stood there, shuddering, and moaning: "I wouldn't have taken the job, if I'd known it was you, Mister Home. I swear I didn't know. Would I've worked for that Ikey Dill ag'in' you, I ask? Would I've done that? I didn't know who it was. Only there was somebody that might have to be socked on the head. That was all he told me, when he hired my brother and me. Don't shoot, Mister Home! You wouldn't kill even Stuffy Mason, and look what I am. I'm only a kid!"

He began to cry, overcome with self-pity. Barry Home shifted his grip and shook him by the nape of the neck.

"What did Ikey do? Which trail did he take?" he demanded.

"Back," said the other. "Back straight to Twin Falls. And, in the morning, he's gonna start ag'in, and get to the railroad across the range, and that's all I know. I didn't get no big stake. I only got fifty dollars. That's every bean. I wouldn't have shot, if I knew that it was you. I wouldn't have shot. I wouldn't have been such a fool. I would've known that I didn't have no chance. But when I heard somebody coming up behind, I got desperate, and the rifle. . . ."

Barry Home was already running out from behind the trees. He had heard enough.

Blackie had not run away. The grass was too long and too sweet for him to get very far. To the amazement of his master, he did not throw up his head and bolt when he drew near. Instead, he waited, calmly, merely made a pretense of being about to flee, and in another moment Barry Home was in the saddle and away. He measured the strength of Blackie for that homeward run, and he used it. It was a sadly worn stallion that he turned into the stable behind the hotel, with only one swallow of water to content the ravening thirst of the great horse. Then he hurried out into the street and straight down it he went to the shop of Solomon Dill, pawnbroker.

He did not try the front door. More expert housebreakers might have known what to do with it, but he was unable to think of any device of opening that front door without ringing the bell that worked by friction above it. Instead, he stole down the alley to the side. There was no door there. But in the rear of the little shack there was a back entrance, and within those closely shuttered windows he heard voices murmuring, sounds so soft that he had to press his ear to the keyhole before he could make out the words. Then all was clear enough.

It was Solomon Dill, saying: "No matter what happens to me, you gotta go and get the thing turned into money, Ikey."

"I'd like to turn it into money, Father," said the younger man, "but then what will happen to you? They'll come with the sheriff. They'll have you imprisoned for the rest of your life. And I'll have to change my name, and go to live in another country."

"You fool!" said Solomon Dill, snarling, "what does it matter what comes to me? But you got your ma and your sister, ain't you, to think of?"

"Yes," said Ikey, solemnly. "I would think of them, too."

"I never liked you none," said the father, again in a snarling tone. "I never liked you none, because you was always too smart for me. I wasn't good enough for you. My hands, they wasn't clean enough to suit you, eh?"

Ikey said nothing, and Solomon Dill went on: "I was only a greasy and a mean man, ain't I?"

"No, Father," said the boy. "I know you helped me to go through school."

"And your sister, don't I help her, too? Why shouldn't she help herself, washing a dish, now and then, and maybe a window? Such things is exercise. Why should she always be spending money and studying? Is that good for the eyes?"

"No, Father," said Ikey.

"But now," said the old man, "what with the value of the stock in the store and the price of the ruby . . . a hundred thousand dollars for that ruby, Ikey! A hundred thousand dollars, if you take it where I say to take it. A hundred thousand dollars! That and the rest. You go to New York, where there is plenty of our kind of people. You change your name. You are Mister Dillingham, then. Your ma, she is Missus Dillingham. Be mighty good to her, Ikey. She is a woman with a loud voice, but she has a good heart. She never is asking for clothes and foolishness."

"And what sort of a life could we lead?" asked Ikey. "How could we live, thinking of you in prison?"

Solomon showed his teeth. "For why not, fool?" he said. "I am an old man, ain't I? And I sit in prison, why not? I pay nothing for board and room. I get my clothes free. The work it is not too hard for old men like me. Besides, I know how to make the best of bad places. It is a little way I have of getting on, Ikey. And all the while, I rub my hands, while I lie in the dark in a good, clean bunk at night, and I think of my fine son, Mister Dillingham, and his mother, Missus

Dillingham, and his sister, Miss Dillingham, such nice people, to write to an old man in a prison.''

Then, hurriedly, he went on: "Now go, go! I have kept you too long, Ikey. I see the morning, it is beginning. And that Barry Home, he is riding on your trail like a fire in the grass. The evil one is eating his heart, a little bit at a time, and there is much heart in him for Satan to eat. Go quickly, my son! And when you ride through the hills, take off your hat when you pass the house of Alvarado. He don't even yet know, the fool, that the ruby in his safe, now, is paste, and that the real one is going fast with you. Go quickly. And be a good boy.''

The door opened, and Ikey stepped straight out into the darkness, and against the muzzle of Home's revolver.

It was a hundred thousand dollars, then, that Barry Home took back into his pocket. But that was not all. He saw, instantly, that he could have nothing to do with the thing. For the simple reason that he knew the rightful owner of the jewel.

Dawn was, in fact, beginning, and the bright sun was up when he rode a very tired Blackie through the plantation of trees, up the winding driveway to the great ranch house of James Alvarado. He still held the kernel of a great Spanish land grant. Only the kernel, a mere trifle of eighty or a hundred thousand acres. In a sense, he was as American as any other citizen of the country, and, in a sense, he belonged in old Castile.

He was American enough to be up like any other rancher at this time of the day, and he was Castilian enough to look slightly down his nose at the tattered clothes and the weary face of Barry Home. The brush had made Barry look like a beggar. And there were streaks of blood, too, here and there on his clothes.

Mr. Alvarado stood perhaps a little too grandly in the hall, resting his hand on the polished, faintly shining back of a chair.

Barry Home pulled out the handle of the broken knife.

"Here, Alvarado," he said. "Here's your ruby. It was swiped out of your safe. You've got something down there that's made of paste. This is the real thing. Good bye. I'm getting back to Twin Falls."

He was at the door before Alvarado caught up with him and stopped him.

"Home," he said, "I can't believe my eyes, or what you tell me. But I know it must be true. By heavens, it *is* true! I see the real fire of the ruby when the sun strikes it, like this!"

It was true. The whole heart of the square-cut stone was blazing. It filled the palm of Alvarado like burning blood.

"You must not go like this," said Alvarado. "I see that you've been through the devil knows what to get it. There's a matter of reward, Home. It's the chief treasure of the family. It's two centuries old in our family . . . something to reward your great. . . ."

Barry Home rubbed a hand across his forehead. He was very weary.

"Look here," he said, "suppose you had a dog that ran away. You wouldn't offer me a reward for bringing it back. I don't want your money, Alvarado."

Mr. Alvarado was almost too amazed to speak: "I don't mean a small sum. I mean that several thousand. . . ."

"I've got to go back. I'm pretty tired," said Barry Home, and got into the saddle.

"But who was the thief?" asked the rancher. "Will you tell me that, at least?"

"A poor devil that's got a wife and a son and a daughter," said Barry Home. "They're sweating enough already. There's no good reason for sending them to jail, I guess." And he rode the stallion slowly down the trail and slowly away toward Twin Falls, for horse and man were very weary, indeed.

Chapter Sixteen
"Food for Talk"

It was well on in the morning when he came to the hotel. He went straight to his room, fell on his bed, and slept.

He wakened with a heavy knocking on the door. The proprietor's son came in when he called. "Here's a note for you, Mister Home," he said. "And there's a long-legged goat downstairs that says he wants to see you. We'll give him the run, if you say the word. It's that Solly Dill, that I'm talkin' about."

"Wait a minute," said Barry Home, for a little tingle went through him, as he opened the note.

"Sure I'll wait," said the boy. "The editor of the paper is downstairs, too. And Mister James Alvarado. He's there, too. Everybody's doin' a lot of talking, Mister Home. You sure wake up this little old town, I gotta say!"

Barry Home was reading:

Dear Barry:

I've been thinking everything over. Everything means you. And everyone else is thinking and talking about nothing else.

I was a silly girl last night. This morning, if you'll come to the gate, you don't have to count out a thousand

159

dollars. Just put your hand on the post. Empty hands are good enough for me.

Judy Sale

He closed the note, crumpled it, straightened it out, and slid it gently into his pocket. Then he stood up.

"That fellow, Dill," he said. "I'll have to see him." And he handed a quarter to the boy.

"I'll have him here in a jiffy," said the youngster and was gone in a noisy scamper.

Not long afterward a slow and solemn step approached, and the lofty, though bent, form of Solomon Dill appeared in the doorway. He held in his hands the round cloth cap without a visor. He held it in both hands, stepped inside, and closed the door gently behind him. His eyes were on the floor. Again he was gripping at the cap with both sets of bony fingers.

"Mister Home," he began, and stopped.

"Well?" said Barry Home, frowning. "And now what, Solly?"

Whatever problem was in his soul, Solomon Dill found it difficult to find proper words. Twice again he essayed, before he was able to say: "About the ruby, Mister Home. I know what you did with it. And I know that the sheriff ain't come yet to my house."

"Oh, the sheriff won't come, Solly. I thought you'd done your share of stewing about it. I'm mum."

A little shudder ran through the body of Solomon Dill, as he straightened his gaunt body. He lifted his eyes from the floor to the knees of the cowpuncher, to the gun on his hip, to his shoulders, and at last, with a final effort, to his face. Large tears ran slowly from the eyes of Solomon Dill, and flowed through the deeply cut furrows of his face. But his voice did not tremble, as he said: "I was always a sort of honest man, for a pawnbroker. I was always an honest man, except that once . . . that once! And now I'm going to be

160

honest all the rest of my old years. Ikey and me, we'll think about you every day, at the end of the day, Mister Home. My little girl, some time I tell her, too.''

He was gone, with a long, backward, gliding step.

And Barry Home stood very still with a humbled heart. It was a sad and yet a glorious world which he was leaving. The worst of men were not altogether hopeless.

Then he went down the stairs, but not the front steps, into the lobby of the hotel. He was both pleased and shamed, when he thought of all the fine fellows who were gathered there, James Alvarado among the rest. But he could not face them. Not, particularly, when he had this horrible foreknowledge of disaster that lay in front of them.

So he slipped out the back way and passed through the kitchen, and so down the back steps to the yard in front of the stable.

"Takes a scared hawk to fly high, I've heard tell," said a familiar voice.

He turned and saw before him none other than Doc Grace. "Hello, Doc," he said. "What are you up to in Twin Falls?"

"Just takin' the air," said Doc, "and a coupla span of mules back to the ranch. The old man has gone batty. He's gonna try to raise some wheat on the bottomlands. How are things with you, Barry? You seem to be holding out, still, in spite of what your hands say."

Not long but keenly did the eye of Barry Home rest upon the other. Then he said, rather slowly: "You didn't think that I took any stock in all those lies you told me about palmistry, did you?"

"Didn't you?" said Doc Grace, frowning a little. "Aw, go on, brother, I had you on the run. You gotta admit that. I run you right out of camp to get ready for your own funeral. You know I did. I dunno the right hand from the left, but you gotta admit that I gave you the cold chills for a while."

And suddenly Barry Home said: "Yes, you gave me the

161

cold chills for a day. But I'm glad you gave 'em to me. It's made all the difference to me.''

Difference? He left Doc Grace, and went down the street like one who is blinded by excess of light. He moved like one overcome by alcohol, pausing every now and then, and going ahead with uneven steps. He was not a very prepossessing spectacle in that brush-torn suit, streaked in so many places with blood where the briars and twig ends had cut his skin. But he was not thinking of appearances when he turned down a certain alley to the next winding street that had grown up on both sides of a meandering cow trail.

It was early afternoon. The heat was white hot. And he had come out without a hat. Now he stood in front of the Sale house, and before he could speak he heard the loud voice of Mrs. Sale exclaiming within the house. Then he heard the patter of rapid footfalls, and the girl appeared in the hallway, looking, behind the shadow of the screen, like something seen deep in water.

Into the bright sun she flashed, and came swiftly to him.

On the gatepost he had laid his empty hands. She took one of them and brought him through the gate.

"You'll be having sun stroke, pretty quick," said Judy Sale. "You come along inside, silly Barry. There's Missus Brewster at her front window, gaping at us. And there's Missus Merrill, too . . . just staring! Oh, I hope they think there's something to talk about. Now I've got hold of you, Barry, they can rest assured that I'll give them a great deal more to talk about in a day or two. Come up here . . . now take that chair in the shade. Isn't that better? Are you dumb, Barry? Can't you speak? No, you don't have to talk. Sit still.''

He said nothing, but he looked out through the showering leaves of the Virginia Creeper and felt that he was inside the cool green wall of heaven.

The Abandoned Outlaw

Among all English authors, William Shakespeare was no doubt the favorite of Frederick Faust. He committed literally thousands upon thousands of lines from Shakespeare's plays to memory, and frequently he would replay a scene from one of those plays in form of a variation in one of his own stories. Faust's original title for the short novel that follows was "The Hand of God." Obviously, this title was changed when the story appeared under the byline John Frederick in Street & Smith's Western *Story Magazine* (5/26/23) because the editor felt "The Hand of God" was insufficiently suggestive of a Western story. Yet that title for this story of the rivalry between two men in everything, including the woman they both love, is perhaps ultimately more apt.

Chapter One
"A Fight to Remember"

They were physically and mentally designed to hate each other and war on each other. Accordingly, the war began as soon as they met. This meeting took place in the school yard and was long remembered, not only by the two boys, but by all who witnessed what happened.

Oliver Beam was the son of old Judge Beam, who owned the major portion of the western half of the county. Oliver resembled the judge in his appearance. That is to say, he was built like a stalwart son of the soil. He was twelve now, but even at that early age a football coach would have noticed with interest the driving power of the big thighs, the square-clipped end of his jaw, and the quiet readiness for battle that was ever in his eyes. He was very blond. In fact, he was still a tow-head at twelve, and it seemed that his hair would never darken greatly. This was the despair of his mother. Also, her heart used to break over the way his hair stuck up behind. The water that served to plaster it down in front was useless against the wiry stubble that pricked up on the crown of his head. And he always seemed to have his back to a high wind.

For all his physical strength, he was not stupid. He had a fine, wide forehead with veritable knobs above the eyes, and into that roomy storehouse he went ahead storing all the fact and theory that the teachers in the little crossroads schoolhouse could give him. But in his studying, like his other work, he was never in haste. He worked slowly, but with astonishing persistence, and he kept on adding one to one until he was close to his thousand.

Such was Oliver Beam, the pride of his school and his family, and a figure upon which the eyes of the entire county rested with satisfaction. Such was the Oliver Beam into whose ribs the shoulder of the stranger went as they played hockey in the school yard. Oliver, when his wind came back to him, eyed the fellow rather with curiosity than with anger. In the first place the boy was a full year younger and definitely more slender. But even had he been of equal size, Oliver would not have felt that it was necessary for him to demonstrate his courage by immediate battle. Oliver had proved the quality of his nerve in twenty strenuous encounters behind the cottonwoods at the corner of the school yard. But his opponents had always been a year or two older and much larger than himself. Therefore, he looked with amazement upon one who was less than himself in every physical dimension, and yet who aspired to battle.

In the first place, the hair of the stranger was a glossy black to contrast with his own straw-colored thatch. And the eyes of the stranger, in opposition to his own pale blue ones, were brown, with touches of yellow in them when he grew excited. Moreover, where Oliver Beam was constructed to lift weights, the other was made to slip from beneath them. In build, he irresistibly reminded Oliver of the stalk of a four-horse whip, perfectly supple and wonderfully strong.

His name was Clancy Stewart, and this was his first day at school. Who the Stewarts were, no one knew. They had settled down in one corner of the old Morgan place, and it was rumored that two thirds of their property consisted of pride and poverty. Clancy had spent the morning of his first day at the school sitting quietly at his desk, watching faces instead of books. He was equally quiet until the afternoon recess. And when that time of play came, he plunged into the game in direct opposition to the hero of the school, Oliver Beam.

It was like the springing up of some new Hector before the eyes of an Achilles. Achilles was glad enough to have a new and worthy victim for his spear, but he was also set back with wonder. Therefore, before at once resenting the insult, he contemplated the young stranger again and again. After this, he went back into the game, deciding that a boy who was actually both younger and smaller than himself could not by any chance have assailed him purposely. Who will insult an Alexander who has already conquered the world?

Such was the reasoning of young Oliver Beam. But hardly had the hockey game begun again when, in the rush for the ball, he felt the same hard shoulder go into his ribs, and this time he was knocked spinning against the side of the school-house. Of course, there was no doubt now. Miraculous though it seemed, the young Stewart was challenging his supremacy.

It was not in the nature of Oliver Beam to fly immediately into a passion and attack. Instead, he retired to the steps and sat down to recover his wind and his mental poise. When this was accomplished and the recess had ended, he gravely retired to the school with the other pupils and calmly resumed his studies. He was not shamed. Every other boy in the school was treasuring up a great heap of pity and malicious expectation at the expense of the stranger. They would see him ground to the dirt after school was over.

Conversely, Clancy Stewart was perfectly contented with himself and his expectations. He quite disdained his books, and, instead, occupied himself with looking around upon the other boys as though he had already established himself as the king of the school. Ah, how great would be his fall. They ground their teeth—but, nevertheless, they did not meet his eye. After King Oliver had crushed his opponent, there would be time enough for the other boys to assert themselves against him.

Every school is a perfectly graded hierarchy. When a new boy arrives he need fight only once in order to fit himself into the ranks; at most, he needs two or three battles. If he thrashes Tommy, it is taken for granted that he can account for Jerry and Joe and all the others who admit Tommy as their superior. And if he fails in his next battle with Mike, it is taken for granted that he is a notch above Tommy and a notch below Mike. Which settles everything satisfactorily. He does not have to fight again until his ambition has outgrown the facts as he knew them a month or a year before. So the other boys in the school endured the fiery glances and the contemptuous smiles of Clancy Stewart until he should have been downed by Oliver.

Clancy, however, seemed to think that all was over. He was utterly astonished when, as he swaggered down the steps after school, he found that only the girls had gone toward the sheds to get their horses and hitch them to the buggies, or else to saddle their ponies. For, of course, nearly every pupil came a distance of many miles to the crossroads. But the girls lingered over their preparations for departure. And the boys did not move at all. They stood in a strangely silent semicircle out of which, as Clancy came down like a king to his subjects, stepped Oliver Beam and approached the swaggerer.

"Seemed to me," he said quietly, "that you ran into me on purpose when we were playing at recess."

"What if I did?" Clancy Stewart's voice held a sneer. "Are you going to tell the teacher on me?"

Oliver regarded him again from head to foot. "There's a good place behind the cottonwoods," he said at last.

"Never mind the cottonwoods," answered Clancy Stewart. "This'll suit me." And his brown fist flashed out.

Oliver ducked. The fist grazed the side of his face and scraped some skin off his cheekbone. "The teacher'll stop us here" he said patiently.

Clancy flushed to the roots of his hair. He saw suddenly that he had competely mistaken this boy. This was not a tame hound to be kicked around, but a silent bulldog, a seasoned fighter. Also, he now understood the attitude of the other boys. They were waiting for him to be beaten to a pulp.

He followed to the cottonwoods. There he imitated Oliver, stripped himself of his coat, rolled up his sleeves, unbuttoned his shirt at the throat, and faced his antagonist. Now that Oliver Beam's coat was off, his shoulders were revealed in their full breadth. Now that his sleeves were rolled up, he exhibited an arm worthy of a miniature blacksmith. The muscles were blocked out in mature masses. Hard work all the year, before and after school and through the summer vacations, had made Oliver Beam like iron, whereas it was patent that Clancy Stewart was above work. His face was comparatively pale, and the arms that he exhibited when he rolled up his sleeves were almost girlishly slender. A chuckle passed around the circle of the spectators. This fellow was a mere braggart. With settled sneers they awaited his destruction.

Perhaps Clancy also expected that the end was coming, but his attitude was by no means one of calm surrender. In the first place, he looked over the ground on which the battle was to be fought. Here was a projecting root—and yonder the sand was loose and deep—and there thrust out some rocks on which one might easily trip. His eye then rose to the faces of the spectators. They were solemnly hostile. His glance settled on Oliver Beam, and in that face he saw a resistless force of patient courage and strength of will. At this Clancy Stewart sighed, shook his head as though to scatter from his mind an idea which was beginning to possess it, and called out: "Are you ready, Oliver?"

"Ready."

And for a reply, Clancy flew at his opponent.

He had won many a fight by that furious onslaught, his hair flying, his lips curling back from his set teeth, his eyes flashing fury, and his fists flying. But Oliver Beam was not one to be crushed by the mere thought of battle. He stood fast. His calm eye marked the opening. His hard fist shot through it and landed on the cheek of Clancy. He was staggered, and, as he reeled away, Oliver Beam methodically pursued him—methodically, although a yell of approbation and encouragement had risen from the spectators. He came closer; he started his left fist, and, when Clancy attempted to ward off the threatened blow, Oliver struck hard with his right. This time it landed toward the base of Clancy's jaw, and he went down like a felled tree. Had the blow landed a little more toward the point of his chin, the fight must have ended there. But he was only partially stunned, and, when he struck the ground, he rolled himself over and over and whipped himself to his feet again.

There was something in that which to the other boys seemed terrible. From what part of the country had young Stewart come that he struggled so desperately to regain his feet once he was down? Had he been in the custom of fighting to a finish, like a dog and a cat? Did he expect to be struck while he was down? A murmur ran around the silent circle. And there was admiration in their faces, also. For Clancy Stewart, half stunned though he was, staggered straight toward his larger opponent.

But Oliver Beam dropped his hands and stepped back. "I guess I'm a lot too big and heavy for you . . . and I'm older, too, Clancy," he said. "I'm ready to stop fighting if you will."

What could have been fairer than such an offer from a conquering champion? But Clancy Stewart groaned through his set teeth: "D'you think I'm licked? Think again! I . . . I'm just . . . trying you out!"

It brought a laugh from the circle of watchers, and Clancy, casting a glance of fury at them, plunged in again. It was not a direct assault this time, however. He had learned a lesson from those pile-driving hands. Just as the spectators held their breaths and swayed sympathetically in expectation of seeing Clancy bowled over, he checked his rush, swerved aside from the shooting fist of Oliver Beam, and cracked both fists into the face of Oliver.

It brought a yell of astonishment from the boys. They were not accustomed to seeing their champion treated in this fashion, but Oliver was not the boy to wince in a crisis. The sting of hard knuckles against flesh was not new to him. He calmly drove a low-swinging left into the pit of Clancy's stomach and saw the young tiger stagger back, doubled up and gasping. This time Oliver Beam followed quickly. He had been chivalrous enough with his smaller enemy. A little crimson trickle was working down from his nose. And his pride was sorely injured. They would remember afterward that, though thrashed in the end, Clancy had drawn the first blood. So he went in with his left hand extended to straighten up his foeman, and his right fist poised for a knock down.

There was no doubt about the ending of the battle in his mind. He had not only size and strength, but also he knew how to box, and Clancy was simply a natural tactician with his fists. He was reeling, gasping for his lost wind, almost helpless on his feet, but when Oliver planted himself and, without the preliminary of a left jab, swung his right back to finish his work at once, the bent figure suddenly straightened. A grin of joy appeared on the face of Clancy, and he struck with all the power in his slender body. The blow landed fairly on the mouth of Oliver. Down he went flat on his back, and with a yell of triumph Clancy flung himself at his victim. He was dragged off by a dozen hands and told sternly to fight fair or receive a mauling from the fists of them all.

Oliver had clambered back to his feet as nearly in a passion as it was possible for him to be. His upper lip was split, and red streaks were rolling down his chin and sprinkling rapidly across his shirt. How very red it seemed to the astonished eyes of the other boys. And, indeed, fury had made Oliver pale.

They rushed together. They clinched. They fell apart.

"When I finish you, I'll start on the rest of the cowards . . . the rest of your gang!" shouted Clancy in a shrill voice.

A swinging left-hander caught him on the chin and plastered him on the ground. He was up, with the same rool and whirl he had used before, and back at Oliver. He avoided a heavy blow, ducked in, and showered slashing punches into the face of Oliver. The mouth and nose of both champions were red. And it was plain to Oliver that he was well matched at last. And matched by a smaller boy!

Shame spurred him on. He plunged forward in an offensive, but it was like chasing a cat. Clancy was out and about him, dodging blows and striking hard in return. The voices of the other boys began to sound faint and far away to Oliver. They rolled upon his ears in deadened waves of sound. He was growing very tired, too, and his arms were swinging loosely, no longer with the straight and snappy action that made his punches unavoidable. Yet, there was Clancy, circling on the outside, as active as ever, it seemed, although his face was reduced to a featureless blur.

The watchers grew quieter. Someone was calling out that it should be stopped. But still they fought on. And whether Oliver received or gave a blow, he staggered with weakness. His split lip had become mercifully numb with much pounding. But his ribs ached, and the pit of his stomach was a sick void. One of his eyes was closed. Through the other he could barely look. And then, when he was milling blindly at the air, he heard the familiar voice of little Sylvia West run in upon them.

"Are you big cowards going to let them kill each other?" she was exclaiming.

Then, at last, hands were laid upon Oliver, and he was dragged away, feebly resisting. He was taken to the shed. There he was bundled into a cart and whirled toward his home, and in his home there were exclamations from his mother and much applying of raw beef to his damaged eyes. Indeed, his condition was so battered, his body and clothes were so black, that even the cowpunchers stared when they saw him pass toward the ranch house.

"A regular bulldog, that kid!" they said for the hundredth time.

But there was an aftermath. That evening, as Mr. Beam and his family sat at the table with open words of disapproval to Oliver and secret pride in his indomitable courage, they demanded to know the name and size of his assailant. But Oliver was ashamed to speak. He took refuge in silence for the first time in his life. And so it was that a knock came at the door. The cook opened it and then exclaimed in astonishment.

"Is Oliver Beam here?" called a childish voice.

"What's run over you?" asked the cook. "Sure, he's here."

"Tell him that Clancy Stewart is here to see him."

"You come in and tell him yourself."

Into the dining room came a strange figure. If Oliver was battered, he was untouched compared to this vision of wretchedness. The red stains had hardly been cleaned from the face of Clancy. The heavy fists of Oliver had slashed his cheeks over the cheekbones, had gashed the tender skin beneath his eyes, both of which were puffed almost shut and colored purple-green-black. His nose and mouth were swollen together, and his lips were split deep in three places. The stained shirt had not been taken from his back. And with a mortal weakness he clung to the wall with one hand, while his body was shaken with strong tremors.

"In the name of heaven, Mother," said Mr. Beam to his wife, "clean that boy up and put him to bed. He's sick. Oliver, is that the boy you fought? He's not half your size."

"Is Oliver Beam here?" asked Clancy.

"He's here, old son. What d'you want with him?"

"My father won't let me come home till I've licked him and made him say . . . 'Enough!' I've come to fight it out."

Chapter Two
"A Contest of Wits"

Of course, after that, it became a proverb. No matter what happened to the Stewart family, no matter what financial reverses they received, men always said to one another: "You can't tell what'll happen when Stewart comes back to fight it out." And, though the poverty-stricken rancher became poorer and poorer with every season, he was never pitied. His son had won the respect of the entire community, for in the West men are still close enough to the soil and to the necessities of life to appreciate the primary colors of a character.

If they found that the Stewarts were somewhat lacking in business ability and certainly far from one hundred per cent in business integrity, and though they discovered that bills owed by the Stewarts were apt to drag and never be paid, and though the family plunged every year closer and closer to complete degradation so far as money affairs were concerned, yet it was recognized that every Stewart had deathless pride and deathless courage, and such things could not be overlooked.

As for Clancy and Oliver, they never fought again. They had tested each other with fists, and neither of them really cared to repeat the experiment. Clancy grew up tall and slender and handsome, fulfilling in every way the promise of his boyhood. Oliver grew almost as tall and much wider of shoulder—a very strong man even in a community where strength was most common. His straw-colored hair had grown a little darker, a little more tractable. His eyes were a richer blue, his face leaner and more like battle than ever. They were still true to their types, both of them, bulldog and bull terrier, equally formidable in different ways.

And all these years they had been rivals. Not in business, of course, for Oliver, at eighteen, had actually taken hold of the huge Beam estate and, accepting advice from older heads, was managing the big property very satisfactorily within six months. He promised to show even more than his father's talents, for in addition to having an eye for business he was able to accept the opinion of another without feeling that he was disgraced. Financially, therefore, they could not compete.

In everything else they were rivals. If Oliver was a dashing and skillful rider, Clancy Stewart was a little better. If Oliver was a rare hand with rifle or revolver, Clancy was a magician with those weapons. If Oliver went to the city and studied for a week, so that his dancing might win more favor in the eyes of pretty Sylvia West, it was of no avail. He could not teach himself the perfect grace of Clancy Stewart. She smiled for Clancy in a certain way that she never smiled at him.

Yet Sylvia was, indeed, the center of life for Oliver, even if he was sure that she was not the center of life for Clancy. Had it not been that Oliver courted her, he felt sure that Clancy would not have thought her worthy of attention. And here they were fighting again for a prize that could only belong to one of them.

Then the elder Stewart died, and the heart of Oliver leaped in spite of himself. Here was his chance. When the estate was settled, it would be found that the debits were greater than the credits by a considerable margin. The place would be sold, and Clancy would be away to other fields and pastures new. Incidentally Sylvia West would see no more of him.

It was at just this point that he met Sylvia, riding by herself through the hills. The wind had blown the color into her cheeks and twisted her hat to a rakish angle and thrown a mist of brightness across her eyes. They did not talk together more than five minutes, but in that time the blow had fallen. She had asked him to help poor Clancy Stewart, and he could no more have refused her wish than he could have denied the command of a goddess. She cantered away, singing back to him a parting word, and Oliver Beam rode gloomily on to find Clancy Stewart. It was tying a rope around his own neck, this act of grace to his rival, but he went through with it as well as he could.

He came at a most opportune time. Clancy was in the midst of a meeting with his principal creditors, and voices had already been raised high as it became more and more apparent that the estate which remained in the hands of the young man after the death of his father was small, indeed. Clancy rose willingly enough and came out to see his old enemy and rival. He was meeting the crisis in his usual manner, with his head held high and his brown eyes steady and grave. The two still retained the old contrast physically, for in his young manhood Oliver Beam suggested the strength of a bull, and Clancy suggested the strength that goes with adroitness of hand and mind and wonderful speed. And Oliver was handsome like a blond Goth, and Clancy had the noble head of a Greek. Their minds were as different as their bodies. And their habits were as different as their minds.

They greeted each other now with a cordial handshake. And Oliver Beam went at once into the midst of his subject. He was a little pale, as who would not be who condemns to futility the dearest of his dreams? But still he kept his mind true to Sylvia West and her happiness, and he spoke with an assurance that was smooth enough.

"I'll tell you what's brought me here at an unlucky time like this, Clancy. I've been thinking over the possibilities of the Stewart place. And it seems to me that it has never been developed quite as much as it might be. There's a quarter section down on the slough that would make good grain land. I'd say you'd knock off ten sacks an acre with any luck."

"Good advice, but late advice," said Clancy with his smile that made other men want to fight. Indeed, he knew the consummate art of saying a mere good morning in such a manner that the person he addressed would follow him for days to return the insult. He was a scant eighteen years of age, but people spoke of him as though he were twenty-five at the least. The dignity of his bearing added something to his apparent age.

Above all, certain things he had done with guns surrounded his name with an atmosphere such as does not ordinarily cling about a youth. Of course, the others had always been in the wrong. In fact, no one would ever have dreamed of laying hand on Clancy for what he had done. Nevertheless, people will begin to look upon such a man askance. Women do not like to have him in a house near their husbands or sons or brothers. And men begin to treat him with a studied courtesy, sweating with concern while they are near him, for, if they are too polite, they may seem to be cringing before a bully, and, if they are not polite enough, they may be brought to time by a slug of lead tearing through them.

It might be said of Clancy that the sheriff thought of him every day of his life, and thought of him with a concern that made him practice a little more patiently with his firearms. Yet, of course, it was inconceivable that Clancy should actually break the law. It was only an outbreak of the terrible temper with which he was born that might eventually betray him.

Oliver Beam, seeing that temper brightening in the eyes of his companion, proceeded cautiously.

"Late advice," he said, "but I've come to try to show you that the advice may be used."

"Good," said Clancy, without emotion.

He was so grave beyond his years, and there was such a courtly condescension in his manner, that Oliver felt more youthful than Clancy by a whole decade, at least. He was a full year the elder of the two, and yet, when Clancy chose, he could always make Oliver feel that he was merely a rude country lout. Oliver felt that he was distinctly in the center of such a rôle at the present.

"In the first place," said Oliver, "there might be a different management. I mean. . . ."

"That we've run things in a bad way over here? Oh, I suppose everyone in the county will agree with you there."

"I didn't intend to insult you, Clancy."

"Of course not."

Oliver bit his lip. He felt that he would be justified if he turned on his heel and reported to Sylvia afterward that Clancy refused to hear his offer. But he was too honest to do that until he had tried his best. He went on slowly and steadily: "I want to make it financially possible for you to experiment with new ways. . . ."

"What's that, Oliver?"

"Clancy, in a word, I want to help."

"The devil," said Clancy.

He actually stepped back a little so that he could view his companion to better advantage, and Oliver blushed. It was as though he were being regarded as a man for the first time in his life by this strange youngster.

"I mean it," he persisted.

"How could you help?" asked Clancy.

"Well, I could float you through."

"What do you mean by float through?"

"I mean I could stave off the creditors until. . . ."

"Listen to me," said Clancy. "It would take ten thousand dollars to stop the mouths of those creditors . . . ten thousand dollars more than the place is worth, even if it sells for all that it should sell."

"Very well," answered Oliver. "That doesn't frighten me."

"You actually mean that you would give ten thousand. . . ."

"Not give . . . lend, Clancy, and it could be paid back when the place is developed."

"There would have to be other money for development."

"I'd give that, also."

Young Clancy Stewart drew out his handkerchief and passed it across his forehead. Oliver noticed for the hundredth time with wonder the slender delicacy of those fingers. If the hand had been seen by itself, it might have been taken for the hand of a woman, almost.

"What's behind this, Oliver?"

"I simply want to help. There's no reason why you should go down. It isn't your fault if the place has been mismanaged. Why shouldn't you have a fling at it? You might bring it around. And the money won't hurt me. My father left more than I know what to do with. I'm simply investing a little of it in my own way."

To this Clancy Stewart did not return an immediate answer. He sat down on the railing of the verandah and rolled a cigarette, all the while deliberating.

"No matter what's made you do this," he said at last, "I'm sorry that it's been done."

Oliver was confounded. But, after all, it was ever this way. Clancy Stewart was sure to do the opposite of what was expected of him.

"I don't understand you, Clancy," he said.

"Perhaps you don't. But you and I have always been enemies, Oliver, haven't we?"

"More or less, I suppose. But never about anything serious."

"Man alive, don't you call Sylvia West serious?"

Oliver blanched. He would never have dreamed of naming the girl so bluntly.

"Answer me!" cried Clancy.

"Of course . . . of course there's something in that. . . ."

"And so I say that I'm sorry this has happened. It's easier to go on hating an enemy, Oliver."

"I suppose it is, but. . . ."

"Look here. You'll be apologizing for having offered to help me in a minute." He stepped to Oliver Beam and dropped his hands on the hard shoulders. "You're a devil of a fine fellow, Oliver," he said, "and I've gone all this time without guessing it." He added, as he stepped back: "It's fine. It's the sort of stuff that's talked about in the Bible, but never gets any closer to reality than print. Why, I begin almost to reverence you, Oliver. Tell me only one thing . . . did anyone put you up to this?"

Oliver could not answer. But under the weight of those straight, keen eyes his head bowed.

"Who was it?" asked Clancy gently.

"I can't tell you that."

"By the eternal . . . it was Sylvia."

The silence of Oliver was taken for an assent.

"You came with a price, eh? That was the price for buying Sylvia. You'd pull me out of my scrape and then go back to her and tell her what you'd done. Wasn't that it?"

He had clasped his hands together. At a distance it might have seemed that his attitude was one of entreaty. But Oliver could see the arm muscles jumping and twitching, and he knew that Clancy was only fighting to keep his hands away from his guns.

"Go back to Sylvia and tell her that I don't take charity

from a hypocrite. Go back to Sylvia. And you bank on this one thing . . . I may lose everything else, but I'll never lose Sylvia. I'll have her in spite of you. Take that away with you!''

So that was what Oliver took away with him. He could not stop to explain. Neither did the insults make him feel like fighting. He was simply saddened and crushed by the knowledge that he could never stand up to this fellow in any contest. Whether with bullets or wit, Clancy was his superior. As for Sylvia, she was lost to him and won for Clancy. There was no doubt of that. If she married Clancy, she would be wretchedly poor, of course. And she would have hard work to do every day and all day. When he thought of that, and, when he thought how she would wither as he had seen other wives of ranchers grow old in a year, the soul of Oliver shrank in him.

As he rode slowly toward his home again, he decided that, if they married, he would solve at least one problem for them by settling upon them enough land and money to remove the wolf from the door, so that the flower-like youth of Sylvia should be preserved. As often as he thought of that, so often he smiled. But when he reached his ranch house, he felt he had left his own youth somewhere on the road behind him.

Chapter Three
"Bill Kensing, Horse Hunter"

When he was left alone, Clancy Stewart sat for a time on the verandah rail, gripping it with his hands to steady himself, for his mind was filled with swirling shadows of his anger. He was not thinking of what had just happened. His thoughts were racing back, leaping wide gaps of years, and calling up the history of his family. There had been Stewarts fighting gloriously by land and sea for the cause which triumphed in 1783. And there had been Stewarts fighting stanchly for the cause which was lost in 1865. Oh, they had done great things, these Stewarts. There had been a Stewart who had represented his country at the court of a great king. And there were Stewarts running back behind the Colonial days into a dim period when, it was rumored, the name had been spelled Stuart, and when some traces of royal blood had stirred in the veins of the clan.

These pictures and these legends were what filled the brain of Clancy as he sat there by himself. When he recalled himself from them, it was to remember that he had just been insulted with a proffered charity. Inside that house were men clamoring for the debts which his father's extravagance had heaped up. And yonder, down the road, was disappearing the man who, he felt, had offered a price for his honor.

He found himself saying over and over, through a haze:

"I've got to be cool! I've got to be cool! I've got to think! I've got to think!"

At last, he made himself go back into the room and face the others. He was even smiling as he stood before them, but he was very far from cool in his heart of hearts. He wanted to feel the butt of a Colt kicking against the palm of his hand. He wanted to be snuffing lives like candles. But he kept on smiling. Unfortunately that forced good humor seemed to the others to be sheer mockery. The young fellow was scoffing at them and their honest bills against the estate. One and all wanted to wring his neck.

They knew tales of this young Clancy Stewart and what he had done in certain crises when he had been assailed even by heavy odds, so they choked back their fury. It was patent by this time, also, that fifty cents on the dollar was all that they could expect. Having this certainty before them, they decided to leave. And, as they went, they all had something to say to the young owner.

There was only one silent man. He had come from the north, and he held against the Stewart estate a bill for certain mustangs that had been brought down from the wilds. It had been a favorite idea of the elder Stewart that the mustang crossed straight upon the Thoroughbred would give a wonderful stock with the leathery endurance and hardiness of the one base and the greater size and speed of the other. He had hardly begun to make the experiment, however, when he died. And all that was realized by the estate was this added burden at the very end. It was not very great, but eight mustang mares at sixty dollars a head—made a total close to five hundred dollars, and, while it was only a drop in the bucketful of the Stewart debts, it was a great deal to this man from the north.

He looked very much like one of the mustangs he had sold. He had a big, bumpish head, with a long, heavy, red nose and little bright eyes set in close to the shadow of it. His forehead was negligible, but what there was of it was obscured by a dense and wiry brush of tawny hair. His huge ears pricked forward and gave an air of peculiar eagerness to him. The neck that supported the great misshapen head was astonishingly thin and short. The shoulders of the horse hunter were narrow and bowed, and his back was crooked, but his arms and legs were long and muscular. Though he looked at first glance like a feeble and rather sickly man, his performance was sure to surpass his appearance by far. And whenever his hands moved, if it were only to make the slightest gesture, he at once seemed formidable.

Since his arrival at the ranch he had not uttered a word, either to the other creditors or to Stewart himself. He had simply gone over the ranch from one side to the other, and, when he had finished with the task, he returned to the ranch house and sat about to listen to the views of the others, turning his head constantly and attentively from speaker to speaker.

When all the others decided that it was time to go, he rose and went with them, and before he had ridden a quarter of a mile something seemed to go wrong with his cinches. He dismounted at once and spent some time fumbling at straps. When he mounted again, the others were far away and out of sight down the road. As soon as he was sure of this, the hunter turned his horse around and jogged back toward the ranch house.

He found young Stewart in the back yard, sitting silently on the stump of a tree, with a bull terrier squatted on the ground in front of him, looking him solemnly in the face. The horse hunter sat hunched in the saddle, with his chin and his Adam's apple thrust out, and his little eyes blinking down at Clancy.

"Hello, Mister Stewart," he said.

"Hello," answered Clancy. "Who are you?"

"I'm the man who got done out of eight mustang mares," said the horse hunter. "Name's Kensing. Most like you don't recollect it."

"I do not," said Clancy.

"Nor the mares, neither, maybe?"

"There they are," said Clancy, and pointed to a big pasture in which the eight were kept by themselves, a sorry-looking group of malformations, but every one of them of the true, tough mustang breed, as strong as rawhide and as hard to handle.

"I see 'em," said Kensing. "What about it?"

"You said that you brought 'em down here?"

"I did."

"Then go and take them again."

At this Mr. Kensing made a quick motion toward his hip, but Clancy Stewart continued to roll his cigarette with the greatest calmness. And, whatever his original intention might have been, Kensing brought forth a dog-eared, sweat-blackened plug of chewing tobacco, one corner of which he worked off between his worn, yellow teeth. He chewed his quid into a malleable consistency and stowed it away—such a mass that it raised a distinct lump in his cheek. Yet he could talk with the greatest ease. He could even have taken a drink of water—or whiskey. The stomach of Mr. Kensing was veritably as tough as the palms of his hands. And these had never been guilty of gloves.

"Nothing was said about bringing them mares down on trial," he declared.

Clancy seemed disinterested. Perhaps he heard the remark, but he made no sign of it, and began to whistle very softly to the bull terrier who continued to look with earnest and wistful love into the face of his master.

"And nothing," went on Kensing, "was ever said about making me wait a year before I got paid." After a pause he added: "I'm talking considerable business, Stewart."

"I suppose you are."

"What I'm wondering is . . . where do I come out?"

"Ask the other men to whom my father owed ten times as much money as he owed you, where they are going to

185

come out. You'll come out the same way, my friend."

"I got no doubt," said Kensing, "that's the way you figure. But you and me have got minds that work different ways . . . different a whole pile."

"Perhaps that's true."

"I come down here with five hundred dollars' worth of hossflesh and get put off with words instead of coin. Now I'm come down again, and I'm going to get the coin. I ain't asking no interest for the time I've waited. I throw that in for luck. But I sure claim to be interested in that five hundred, and every last cent of it."

The words were emphatic enough, but the voice in which they were uttered was the calmest of calm drawls. However, Clancy now at last looked up.

"Well?" he said.

"I'm talking turkey, son."

"Well?" repeated Clancy.

"Maybe you ain't old enough to know who I am. I'm Bill Kensing." He waited, then flushed deeply when he saw that his shot had failed to strike between wind and water. "In my part of the country that name means something," he said. "It means that the time for fooling and beating around the bush has gone past when they hear that name. Might be that even a youngster like you has got sense enough to understand me."

Clancy Stewart looked up with a most engaging smile. Nothing could have been more obliging. Nothing could have been more misleading.

"Like to do anything I can to make you happier," he said.

"I hope you would, my son, so I'll just tell you what I mean. That five hundred dollars will make me pretty happy."

"But," said Clancy, "there's a difficulty."

"I'm agreeable to talking things out. What stands in between?"

"I'm only paying fifty cents on the dollar to the others,

and, if they heard that I'd paid you off in full, they'd be rather angry, eh?''

"D'you think I'll hang around and talk about what I got?" the other grinned. "I ain't that kind, son. I come for what's mine. I ain't come for no more, but I sure enough ain't going to go back with no less. There's a half dozen gents sleeping deep and cold that thought they could sneak past me without giving me what was my due. And I sure hope that you ain't going to be the seventh.''

"But," said Clancy mildly, "you think I should pay you in full? Wouldn't that really be cheating the other creditors?''

"I ain't here to split hairs," said the horse hunter. "I'm here for action . . . which action is my middle name.''

Clancy looked up with a smile that showed all the whiteness of his teeth.

"Is that sixty-acre lot big enough for you to warm up in?" he asked politely, "because if it isn't, there's a quarter section across the road that you're welcome to try your stunts in. But please don't scare the cows.''

The horse hunter shifted his quid. He had set his teeth and pressed his lips together so that his mouth was outlined by a white, oval mark.

"Maybe you're laughing at me?" he murmured.

"Maybe some folks might think that," said Clancy. "I don't know, I'm sure.''

"Son, you're taking up fire into your hands.''

"Friend," said Clancy, "I love fire,.because I'm cold by nature.''

"And," said the horse hunter, "there ain't nothing that I like no better than to warm up one of them cold gents.''

Clancy smiled again. "As I said before," he remarked, "there's a great deal of room here for you to do as you please, and a perfectly good dog to watch you do it.''

There was a snarl from Kensing. "Kid, grab your gun!''

But the hands of Clancy were employed in negligently juggling a pebble. "If you draw a weapon," he said, "I'll kill you, Mister Kensing, and heaven have mercy on your bones.''

"You? Devil take. . . .''

And he reached for his gun. There is no word for what happens when a gunfighter reaches for his Colt. A light winked at the hip of Bill Kensing, and the gun exploded at the same instant, but it was fired too soon. It merely kicked up the dirt at the feet of Clancy. As a matter of fact, the trigger had been pulled by an involuntary contraction of the finger, which occurred as a forty-five-caliber slug from the gun of Clancy crashed home in the body of Kensing. He stooped forward out of his saddle, landed like a professional tumbler on the back of his shoulders, and lay still. The mustang he had been riding was not frightened. It merely stepped a curious step forward and sniffed at the face of its master. Then with a squeal of terror it wheeled and fled wildly down the road.

Chapter Four
"A Coward's Cunning"

As for Clancy, he did not rise at once. He stared at the body of what had been Bill Kensing, like one who has fallen into a daydream. When, at length, he rose and looked down into the face of the horse hunter, his own expression was not of dismay or fear, but a sort of horror, as if he had not really known that life could be snuffed out so suddenly and the dead thing which remained could be so repulsive. He took up the hat of the man and dropped it over his face. This seemed necessary. Then he looked to the bull terrier. That wise little fighter had not stirred during the combat. He had seen a flash of lightning with two prongs, one of which had entered the earth and the other had dashed out the life of a human being. But, since he could not understand it at a distance, he seemed to feel that it was useless to try to acquire information with his nose. He merely looked at his master and waited for instructions. If there were more trouble, he was begging mutely to be used.

But Clancy now went back toward the house. Sam, the terrier, ran on ahead, scratched open the screen door, and held it wide with his rump while the master passed. The instant Clancy was through, Sam allowed the door to close swiftly, but without a loud noise, and darted ahead to the kitchen door itself. It opened to the blow of his shoulder, and then he stood aside and looked up with a madly wagging tail as the master walked past him. But there was not a word or a pat for poor Sam now. Clancy went on to the telephone, and there he called the sheriff. In a moment the familiar voice of Newt Winters was booming at him down the wire.

"Hello, old son. What's busting out your way?"

"There's some work out here for the undertaker," said Clancy at once.

This brought a long silence. "I hope that's your way of making a joke, Clancy."

"Sheriff, I'd rather be hung than have that sort of a sense of humor."

"Then tell me what's up?"

"First, did you ever hear of a man named Bill Kensing?"

"Bill Kensing? Did I ever hear the name of Julius Cæsar? Of course, I know Kensing. It's his work, is it? I was afraid that it might be. . . ."

"Newt, I killed Bill Kensing."

The sheriff was an old-fashioned man with old-fashioned oaths. "Blue blazes and tiny fishhooks," he murmured down

189

the wire. "But what of that, Clancy?" he added in a moment.

"That's what I want to know from you. What of it?"

"Nothing at all except a vote of thanks from about a dozen sheriffs that I know. Your place was full of folks all today. Of course, a lot of them saw the fracas and seen Bill go for his gun. I guess you gave him an even break, Clancy?"

"He made the first move, Sheriff."

"The devil he did! Well, you've picked up a lot of talent, Clancy. I'd rather for your own sake that you didn't know one end of a Colt from the other. But let that go. The point is that you killed Bill Kensing in a fair and square fight. That's all there is to it."

"Then what shall I do?"

"Ride into town and put yourself in my hands, of course. You'll be admitted to bail mighty quick."

"Sheriff, I have a lot of enemies in town. You know that."

"They can't touch you in this play, Clancy."

"You're sure I'm safe?"

"Absolutely! All you need to do is to trot out your witnesses."

"Not a man saw the shooting."

There was a gasp from the sheriff. "What's that?"

"No witnesses for me. The whole crowd had gone, and then Bill Kensing came back. He wanted me to pay him in full. I told him he'd have to take his luck with the rest of the people my father owed money to. He got ugly. I joked with him. That made him furious. He reached for his gun. . . ."

"Good Lord, Clancy . . . no one saw him do that?"

"Nobody. Will it count against me?"

There was a pause. "No, I'll see that you get a square deal."

"How can you see to that, Newt? You can't be a judge and twelve men."

"Clancy, what have you got in your mind?"

"I've got in mind to saddle a horse and start on an out trail."

"Son, are you plumb out of your wits? Now is your best time to stand a trial."

"No time is good for me to stand a trial in that town."

"How's that, Clancy?"

"You know as well as I. They're against me. They've already written me down as a gunfighter. And I've heard that a lot of them are simply waiting for an opportunity before they bring me to time."

"You're wrong, Clancy. I swear that you're wrong!"

"Newt, I'll never stand trial for this."

"You'll ruin your life, then. I'm your friend, Clancy. I'll do whatever I can for you if you come into town and surrender. But if you refuse to come in, I've got to treat you as an enemy. I've got to call out a posse and chase you down. It means, too, that because you've run away, people will take it for granted that you're guilty."

"Let them think what they please."

"They'll take it for granted that you took Bill Kensing by surprise and shot him!"

"What?"

"I'm telling you the facts, Clancy."

Young Stewart groaned. And the terrier whined softly in his terrible anxiety to read the mind of his master and fly at the throats of his enemies.

"They'll think that I . . . murdered him?"

"Of course!"

"Then I'll come in."

"Right away, Clancy."

"Straight down the road as fast as my horse will take me." And he hung up the receiver.

As for the sheriff, at his end of the line, he rang off with a sigh of the profoundest content. "If I die tomorrow, Jerry," he said to his nearest friend, "I'll have done one good thing.

I've kept young Clancy Stewart to the straight and narrow. He's killed Kensing!''

"Not Bill?''

"That same. The kid done it.''

"From behind, then. No, that's not Clancy's way. But it's hard to believe.''

"It's all of that.''

"He's coming in?''

"I've persuaded him to. How will his trial go?''

"Close,'' prophesied Jerry, "but, seeing that he came straight in and gave himself up, they'll acquit him, I think. He has his enemies, but I don't think that murder is the thing they'd write after the name of Clancy Stewart.''

So they sat down to wait the arrival of their prisoner-to-be. In the meantime all that they had said had been overheard by the man of all work who cleaned up the jail courthouse, swept the offices, sprinkled the lawn, and on occasion acted the part of cook for the prisoners when there were any in the jail. And he was allowed to come and go as he pleased. People thought no more of talking in the presence of Lank Mackay than they would have thought of speaking before a dog or any other dumb beast, for Lank Mackay seemed to have no eyes, no ears, for anything but his work. He was a man without a country, without a soul. In fact, he was one of those strange monsters who are often talked of but very rarely found in the flesh—a born coward.

By this it is meant that courage was in Lank Mackay at absolute zero. He literally had none. If a child yelled at him, Lank Mackay shrank. His only pride, his only love and solace, was the courthouse. He had been a youngster when it was built. It was the pride of the county and the community. And Lank Mackay, watching the foundations dug deep and strong, and then seeing them filled in with imperishable concrete, expected to see rising from that start, some day, towers that swept the sky.

He was not disappointed. The big, quarried rocks were

piled one on the other. The walls lifted and lifted—one, two, and three stories were attained before the roof began to go on, and still the full height was not reached. It already stood enormous over the squat structures in the town. But now a tower was added, which climbed up and up for two short stories more, and in the very top there was an open belfry. In the belfry was placed a bell. Why it should have been hung there, no one knew. It was never used. But to Lank Mackay it seemed that the big bell was the perfect touch. When the structure was completed, it was given a voice. To Lank Mackay the courthouse was a living thing.

He had grown up adoring and wondering over it. Finally he achieved a great ambition and was allowed to work in it. He became the assistant janitor. And when the old man who cared for the building died suddenly, Lank was elevated to the dizzy eminence of head janitor himself. But he had no assistant. He wanted no hands but his own to perform the work around the courthouse. He would stay up late at night to burnish the doorknobs and polish the windows. He had no Sundays or holidays. Every moment was spent cherishing some corner of the courthouse, or else he was busy on the grounds. He dreaded the outdoor work. It exposed him to his mortal enemies, the boys of the blocks around the square. They stole out behind the palm trees on the lawn, and they made rushes at him in little groups, for every one of them had become familiar with his cowardice.

That was not all. One terrible day a boy had stolen behind him and roped him. Then he had been mobbed by a dozen willing hands. He had been dragged, screaming for help, to the water troughs and soundly dunked. After that, the boys had retreated, having rolled him in the dust and left him a mud-blackened cartoon of a man.

Lank Mackay never recovered from that exploit. In his pitiful heart it was like a death stroke. It was not that it encouraged the boys to skirmish more and more close to him, but it was because he could no longer drive them back by threats and a waved rake. They had merely been teasing him before, ready to run if he chased them. Now they knew that they were actually his masters, and they would not give him peace.

The other men around the courthouse had to come to the rescue of Lank. Once or twice the sheriff himself had collared a boy with either hand and dropped them unceremoniously into the trough. More than once a deputy had come out and kicked sundry young scoundrels into the hedge. But all would not do. Boys are like red Indians, not less cunning, far more cruel, and with a devilish patience. They lingered like black clouds on the horizon of Lank Mackay's mind and life.

And so his shame was exposed to the world. Here was a man who was afraid of children. He was so low that men and women refrained from pointing him out. Men never smiled when they spoke of Lank, but, when it was necessary to name him, men scowled upon the ground. The whole human species was impeached for having produced one such member.

And Lank? He could not hate the world. There was not strength in that poor, trembling heart of his to support a passion against all of society. He had only power and room for one rage and one love. The courthouse was his love; and his hate was saved for the head of Clancy Stewart.

Clancy had no more idea of the hatred of the janitor than the stones of the courthouse had of his love. Yet it was not strange that Lank should hate young Stewart, because here was his perfect opposite. Here was a man who carried in his face the proof that he had never known such a thing as fear. His eye was as bold as the eye of a bull. He could stare down ten men as readily as he could outface one. The first time Lank heard the careless laughter of Clancy Stewart he had shuddered, for it seemed to him that the sound was like a tide of sunshining strength and self-confidence. He would have sold his life for the ability to laugh like that just once.

So he had begun to hate Clancy. He had never spoken to him, but whenever he passed him on the street, he trembled with aversion. Once, when three young demons were pursuing Lank across the lawn of the courthouse, he had seen Clancy, standing across the street, convulsed with laughter. And that vision was enough to poison the mind of poor Lank. From that moment he waited to stab Clancy with his vengeance.

On such little things he had built up this consuming passion, but, terrible though his hatred was, it probably would have been dissolved by half a dozen kind and considerate words. But as it was, he was biding his time, and this day it came to him.

He had heard the words of the sheriff over the telephone and afterward to Jerry. And Lank stole out of the room, jammed a hat upon his head, and fled out of the courthouse and over the spongy softness of the lawn. A little later he was still running and gasping down the northwest road. He was half a mile from the edges of the town when he saw a cloud of dust rolling toward him, and then the form of Clancy on his well-known bay mare. He stopped Stewart with a wildly waving arm. Then he had to lean with one hand against the shoulder of the mare, gasping in his wind and staring into the face of Clancy before he could speak.

"Don't go to town. They got a plant. They got you framed!" he was wheezing.

"Look here," said Clancy, "do you know what you're talking about, Lank?"

"I heard the sheriff and Jerry. They aim to get you into the jail, and then they say that it's all over with you."

"How could it be?"

Lank hesitated. He had not dreamed that he would be cross-questioned. His whole purpose was to scare Clancy Stewart into flight, knowing that, once he had become a fugitive, it would be almost impossible for him ever to come back. Yet here was a man who, hearing that he was in peril of his life, still dared to linger and debate the question. It was utterly amazing. And it increased, if that were possible, the distance which poor Lank felt between himself and Clancy.

"I dunno how it could be," he said, "but if you want to keep a rope off'n your neck, I'd say that you'd better keep away from that town and Sheriff Newt Winters!"

The youthful rider looked curiously down into the face of his informant. And from behind the horse the bull terrier, Sam, slid quietly to the front and squatted before the janitor, ready to attack if his master so much as whispered.

"D'you know what would happen to you if the sheriff found out that you had warned me, Lank?"

"What?" breathed Lank.

"Why, about five years in prison, I guess."

"Oh, Lord!"

"I didn't mean it, Lank. But just the same it took nerve to come out here and tell me. Only, I know Newt. I can't imagine that he'd double-cross me."

He shook his head decidedly, as though the full picture of the character of the sheriff returned on his mind's eye. Lank was paralyzed with fear. *What if this man actually rode in to the sheriff and there confronted him with the lie told by Lank?* To Mackay the thought was just as dreadful as the thought of death.

"Look here," said Lank, sweating with terror and fighting for his life, "ain't it in your head that the election ain't so very far off?"

"What the devil has that got to do with me?"

"Think again, Mister Stewart."

"I'm thinking, still, but it leads me nowhere."

"Wouldn't it be pretty good for the sheriff if he made a slick capture just before the voting?"

There was a growl from Clancy Stewart. His mind hung in a doubtful balance.

"Especially of a gunfighter," added Lank in such a whisper as might melt into the thoughts of Clancy without rousing him from his reverie. "They sure hate gunfighters in this here county."

He had struck the theme on which Clancy had already harped in his conversation with the sheriff over the telephone. And this mention of the subject by the janitor was enough to give him proof.

"What can I do to show you that I'm grateful for the tip, Lank?" he asked suddenly.

"Just take care of yourself . . . that's all."

"But what made you warn me, Lank?"

"I hate to see folks stepped on when they're down. That's all."

"Lank," said the youngster impulsively, "you're true blue, after all."

He leaned from the saddle, wrung the hand of Mackay, then whirled the bay mare and cantered down the road, with the dust boiling up under the hoofs of his horse and rippling into a great, white cone behind him. And Lank watched the dust cloud grow dim and dissolve with profound content. Now that Clancy had fled, he would come back at the extreme peril of his life. Lank had the satisfaction of having stabbed with perfect security. From this moment all the forces of the law would unite to beat down the man he hated.

Chapter Five
"Sylvia Experiments"

The sheriff waited a full hour, then he climbed into the saddle and went to investigate. He went out on the road without finding a trace of his man. He went on to the Stewart house, and there he found the dead man lying on his back, looking peacefully up to the sky, with a jet black crow standing on his forehead and watching the sheriff ride in with keen, beady little eyes. The crow flapped away, and the sheriff shouted for Clancy, but no one answered. He opened his bull throat and shouted again, but only an echo, struck back from the face of the barn, made a response. So with perfect certainty he knew what had happened. The heart of Clancy had failed him at the last minute. His guilt had risen and stared him in the face, and he had not dared to brazen the matter out by surrendering to the power of the law.

He was not impressionable, this stalwart sheriff, but, as the full force of all of this came home to him, he groaned and sank down upon a tree stump. He had known Clancy Stewart from the boy's infancy, and he knew that he had in him the making of an outlaw capable of thrilling every adventure-mad boy in the country. Then he ground his teeth with mingled sorrow and rage to think that the duty of capturing such a man should have fallen to his lot.

They buried Bill Kensing the next morning, and the minister was able to think of something pleasant as an epitaph.

But the sheriff was not there to witness that touching ceremony. While the clods were falling on the coffin of bad Bill Kensing, the sheriff was spurring on the out trail after the killer.

The first part of that trail was clearly blocked out, for, from the meeting with Lank, the killer had ridden straight to the West ranch, over the Tufter Hills, and down into the valley. There at the ranch house he had seen Sylvia herself sitting on a rail of the verandah and talking with Charlie Parsons.

He reined his horse to a jog. It would not be hard to tell if the news of the killing had come to them. Their first gestures would betray them. But when he came up, they greeted him as pleasantly as ever, and Charlie Parsons, as though recognizing that he made their gathering a crowd, left at once.

The sound of his galloping horse was still beating back to them when Clancy broke his story. Indeed, he had barely turned to Sylvia with a smile when he found her soberly searching his face with a frown.

"Now," she said, "what has happened?"

"What could happen?" said Clancy. "The creditors think that the Stewarts are not only poor but crooked."

"The cowards," said Sylvia fiercely. And then: "But, oh, they didn't say such a thing before you? Yes, that's it, and you. . . ." She could not complete the sentence, but caught her hand to her lips as if to check terrible words.

"No one said that to me in so many words," he answered.

"But what is it, Clancy?"

"I've come to say good bye."

"Good bye?"

"I'm taking a long trip, Sylvia."

"But where, and why, Clancy?"

"Because there's nothing to keep me here, except one thing. It's bad luck for the Stewarts, this country is. I'm through with it, Sylvia."

"But the one thing, Clancy?"

199

''Of course, you know what I mean. It's you.''

Sylvia was seventeen. She looked older, of course. She had ranged through the mountains with her horses since she was large enough to sit in a saddle. The winds and the sun that had darkened her skin seemed to have made her mind stronger also. She was like Clancy Stewart in this. And if he seemed twenty-five, she seemed not more than four years his junior. Above all, she had a fine, frank, confident way of approaching situations and persons, that spoke of a thousand times as much experience as she had actually had. She never stopped to hesitate and think. The first impulse was always good enough for Sylvia to act on, since that first day when she had run between Oliver Beam and Clancy Stewart and made the other boys draw them apart. She was still just the same Sylvia, only there was more of her.

If one had asked which was the loveliest girl on the ranges, the answer would have been Sylvia's name without the slightest hesitation. She was not beautiful, really. There were imperfections in her features. But it was hard to see them except when she was very tired and looked down to the ground. Then one could see the physical truth about her face, but as a rule there was so much spirit and expression, there was so much life in her eyes and in her smile, there was such a wealth of melody in her throat, and such good will in everything she did, that men accepted her almost as another man at first and were astonished to find, a few minutes later, that to part with her was to tug hard at a string that was set deep in the heart.

Such was the Sylvia who heard Clancy Stewart confessing that he loved her. At least, she knew that it was the nearest he would come to such a confession. And she valued him just as much as if he had fallen upon his knees and protested that she was dearer than the breath he breathed. She valued him very much more, indeed, for she knew Clancy very well—so very well that she was quite aware she could never understand him entirely. Perhaps that was what most fascinated her.

Other men laid their characters plainly before her. They revealed themselves in half a dozen words, or by too much foolish smiling, or in a thousand, small things which could not be fitted into words, but Clancy she found to be a little removed from her. Indeed, he made no effort to conceal anything from her. And yet, he was never entirely revealed. Sometimes she felt it was because he cared for one thing in the world more than he cared for her. Just what the other thing was, she could not decide. Sometimes she named it pride. At least, there was something between them. And, striving to surmount that barrier, she was beginning to find that she could not do without seeing Clancy quite frequently. She had not known how much he meant. But now came the confession from his lips, and her mind was made up on the instant.

"That means what?" she asked.

"Why," said Clancy, "I'm no good at riddles, Sylvia."

She could have smiled. That stiff answer was exactly what she had expected, for, though he could be poetic enough about small things, she knew that he always made a point of being rather noncommittal on great occasions. Instead of smiling, she went a little closer to him.

"Do I dare guess your motive in leaving, then?" she asked.

A sudden color rose to his face. Just for an instant his eyes were directly before her, with such emotion flaming in them that she was bewildered. Then he glanced down and set his teeth.

"I have to say something now, Sylvia, I've. . . ."

"Don't say a thing more," she broke in. "What you have done hasn't a bit to do with what you are, because I know you, Clancy. . . ."

"I'm afraid you don't," he said. "Because . . . Sylvia, about an hour ago I killed a man."

Sylvia kicked a pebble and then watched it roll. He waited for her to say something, but she seemed to have fallen into a dream.

"I supposed that would come," she said at last. "It was always in you."

"I suppose it was," he answered as stiffly as ever. "And so I've come to say good bye, Sylvia."

"You're going to run away, then?"

"I am. They wouldn't give me a fair trial. They know that I love my gun too well."

"That's true."

She was like a noncommittal friend.

"What do you plan to do, and where are you going, Clancy?"

"I've no idea. Any road is a good road to me."

"And when do you come back?"

"I can never come back."

She waited a while and then raised her eyes to him. "You can't mean that," she said.

"But I do."

"Then you're a coward, Clancy."

"I tell you, Sylvia, that it takes every bit of courage I have for me to keep away from you."

"But why do you give me up?" And she added suddenly: "I do love you, Clancy."

He clasped his hands behind his back as though to keep them from going around her; he lifted his head and his glance went quite past her.

"I wish," he said, "that I knew what was the honorable thing to do."

"Clancy, are you a stick of wood?"

That swept them into an embrace. And when, a moment later, her mind cleared, she knew that she had been right in making the experiment, for, after all, it had been an experiment. She had not really known that she loved Clancy Stewart, but, now that she had taken the one step forward, it seemed to have carried her a thousand miles. He had passed into her life, and she into his, so that, as she looked up to him, it seemed to Sylvia that he was far closer to her than her father or her brother. And, at last, all the barriers were melted away in Clancy. He was not too proud to tell her a thousand foolish and tender things until she broke away, half laughing and half weeping.

"But you have to go," she cried to him. "Oh, Clancy, every second I've kept you here...."

"I'll be back in a week. And then I'll take you, Sylvia. But I have to have money...I have to have a horse...I can't let you ride a step on a horse of your father's. And you'll be ready to go?"

"In five seconds, day or night, whenever you call me, Clancy."

Chapter Six
"Oliver Starts a Trail"

The sheriff did not catch young Stewart. That knight of the range had vanished like a ghost among the upper hills, and people neither heard of him nor saw him. Talk was made about him and his wild exploit for a month and then the topic died down, for, though legends are cherished on the mountain desert for a long, long time, it generally requires something remarkable to start the story. And what Stewart had done had been simply one flash.

Once Stewart was gone, as was generally noticed, Sylvia

West lost all interest in social pleasures. Time had been when she would gallop her horse thirty miles with the utmost cheerfulness and dance the sun up out of the east, but now she seemed to care nothing for such affairs. What she wanted was to be left alone on the ranch. Her father said that these were beginning to be the happiest days of his life.

No one, as a matter of fact, connected her change of habits with the disappearance of Stewart, because she was perfectly poised and cheerful whenever his name was mentioned. She did not blame him, and she did not pity him. She spoke as if his actions were a matter of indifference. So people quickly forgot that she had been intimate with him ever.

That is, all forgot it save Oliver Beam. But, though his mind worked slowly, it worked just as surely. At about the time when the rest of the world admitted that Sylvia West was heart and fancy free, he determined that she must be watched, so he began operations on the dam in Gunter Valley.

This was his own and favorite project. His father had always laughed his idea down. He had waited for a time after the property came into his hands before he began the task. But, at length, he was ready. He secured the engineer who would talk over the plan with him, and then he found a construction company that would undertake the work. It was not a very large scheme, but he could back enough water into the valley, he hoped, to irrigate a tract of five thousand acres of rich, sandy loam which belonged to the estate, also, and which was known as Gunter Flats. As reclamation projects go, therefore, it was not a very great thing, but, if he succeeded, he might boost the price of that tract from fourteen dollars an acre to three hundred. Best of all, if he could accomplish that, the ranchers would no longer be able to say that his father had made the fortune, and that young Oliver Beam was only saving it.

These were all good reasons for starting work on the dam. There was a second reason which was even more important, and it was that the work on the dam brought Oliver near the West ranch. As a matter of course he was asked by the hospitable cattleman to spend his spare time in their house. Oliver accepted. It was exactly what he wanted. In the first place, he desired to find out whether Sylvia had lost her interest in him. In the second place, he wished to keep a close eye on her and make sure that she was not meeting Clancy Stewart clandestinely.

About the first question there was no room for doubt. She was perfectly cheerful and merry and kind with Oliver. But something—the absence of which was what made it for the first time noticeable to Oliver—was gone. He had not even realized that it existed until he found it vanished, but now he could remember certain signs of voice and eye which had seemed to indicate that she was aware of him when he was in a room with her, a tingling awareness something like that which he felt when even the thought of Sylvia passed through his mind. That slight widening of the eyes, the faint change of the voice, was no longer there, and all he saw, instead, was a sort of sisterly affection.

She was very fond of him beyond a doubt. It was the certainty of that fondness which, in some way, made her positive that every germ of real love for him was actually gone. The contest was over. There was no longer any rivalry between Oliver and Clancy. Sylvia knew that, and so did Oliver, but, though he knew that his own cause was lost, he was not so entirely sure that Clancy's cause was won. At least, he wanted to have some tangible proof of it before, like a level-headed man, he convinced himself that he was simply wasting too much time, and before he gave up Sylvia and the thought of her.

So he had Thanksgiving dinner with the Wests. Time sloped on into December. It was two months and a half since Clancy Stewart had ridden away and left Bill Kensing dead behind him, but still there was no word from Clancy, and there was no sign of him near Sylvia. It was freely reported through the countryside that he must have been killed in some accident among the mountains. Perhaps an accident with a gun had dropped him among the rocks, and the coyotes and the buzzards had long ago done their work on him and left him to whiten in the winter weather. But Sylvia seemed not at all unhappy, so that Oliver began to feel more and more uncertain about her. If she had stopped caring for him, it seemed equally probable that she had stopped caring for Clancy Stewart. And with this Oliver began to hope again.

In mid-December a northwester came combing over the mountaintops and brought with it a driving fall of snow. It was not cold weather. The snow whipped down to the earth in a soft slush just too firm to run. For three days it was packed down in a soggy mass of increasing depth. Then came a freeze and mountains and plains and valleys were sheathed with an equal coating of ice. A horse, even when specially shod, could hardly keep its feet on such going as this. And a man could not walk fifty yards without taking a risk of breaking his neck.

Then there was another fall of snow. It served to mask the most slippery places, and travel through the mountains was quite shut away, yet even on this night Oliver Beam did not give up his midnight vigil. He had formed the habit of rising promptly at twelve each night, stealing down from his room in the West ranch house, and then throwing a circle around the house, through the woods, past the nearer sheds. He hardly knew why he did this. But every night, after his coming, he wakened with a start at about that time and felt in his mind a heavy weight of expectation. It was a very definite feeling. Somehow it seemed impossible that the Clancy Stewart, whom he knew so well. could have given up all hopes of Sylvia, and without a battle to see her at last to say farewell. And since it would be dangerous to return by day, was it not probable that he must steal back at night?

As a matter of fact he was ashamed to confess that he

actually hoped to find, or feared to find, Clancy wandering about the house by night, but at least he could not lie awake the rest of the night with a leaden heart, so he would rise, put on his clothes, and go out for his stroll around the house. When he came back, he was instantly asleep.

On this night of mid-December he rose as usual, dressed, buckled on his Colt, and started out on his tour of inspection, stealing cautiously down the stairs and opening the door with the utmost care, for he was rather childishly proud of the fact that he had been able to go out from the house every night without alarming a single one of the many sleepers under the roof.

He found outdoors a rare and lovely night. The last clouds from the storm were blown over. The sky was an infinite depth of midnight blue and quivering with stars. There was light enough to show the host of the pines sweeping up the sides of the mountains, and the mountains themselves walking away into the horizon. To enjoy all that beauty Oliver gave himself a long moment at the edge of the verandah. Then the dry snow crunched loudly under his feet as he stepped down.

He went, as usual, straight into the thicket that lay west of the house and through it by the winding path which the cattle had beaten on their way for water. From the thicket he made a turn around the sheds and corrals where part of the hospital bunch was kept. He had rounded the last of the sheds when he saw the figure.

It came from the big barn where the saddle stock were kept in this bitter weather. It passed into the second copse which stood near the house, throwing a jetty shadow on the snow. At first sight of the rider on the horse Oliver made sure that his vigils had been rewarded at last, and that he had seen Clancy himself. But another glance assured him that it was a woman, and a third look gave him proof that it was Sylvia.

Sylvia was riding alone toward the mountains on her favorite little paint hoss. He regarded that miracle with utter amazement. But a little later it seemed to him that everything was clear. This was the meaning of her quiet content, her indifference to dances and parties, her mild coldness to himself. She had been making these trips night by night into the hills to meet her lover, who had hidden himself in the thick tangle of caons and forests which turned the district into a hole-in-the-wall country.

He did not wait to saddle a horse. Over this slippery going, a man on foot could outrun the finest horse that ever stepped. He set out in pursuit as he was.

Chapter Seven
"Oliver Interrupts"

He could have called her back. She was still in easy range of his voice. But if he called, everyone in the house would hear. And if they wakened, what would come to Sylvia out of the flood of questions? And what would that stern old father of hers think and do? Besides, the thing to do was to get rid of the evil by striking at its source, and that source was the outlawed Clancy Stewart. On this very night, perhaps, he would attempt to persuade Sylvia to run away with him and share the wild life of a hunted man.

So Oliver drew his belt a notch tighter and started ahead. As he started, the wind began to rise out of the north. It was a fortunate thing for Oliver. It promised him snow in the face before long, unless the wind changed its quarter. It was

better to face a storm wind than to have to dread the sound
of his footfalls on a silent night. The rush of the wind covered that. He could come as close to the fugitive as covert
allowed him to do. And, since there was a dense and denser
growth of trees in the direction which she took, that meant
that he could travel at her very heels. If perhaps a twig
snapped under his foot, she would think it a branch snapping
under the united pressure of snow and wind. And if his foot
crunched noisily in the snow close behind her, she could only
call it the falling of other snow, blown from the boughs
above.

So he kept well up. The sky overhead grew steadily
darker. Section by section from the north, the stars were blot-
ted out. And where the trees were thick, it was impossible
to see his way clearly. He had to be more or less guided by
the grunting and snorting of the horse, as the gallant little
broncho worked into the teeth of the wind in spite of the bad
going underfoot. They climbed to the first low ridge, slid and
skidded into the hollow beyond, and then toiled up the next
slope. At the crest Oliver saw the girl and her horse blown
to a standstill, a faint outline against the sky. Then she disappeared on the farther side, and Oliver hurried in pursuit.
He was cuffed to a standstill, in just the same fashion, by
the tearing wind out of the north when he reached the sum-
mit. But, gasping and then setting his teeth, he fought his
way down to the nearest copse.

There he paused to reconsider. This night brought as black
a storm as he had ever faced, and it seemed to him madness
that a girl like Sylvia should have ventured out into it. The
snow was coming again. Now it was frozen sleet which rattled like bullets among the branches of the evergreens. Where
it struck his face or his hands, it stung him bitterly. He
ground his teeth when he thought that Clancy Stewart had
allowed the girl to come to meet him through such weather.

No doubt the fellow had degenerated even from his old,
happy-go-lucky standard of manners and morals. And more

than once, as he continued, Oliver beat his hands together to keep the circulation warm beneath the gloves, and to keep some nimbleness in his fingers. He felt a shrewd certainty that he would have to reach for a gun before dawn came on this night. And, indeed, no matter at what price, he was determined to bring Sylvia safely back to her father's house. He could not see her life thrown away on a hunted man. That Clancy was infinitely more gifted in the use of all manner of weapons made no real difference. He could take a gambling chance.

The roar of the wind had risen to become like the voice of a waterfall quite covering the noise of Sylvia's horse, and the night was a great blot of darkness, so that he had to press close, close upon the heels of the laboring horse. But the trail ended at last. It could not have continued much longer into that wind.

Presently he saw a ray of light ahead of him, often broken away by intervening tree trunks as he advanced, but shining again as he went ahead once more. The girl directed the horse toward it. As he came closer, Oliver could see that it was a hut under the trees, and that the light was pouring through a crack in the one door, which was on the leeward side of the shack. Before this door Sylvia dismounted, called in a voice which blew wildly back upon Oliver, and then the door was thrown wide before her. Oliver saw the form of a man black against the firelight inside. He saw Sylvia taken in the arms of the stranger and drawn into the house. Then the door was closed, and Oliver was left in the dark of the storm and the deeper dark of his thoughts.

He so far forgot that even the danger of the cold passed from his mind. He roused himself, first of all, on account of the chill that was invading his right hand. It made him remember that his life might hang on the agility of that hand on this night. He began to beat the warmth into it with a great effort. He worked the fingers vigorously against the palm of his left hand. When the circulation was finally restored, he went ahead toward the house, keeping his right hand under his coat.

At the door he pressed his face close to a rent in the wood. The remnants of an old, cast-iron stove were there, with the front torn out and a fire weltering on the inside, cramming the rusted chimney with more smoke than it would take, and sending a surplus curling out into the room. By the light of the fire he saw that it was, indeed, Clancy Stewart who had met the girl here. He was not greatly altered from the Clancy he had always known, except that his face was a little leaner, a little older, than before. Though this was doubtless the effect of the glancing firelight, it appeared to Oliver that there was a singular wildness in the eyes of the exile. The rapture of their first greeting had subsided a little. They stood away from each other with their hands still clasped.

"I saw the signal yesterday afternoon," said Sylvia.

"I've been praying that you'd fail to see it. I've been half mad since the storm began."

"It started as I left the house almost. . . ." She paused.

"Almost as though nature itself were against us. Is that what you mean, Sylvia?"

"I suppose I do. But it was strange to feel that wind rise just as I started out to find you."

"But you kept on, Sylvia."

"I wouldn't let myself be startled by such a thing as the wind. Of course not."

"We're going to trek straight across the mountains," he said. "I've planned everything. I've found the minister to marry us. I've planned the way we'll get to the sea. . . ."

"The sea, Clancy?"

"Of course! We're going to put an ocean between us and this range."

"We can't travel on nothing. I'll be able to bring some money, though. . . ."

"Money from your father's house?" He laughed with a furious happiness. "I'll take no help from any man. They've started fighting me, and I'm going to fight back. I've been winning so far, and I'll keep right on winning. Are you afraid to go with me, Sylvia?''

"I'll go to the end of the world with you, Clancy."

"Heaven bless you. Money or no money?"

"Money or no money."

"But what have you been thinking all of these days of silence?"

"It has been hard, Clancy, but I've kept my faith every instant. I knew that you would not fail to come back."

"Dear old Sylvia."

"And here you are. But you've been starved, Clancy. You're thin as a ghost. Poor boy."

"Starved with hard work," said Clancy, and, still laughing, he showed her the palms of his hands. They were covered with brown, leathery calluses which looked like the growth of two years instead of a tenth of that time. "Hard work did it," went on Clancy. "Took some of the fat out of my face . . . and my head, too."

"But where have you been working, Clancy, and for what?"

"This." He scooped a leather bag from a corner of the room. He dropped to his knees, spread a piece of paper, and upon it poured out a mound of yellow dust.

"Gold!" cried Sylvia.

"Thirty pounds of it."

"Clancy, how did you do it?"

"With these!" He held up his two hands to her. "But it's enough to start on."

"We can go anywhere in the world and start with that."

"I intended to keep the secret, Sylvia, but I couldn't. Oh, how happy I am."

It seemed to Oliver Beam, watching and staring with an aching heart, that Clancy had been transformed. Half of his pride was gone. Half of his coldness was lost. He had grown wild, indeed, but his heart was a thousandfold warmer.

"And I, Clancy . . . my dear . . . but how did you do it?"

"While I was wandering, I found an old claim with an old prospector working at it. He was getting nowhere, chiefly because he was too old and feeble to swing his single jack. I got him to sell out everything as it stood. I gave him my last penny, and let him ride away on my horse. Then I began to tear the heart out of that rock, and I got this for a result. That's all there is to the story."

"It's a lovely story, Clancy. But it's like a fairy tale."

"It is."

"Because there seems to be magic in it . . . it's magic, you see."

"White magic, Sylvia. It'll make you happy, I hope, for the rest of your life."

"But if it were black magic?" she said.

"How could it be? But you look half sad, Sylvia."

"Because I begin to wonder. . . ."

"What?"

"If this can last. I feel as if we were stealing happiness."

"That's silly. When we're ten thousand miles from here. . . ."

"Clancy!"

"Is that too far?"

"Only, it takes my breath."

"Well, you'll find that we'll be happy. Or we could stay closer. Suppose we found some little place in Italy. . . ."

"Down by the sea. . . ."

"And in the hills. . . ."

"With a river running near it. . . ."

"Close to the edge of a lake. . . ."

"With that blue sky reflected in it. . . ."

"Would you be happy there, Sylvia?"

"It would be heaven!"

"I could buy some land and farm it."

"You, a farmer! Oh, silly."

"But you don't know what a sober and serious character I've become, my dear."

"I know you a lot better than you think, Clancy Stewart. I'm going to be the business head of this family."

"You shall be, and a thousand times welcome to the post. But wherever we go and whatever we do, it doesn't really matter."

"Of course not. We could be happy on a desert island."

So, with laughter, they fell into each other's arms. And Oliver Beam staggered back from the door with blackness swimming before his eyes. He had lost her, then, completely. But now the wind curled in around the house and caught at him. He came resolutely back. It was necessary to get in there and face them, so he struck heavily against the door.

In an instant it was jerked open. He strode in and found that the revolver was in the hand of Clancy, while Sylvia stood back by the stove with clenched hands and staring eyes. His mind leaped back to something else he had seen—a male and female wolf he had once caught in the same circle of traps some years before.

Chapter Eight
"A Strong Man's Stand"

It was Clancy who recovered first, but, although he addressed Sylvia, his gaze was fixed steadily upon Oliver.

"I thought a minute ago," he said, "that there was no one in the world I could trust near us. But here comes the one man of all. Oliver, if you're half as happy to see me as I am to see you, we'll begin by shaking hands.''

And the hand of Oliver took the slenderer fingers of the outlawed man. As he held them strongly, he reflected that now his great opportunity to crush Clancy had come at last. No matter how superior in speed and nimbleness, there was no crushing strength in Clancy to match against his own. It seemed that the same thought came to young Stewart himself, for a fear flickered for an instant in his eye and then went out, but only as the grip of Oliver was relaxed.

''And yet,'' went on Clancy, ''I can't help wondering at you rambling through the hills helter-skelter at this time of night . . . and such a night, Oliver.''

But Oliver Beam was not the man to maintain a pretense. He shrugged his big shoulders. ''You know that I haven't been rambling,'' he said.

''You haven't?''

''Of course not. I've followed Sylvia.''

''I can't quite make that out,'' said Clancy.

''Oh,'' muttered Oliver, ''I suppose you can't. But. . . .''
He halted, and Sylvia herself came smoothly to his rescue.

''He feared I was going to get into trouble. That's why he trailed me here. He was afraid that I was keeping bad company at night. So, of course, like an old friend, he came along to find out what was what. Is that it, Oliver?''

Her easy sarcasm made him flush, but although he drew his jaw into a squarer line, he did not flinch.

''That's it,'' he said.

''But now you find me in good hands, I suppose you'll be remembering that you have a soft bed waiting for you in my father's house?''

He shook his head.

''Ah,'' said Clancy, ''is that it?''

''It is,'' said Oliver.

''Then let's step outside at once.''

''Willingly!''

They had both turned toward the door when Sylvia ran before them.

"What is it?" she cried.

"I have something to say to Oliver that even you must not hear, Sylvia."

She eyed them shrewdly. "I think I know," she said at last. "You . . . you were going outside to fight."

"Fight? Old friends like Oliver and I?"

But the dancing devil was in his eyes, easily to be seen.

"Clancy, on your honor, do you mean no harm?"

"You are too solemn, Sylvia. It's an old affair between Oliver and me."

"You are going to fight?" she insisted, and then she cried to Oliver: "Have you come to steal all my happiness the moment it begins?"

"Happiness?" he echoed.

"What else could it be?"

"Do you want me to tell you?"

"No, no! I can read your mind, and what I read I hate the sight of!"

"Very well. I shall say nothing, then."

"And you are going back, Oliver?"

"It's a tough night for the walk home, don't you think?"

He had put it mildly enough, but his meaning was plain. He was there to stay with them.

"Let's hear everything he has to say," said Clancy. "Sit down, everyone. There's the remains of the old, homemade chair for you, Sylvia. Take that box, Oliver. And the stump will do for me. Now let's hear all you have to say. Time is nothing."

He sat down and locked his hands around one knee, smiling, but there was no mirth in the smile, and his eyes were glaring straight at Oliver like the yellow eyes of a great cat.

"What can talking do? Are you mad to try to persuade me?" asked Sylvia.

"I suppose I am. But I'd rather save you and have you hate me."

"Save me?"

"Yes."

"And from what?"

"From utter ruin, Sylvia."

"That sounds like a book. But what does it mean?"

"It means a wrecked life."

"Do you think so? But to cut the whole matter short, it's my life, and I'm ready to throw it away, since you wish to call it that. I have a right to do that if I choose."

"I don't think you have."

"Really?"

"No. You haven't the slightest right to break your father's heart, for one thing."

"All fathers' hearts are broken when their daughters marry. And all fathers recover."

"You can't laugh me down. I say you have to consider your friends. If you were willing to have their friendship, you have to be willing to have their advice, too, now and then."

"Only when I ask for it."

"Did you ask to be brought into the world? Did you ask to see the light or breathe? Did you pick your friends out of the thin air? You took what you found. You made nothing. And I say they have a claim on you. Besides, Sylvia, you're too pretty to belong entirely to yourself."

It was rather a neat turn for Oliver. He usually spoke seldom and bluntly to the point. In fact, he was altogether eloquent on this subject, beyond his precedents.

"That's well put," said Clancy carelessly.

"You'll care for other things I have to say a lot less than for this one, Clancy."

"And how the devil do you know that I'm going to sit here and let you rave along?"

"If you love Sylvia, you'll want her to hear every word I can say."

"How's that?"

"If your marriage is the right thing, nothing I can possibly say can shake either her or you."

"That's true."

"Then let me finish what I've come to say."

"But by what authority do you come to interfere, and to hound, and make us unhappy?"

"Will you be unhappy? If what I have to say can make you unhappy, then you admit that what you intend to do is wrong. And that's my authority for coming."

"I didn't know you were such a logician, Oliver. Talk ahead, then."

"Oh, it won't take long. In the first place, Sylvia, you realize that the rest of your life will be wasted?"

She smiled knowingly at Clancy. "I think not, Oliver."

"I understand what you mean," he said gravely. "I was outside the door when the gold was poured out of the sack. But it isn't the money I speak of. I'd give you ten times as much money as that if gold would make your happiness. Will you believe that?"

Such was his simple directness that half of the bitterness and the scorn and the anger passed from their faces, and they were able to see that he meant what he said. It was for her happiness primarily that he was talking. And from this point they both leaned forward, seriously, to listen.

"But you see, it could never in the world be managed with more money."

"Explain yourself, Oliver."

"You could never get away from them. They never sleep. They'd run you down, you know."

"I've been perfectly safe all these weeks in the mountains. How do you account for that?"

"Because you were living by yourself. But the minute you come into the world again and take away a wife, they'll be after you. Not with polite questions, but with blunt bullets, Clancy.''

Clancy flashed a glance at Sylvia. She was standing the torment admirably. She had flushed a little and then grown pale, but her head was as high as ever, and her eyes fixed as steadily upon the face of Beam.

"Look back over history," said Oliver. "You know the stories of a hundred men who tried to get away from the law. And they've always failed."

"Man-killing, cruel, wolfish men, all of them," put in Sylvia.

"And what would Clancy be after six months of being hunted? What would he be after having dodged a few bullets? He'd be shooting to kill, Sylvia, and he shoots too straight not to do what he wants with a gun. And with three or four dead men behind him. . . ."

"Stop," gasped Sylvia.

For the first time Clancy became really alarmed. He had felt that he could count on Sylvia as he would have counted on himself. He had attributed to her a nerve of iron like his own. He could hardly believe his eyes when her courage was suddenly shattered. She began to tremble, and her glances roved over the cabin. Clancy stepped near her, as though he were actually shielding her from physical punishment.

"No more ghost talk, Oliver!" he commanded.

"That's for Sylvia to say."

"I think not."

"I say it is. She's taking a step now that she can never draw back from. She's either got to be back at her father's house before morning, or else she has to marry you. You know that. But where is there a minister? And how can you get to one before morning?"

"That's my affair," exclaimed Clancy with the indignation of one caught in the wrong.

"It's my affair, too, and the affair of everyone who cares about the honor of Sylvia."

"That's enough!" said Clancy fiercely.

"I've only begun. Are you afraid to have her hear the truth about her position with you?"

"I'm afraid of nothing, but I don't choose to stand quietly by while you insult me. I say that the time has come for you to leave the shack, Oliver."

"And I say that I shall not stir a foot until I know that she is going back with me."

"Back with you? Look here, Oliver, have you gone crazy with jealousy?"

"I've never," said Oliver, "made a secret of my love for Sylvia. But I think I'm not jealous now. I'm simply trying to work for her best happiness. Will you believe me, Sylvia?"

"I . . . ," she began, but Clancy cut in sharply.

"Talk to me, not to her," he said sternly. "And I'll answer you in any way you want to start talking."

It was plain enough now that he would fight, and fight soon, unless Oliver withdrew. And the latter, measuring his chances with a great, sad heart, knew that he could not hope to win. And he knew, also, that he could not withdraw.

"I can't go," he said frankly. "I've got to take her back with me, Clancy."

"Do you stick to that?"

"Yes."

"Then . . . ," said Clancy significantly.

"Whatever you say."

"We'll go outside. . . ."

"Clancy . . . Oliver!" cried Sylvia and started forward.

"Now," shouted Clancy, sweeping her back with one hand and reaching for his revolver with the other.

Oliver, desperate with eagerness, tore out his own weapon. The cold had left his fingers now. They were flexible and agile. Never had he made a draw so smoothly or so deftly. Yet it seemed that his hand was weighted down with rounds of lead. A gun darted into the grip of Clancy. With one bullet he ripped a long splinter from the floor. With the second he shot Oliver Beam fairly through the body, and the latter sank by slow degrees, down and down, like a snowman melting with terrible swiftness.

Sylvia and Clancy reached him at the same instant. What he said, before his eyes closed, was: "Marry her, Clancy! In the name of heaven, marry her, and I'll die happy!"

"I promise!" cried Clancy, and a faint smile touched the lips of Oliver.

But he was not dead. He had merely fainted away. They found the weak and fluttering beat of his heart. They ripped away the clothes and found the purple-edged wound against the staring white of the flesh. In frantic haste they began the bandaging. It was done at last. He had not yet opened his eyes. Beside him crouched Clancy, holding the head of his fallen rival. Then Sylvia rose to her feet and took command.

"He needs food," she said. "You have to get it for him. I'll nurse him and cook for him. You'll hunt and bring in the supplies."

"A doctor . . . ," began Clancy.

"It would take a whole day to cross the ice and bring a doctor back. It won't do, Clancy. And in the meantime everyone will think that I've run away with Oliver Beam."

Chapter Nine
"Lank Does the Unexpected"

This, of course, was the interpretation that everyone put upon the disappearance of Sylvia and Oliver. It was an elopement. The only strange thing about it was that Oliver Beam should have been one of the pair. Such a steady-going and solid fellow as Oliver—but, of course, it was Sylvia's work that had swept him away.

She came in for a great many unkind remarks. It had not taken long, people said, for her to see that it was foolish to grieve for a lost lover. She had changed her mind and taken the second best. Her father's consent, of course, would be given instantly to such a match as that with Oliver, for he was the matrimonial prize of the whole district. But Sylvia, for a dash of romance, had decided upon a runaway marriage. So the ladies shrugged their shoulders, and the men grinned. Sylvia's father grinned most of all. He did not care what other folks might say about Sylvia's marriage with Oliver. In his estimation such an alliance with the Beam fortune could be nothing but a magnificent diplomatic triumph for Sylvia.

There was one person in the county, however, who was even more delighted than Mr. West, and this was none other than Lank Mackay. For Lank saw, in the marriage of Sylvia, the dissolution of the last power which might attract the gunfighter back to that region, and, accordingly, the end of his fears that Clancy might return like an avenging whirlwind and sweep him out of existence. He would never come back, even if he knew the truth concerning that tale which Lank Mackay had told him as he was riding toward the town to give himself up to the sheriff and so escape the danger of the law. Even if he knew this, it would not help Clancy now. He was formally outlawed, and his head would soon fall for the sake of the price which was resting on it. Yet the beautiful part of the whole affair, it seemed to Lank, was that he had accomplished his purpose without a touch of real danger to himself.

He had gone about for days and days hugging to his breast this consciousness. It gave him a sense of power, also. These men who so openly scorned him, who treated him gently, as they would have treated a cowardly dog—who could tell when he might have a chance to destroy one of them just as he had destroyed the great Clancy Stewart—and all by words. At this thought he would laugh with such infinite relish that he quite exhausted himself. Sometimes, when he saw one of his tormentors on the lawn of the courthouse, he would mark down the boy with so fixed and malignant a glance that the child dreamed of it that night and would decide to give up that delightful pastime of baiting the janitor of the courthouse.

Indeed, a change was gradually coming in the character of Lank Mackay. So great had been the feat of toppling Clancy Stewart to ruin that he would often look around upon other men with so hungry an eye that they shivered under it and found them regarding Lank for the first time as a man. In fact, Lank was growing with an astonishing rapidity.

The greatest day came when he was charged by four wild young ruffians, all yelling like Indians, while he was at work, raking the lawn. He had leaned passively on his rake and watched them sweep upon him, for he was too busy marking their faces to have time for fear. He was too busy deciding what cruel torments should be the fate of each, to draw back a step from their charge. Like Indians, when they found that he did not shrink from them, they swerved aside at the very moment of the meeting and swooped away on either side. Then they danced off from him in a loose circle, encouraging one another with shrill cries to attack the enemy, but not one having nerve enough to make the assault.

"I'll tell you what I'm going to do," said Lank Mackay at last. "I'm going to wait for night. And one of these nights I'm going to sneak off to your homes. I'm going to push open your windows without making no noise . . . oh, I know the rooms that every one of you sleep in. And I'm going to sneak through the window and come over to your bed . . . all in the black dark that you can't see nothing in . . . and then I'm going to go . . . so! I'm going to grab you just like that by your throats. Ah, you've no guess what a lot of strength there is in my hands. They'll cut right through your windpipe. And there won't be no sounds . . . there won't be even no kicking, because I'll sit on your legs while I throttle you. That's what I'm going to do, and, in the morning, when your ma comes in to look at you, she'll find you lying real pretty, with your tongue and your eyes sticking out, and your face all black! Ha! ha! ha!"

The ringing laughter of Lank Mackay made the four boys jump back. They eyed him for another awful instant, and then they whipped around and took to their heels, and each one fled as fast as his legs could carry him until he found himself safe in the house of his father.

Lank Mackay was still leaning on the rake on the lawn of the courthouse and grinning after them, until suddenly he was aware of what had actually happened. They had rushed upon him, and he had stood his ground without fear. Without fear! He had waited for them, and then they had shrunk away before him. It had not been natural. There was something unearthly in it. By the mere power of his mind he had checked them. Then, when they were checked, he had beaten them with terrible and cruel words, and he had routed them before him. At that delightful recollection he drew in his breath as though he were drinking.

There was no more work for Lank Mackay that day. He was paralyzed. Joy had numbed all of his mental faculties. He sat apart and wrapped his long arms around himself and brooded upon the delightful and strange victory. By the next day he found himself surrounded by an entirely new atmosphere. He could sense it the instant he stepped into the street. He could feel it when he passed the first urchin. Instead of elbowing him off the sidewalk, the boy fled, round eyed, to the other side of the street and passed him sidling, as though he dared not take his eyes off the monster. Other boys acted in the same fashion. There was no doubt that the word had been passed around by the four who had been frightened. Every youngster in the town shared in the reign of terror that now began. In fact, his strange cowardice had prepared them for an equally unnatural strength.

A rumor passed about that a Mexican had given him an amulet which removed all fear from his body. That story was widely believed. In fact, Lank had always been so strange that people were prepared to see him remain a freak. They were all confirmed in their certainty that something queer had happened in the mind of Lank Mackay when the adventure of Wild Charlie Appleton occurred.

Charlie was a famous character in seven counties in which he had killed seven men. And though he had been saved from hanging by that strange reluctance of a Western jury to convict men for killings they do in gunfights—on the theory, no doubt, that every juryman may find himself one day in need of similar leniency—yet the repute of Wild Charlie was so black that he could no longer find work as a cowpuncher. No one else would work on the same ranch with him. He was reduced to eking out his living by means of cheating at cards and similar employments. When his pocket had enough money in it, and when he had brooded long enough upon his grievances and the debts owing to him from the rest of the world, he was in the habit of filling his stomach with bad whiskey and then throwing himself into the saddle to career through the town looking for trouble.

He rarely found it, however, for no one cared to cross him. Brave men ran when they saw Wild Charlie on a rampage. Not that they would have dreaded to face him if there had been stakes worth fighting for. But who will risk his life to kill a mad dog, unless the dog is actually threatening someone with its teeth?

So on this day Wild Charlie, with a gun in one hand and a quirt in the other and the reins of his horse between his teeth, with his hat blown off, and his long, pale hair flying, rushed across the town, reached the courthouse square, and didn't hesitate to gallop on over the lawn itself. The sacred lawn of the courthouse, whose leveled surface filled the heart of Lank Mackay with Homeric pride. He saw the terrible gunfighter approach, a figure dimmed by shadowy anger in his eyes, for he saw the hoofs of the cow pony falling fetlock deep, muffled in their fall by the spongy surface from which, at every stride, great, raw clots of turf were thrown up behind to hang in the air. And they were to Lank more precious than drops from his heart.

He rushed from behind a palm and stood in the path of the onrushing badman with his rake poised in his hands. He shouted, and at the shout the trained pony halted. It halted with such suddenness that Wild Charlie was jerked far forward in the saddle. Before he could straighten himself, the prongs of Lank's rake were fastened in his tangled hair. He was jerked ignominiously from the saddle and fell upon the turf on his face.

There he lay, stunned, while his gun was taken from his nerveless hand, and, then, viewed by the many eyes which were crowding the courthouse windows to follow the approach of spectacular Charlie, Lank Mackay kicked his victim to his feet, kicked him again into full speed, and ran Wild Charlie, yelling for help, off the lawn, out of town, and out of the sight and the minds of everyone in the county and its six neighbors.

Such was the famous fall of Wild Charlie. Men were spellbound for days and days afterward. There were no real attempts to explain the miracle until the sheriff stepped to the fore. He had ever been the benefactor of Lank, and he declared that Lank had simply passed from childhood to manhood some twenty years later than the average person. But now that he had taken the step, he would prove himself to be as good a man as any.

Such was the opinion of the sheriff, and such was the gradually spreading opinion among the other townsmen, and Lank Mackay was on the high road to consideration not only as a man but a man of the very first quality. Such was his condition when the catastrophe came. He was struck down in the first flower of his new repute, and the blow came from the one thing which he loved in the world, and that was the courthouse itself. From the lofty eaves a fragment broke away and struck the head of Lank a glancing blow as it fell.

A doctor was with him in two minutes and examined him as he lay on the table in an office, but the doctor's opinion was that he would die within five minutes or five hours. As a matter of fact, the minimum was a little too liberal. Lank Mackay presently opened his eyes and looked wildly around him.

"I don't see the sheriff!" he cried.

The sheriff leaned above him. "Steady, Lank!" he said. "Steady, old boy. I'm right here to the last. . . ."

"It is the last, then?" asked Lank with narrowing eyes.

The sheriff strove to lie, but the truth was in his face, and Lank saw it. He closed his eyes for an instant with a grimace, then looked up to the sheriff.

"How long have I got?"

"Not long, Lank. Lord knows I'm sorry to say it. And just when. . . ."

"I was getting onto my feet," said Lank sadly. "I was

227

making them see that I wasn't plumb skunk."

"Poor Lank," said the sheriff softly.

"Tell me one thing . . . they'll respect me, Sheriff?"

"They will, Lank."

"Then I'm going to make a clean breast of the one thing that's chalked up against me. It's about Clancy Stewart. Lean close, Sheriff. I begin to hear a roaring in my ears."

The sheriff leaned obediently closer. As he listened to that dying whisper, his expression changed to horror and amazement. Lank Mackay died midway in a sentence, but he had told enough to make the sheriff shout his tidings to the men in the room. Clancy Stewart had not fled from justice until this dead man had warned him that there would be no justice for his share if he dared to put himself into the hands of the law. They had hunted Clancy for the price on his head; they must hunt him now to tell him that his outlawry was ended, and that he was invited to come in for a trial which would be a mere mockery, for his innocence was proved.

Chapter Ten
"Sylvia Is Married"

The thaw had come with a wonderful suddenness. A warm south wind breathed on the ice and turned it to water. A short and heavy rain washed the snow from the slopes. The mountains were white and dazzling when the evening came, but in the dawn they were dark again, except where the clear sunlight was pouring on the evergreens and making them glitter. It was like the coming of a false spring. The hoofs of the horses sank deep in the mud, and the earth still was giving up crinkling sounds as though it had drunk deep but could drink still deeper.

Through this difficult and heavy slush Clancy Stewart had ridden to the top of a slope with a companion on horseback dressed in a clerical garb. He pointed down the slope to a wrecked cabin, a mere ghost of a shack from which a wraith of smoke was rising.

"Now, sir," said Clancy, "I can explain why I have brought you here."

"You may explain as well as you can," said the other in anger, "but there will be still another explanation due to the sheriff."

Clancy Stewart shrugged his shoulders. "In that cabin," he said, "is a girl who left her father's house and came out into the wilderness to marry me."

"You may burn me alive," said the stern old man, "but you can never persuade me to officiate at such a marriage."

Clancy smiled. "In the same place," he said, "you'll find a man who came out to persuade Sylvia to ride back to her father's house with him and not ruin her life. . . ."

"A worthy man."

"He is lying in that shack badly wounded."

"Murder, then," cried the minister.

"Be quiet," said Clancy. "You chatter like an old crow. I say that Oliver Beam is lying in that shack wounded. Sylvia is expecting you to come to marry her to me. You must ride down there without me. You must tell Sylvia that I have no intention of marrying her, that I have sent you down there to marry her to Oliver Beam."

"I am astonished!" exclaimed the clergyman. "I cannot know what to say."

"Say nothing," said Clancy.

"But how will I explain things to her? Ah, I see. You no longer care for her."

Clancy paused a moment. "That is it," he said at last. "You must persuade her that I no longer love her. You must point out to her that, if her honor is to be saved, she must marry Oliver Beam. Can you do that?"

"One would think," said the clergyman, "that you either despise the girl or else you really have a friendly feeling for the man you have recently shot down."

"You may think what you please," said Clancy, "but I want you to remember that some people do their thinking *afterward* and not before an event. Will you go down to the cabin?"

"I see no reason against it. Oliver Beam is a good man."

"And able to endow your church."

"That, of course, is nothing."

"Of course," said Clancy, "that would never enter your head. Good bye, sir."

"But what," said the minister, "is your profit out of this transaction? You ride all night. You kidnap me from my bed at infinite risk of being discovered and shot by other men in the house, and then you bring me here simply to have another man married . . . ?"

"To save the honor of a girl, sir!"

"But you . . . ?" The minister bit his lip and did not proceed with his speech.

"I am outlawed and, therefore, without honor?" suggested Clancy.

The minister returned some unintelligible answer and then hurried his horse down the slope and toward the cabin. Clancy did not pause to watch him, but, reining his horse around, he struck out due south, or a little to the west of south, crossing another bridge and dropping at length into a valley, the floor of which was so covered with gravel that it held up under the weight of his horse easily and let him continue at a good rate. He had journeyed on perhaps an hour from the time he had left the minister to descend to the hut, when the patter of a horse's hoofs before him made him draw back into a dripping wood. There he waited, cursing the water which trickled down his back.

The man who approached showed no eagerness to push on in his journey. Instead, he dismounted at the crossing of the trails, and, going up to a well-squared fence post, he nailed a large placard against it, mounted, and proceeded on his way. Clancy waited for him to pass out of sight. Then he swung into the road and was on the point of galloping on when his eye caught on the central word of the placard. That word was "Stewart".

A moment later he had reined his horse to the side of the road and was reading the following:

The reward offered for the apprehension of Clancy Stewart is hereby withdrawn, the confession of Arthur Mackay having proved that Stewart was deceived into fearing the justice he would receive if he surrendered to the law. Clancy Stewart is hereby assured of a square deal.

That proclamation was signed by the sheriff, and it seemed to Clancy that he could hear the ring of Newt Winters's voice as he uttered the words. He was a free man, then. If he was invited back in this manner, it simply meant that his trial was a foolish formality. But now his was the position of a man who has seen heaven and voluntarily turned his back on it. He had given the woman he loved to another man at the very moment when it had become possible for him to marry her in all safety and honor for both of them.

There was a ghost of a hope that the minister might not yet have completed the ceremony. It would take more than a little persuasion to break down the stubborn spirit of Sylvia, and if she were still holding out . . . ?

He whipped the bay mare around and rode like mad up the slope. Off the floor of the valley he struck the soft mud again, and in it the good mare labored heavily. They dragged along at a pace so slow that it was heartbreaking. Even so, the little mare was exhausted halfway up the last slope, and Clancy was on the point of throwing himself from the saddle to the ground to complete the journey on foot when he had sight of the minister, riding over the brow of the hill and coming slowly down toward the hollow. At sight of him the clergyman raised a hand in greeting and hurried down.

His face was beaming. His eyes were shining with perfect happiness.

"Has the ceremony . . . ?" began Clancy.

"It has been such a battle of words as I never hope to enter on again!" said the minister.

"But have you married them?"

The other would not be hurried.

"She would not even listen. The thought of marrying Oliver Beam was, she swore, abhorrent to her. It was like talking to a pillar of stone."

"Heaven bless her," breathed Clancy Stewart. "She was steadfast, then?"

"Until the very end."

"Then she is still free?"

"Until, I say, the very end. But constant dropping of water will wear away the stone."

"She changed, then? She gave way?"

"I conquered in the end. She is now the wife of Oliver Beam. In a week she will be mistress of his house as well as of his heart."

Clancy Stewart was still as a dead thing in the saddle.

"She is the wife, in fact, of the richest and most honored man in the mountains. What could be more fitting than their union, my dear friend? All that I wonder over is that you could have been the instrument which has brought about such a great work."

And still he rattled on. He was so impressed, in fact, that he would himself intercede for the outlaw with the sheriff.

So, at length, he started away, and Clancy Stewart found himself at last alone.

He had closed the door to heaven in very fact, and yet, as he pondered, he wondered if he had not done what was best for Sylvia. She would be, as the minister had said, the wife of the richest man in the district. She would be the queen of all the married women. She would have at her service a great fortune and all the comforts which a great fortune connoted. And so, as he summed up all the details of the thing he had accomplished, Clancy Stewart decided that, after all, it had been for the best. No matter how close his own heart might come to breaking, it was well that Oliver Beam had won her.

He found that his mare had been toiling slowly up the slope during this interval of thought, and now his head came above the top of the ridge and allowed him to look down into the hollow where the shack stood, in which lay wounded Oliver Beam, victorious in his long struggle against Clancy. On a log in front of the house sat Sylvia West, with her head bowed and rested on her hands. This was no posture, certainly, for a newly married woman. And something told Clancy that what he felt, she felt, also.

He reined the mare back quickly. Certainly he must not be seen. He rode slowly down again and headed east. In the mind of Clancy there was a shadow of bewilderment. If he had been crushed by superior strength, he could have understood. But a man he had never injured had struck him down with a random blow. It was Lank Mackay who had beaten him into the ground. And what was Lank Mackay but an outcast?

He checked his horse and listened to the stillness of the morning. A bird whistled in a treetop. Then the silence shut in solidly, and it carried home to the mind of Clancy a new thought, that all of these things might have been predestined. And Lank Mackay was the instrument of the unseen director.

ACKNOWLEDGMENTS

The Lightning Warrior

The Indians call the great white wolf the Lightning Warrior because of the swiftness of his attack. But even the giant Colbolt isn't interested in the massive wolf until Sylvia Baird makes the beast's pelt the one condition for her hand in marriage. She thinks she is safe, but when he returns with not only the pelt, but the wolf itself, and demands his prize, Sylvia's only hope is a desperate flight for freedom. Colbolt sets out in determined pursuit, but he's forgotten Sylvia's newest ally. . .the Lightning Warrior.

___4420-X $4.50 US/$5.50 CAN

Dorchester Publishing Co., Inc.
P.O. Box 6640
Wayne, PA 19087-8640

Please add $1.75 for shipping and handling for the first book and $.50 for each book thereafter. NY, NYC, and PA residents, please add appropriate sales tax. No cash, stamps, or C.O.D.s. All orders shipped within 6 weeks via postal service book rate. Canadian orders require $2.00 extra postage and must be paid in U.S. dollars through a U.S. banking facility.

Name_____
Address_____
City_____State_____Zip_____
I have enclosed $_____ in payment for the checked book(s).
Payment <u>must</u> accompany all orders. ❏ Please send a free catalog.
    CHECK OUT OUR WEBSITE! www.dorchesterpub.com

OUTLAWS
ALL

From Alaska to the Southwest, Max Brand, the master of the Western tale, brings the excitement of the frontier to life like no one else. His characters live, breathe, struggle and triumph in a world so real you can hear the creaking of the saddle leather. Gathered in this collection are three classic short novels by Brand, all filled with the adventure and heroism, the guts and the gunsmoke, that made the West what it was.

___4398-X $4.50 US/$5.50 CAN

Dorchester Publishing Co., Inc.
P.O. Box 6640
Wayne, PA 19087-8640

Please add $1.75 for shipping and handling for the first book and $.50 for each book thereafter. NY, NYC, and PA residents, please add appropriate sales tax. No cash, stamps, or C.O.D.s. All orders shipped within 6 weeks via postal service book rate. Canadian orders require $2.00 extra postage and must be paid in U.S. dollars through a U.S. banking facility.

Name_____
Address_____
City_____State_____Zip_____
I have enclosed $_____ in payment for the checked book(s).
Payment <u>must</u> accompany all orders. ☐ Please send a free catalog.
     CHECK OUT OUR WEBSITE! www.dorchesterpub.com

MAX BRAND

TROUBLE IN TIMBERLINE

"Brand is a topnotcher!"
—*New York Times*

Barney Dwyer is too big and too awkward to be much good around a ranch. But foreman Dan Peary has the perfect job for him. It seems Peary's son has joined up with a ruthless gang in the mountain town of Timberline, and Peary wants Barney to bring the no-account back, alive. Before long, Barney finds himself up to his powerful neck in trouble—both from gunslingers who defy the law and tin stars who are sworn to uphold it!

_3848-X $4.50 US/$5.50 CAN